MADELINE MISSING

Jack Dillon Dublin Tale 7

Second Edition

MADELINE MISSING

Jack Dillon Dublin Tale 7
Second Edition

Mike Faricy

Library of Congress Control Number: 2023920425
paperback ISBN: 978-1-962080-73-6
e-Book ISBN: 978-1-962080-74-3

MJF Publishing books may be purchased for education, Business, or promotional use. For information on bulk purchases, please contact the author directly at mikefaricyauthor@gmail.com

Published by

MJF Publishing
https://www.mikefaricybooks.com

ACKNOWLEDGMENTS

I would like to thank the following people for their help & support: Special thanks to Nick, Roy, Julie, Mittie, and Toui for their hard work, cheerful patience and positive feedback. I would like to thank family and friends for their encouragement and unqualified support. Special thanks to Maggie, Jed, Schatz, Pat, Av, Emily and Pat, for not rolling their eyes, at least when I was there. Most of all, to my wife, Teresa, whose belief, support and inspiration has, from day one, never waned.

“May your enemies never meet a friend.”

ONE

He watched her as he stood in the dark, looking out the sitting room window. She climbed out of the back seat and staggered for a couple of steps attempting to regain her balance. The three women in the car laughed, screamed good night, then drove off and disappeared around the corner. He took a final drag off his cigarette and stubbed it out on the white windowsill.

Aideen Suel waved goodbye as the car disappeared. She took a deep breath and attempted to make her way toward the front door, staggering along the sidewalk. She pulled out her keys, took a long moment to focus on the proper one, then struggled to insert it and unlock the door. It had been a fun night out with the girls, trading stories with way too much to drink. She unlocked the door, stepped inside, dropped her purse on the floor, and kicked off her heels, nearly falling in the process. She giggled, decided one more glass of wine couldn't hurt, and just might help her get to sleep. She staggered into the kitchen and made her way to the cupboard where she kept the wine glasses.

The bottle was on the granite counter next to the tea kettle. She emptied it, filling her glass almost to the rim, took a large sip, and headed for the staircase. As she stumbled out of the kitchen, she put the glass to her lips.

"Aideen, my love, imagine my surprise, you're jarred."

Her scream was cut off by the mouthful of red wine she spit onto the carpet leading upstairs. "What are you doing here? How in the feck did you get—. Get out of me house. You're not supposed to be here."

"Well, aren't you just the cute hoor. In case you hadn't noticed, I am here. Come on, I heard you've been out on the prowl again after your man left for greener pastures. It may have been a couple of years, but I'm guessing an old slapper like you still loves a good ride after a night out. I think—"

"Did you not hear what I said? Get the hell out of this house."

"Oh, I heard you all right."

"I'm gonna call the Garda, you limp—"

His fist caught her on the chin, spun her around, and slammed her against the wall.

Her wine glass shattered, spraying red wine down the wall, across the carpet, and over her blouse. He grabbed a fistful of her blonde hair, yanked hard, and spun her around. As she turned, she brought the broken stem of the wine glass up and slashed him across his nose and cheek.

"Go on. Get your worthless arse out of me house, you no good bastard. Do you—"

The uppercut to her chin caused her eyes to disappear into the top of her skull. He grabbed hold of her arms as she began to fall, pulled her back up, and gave her a solid head butt between the eyes. He let go, hit her with a right cross, and she bounced across the stairway landing. He took hold of her ankles and pulled her from the landing. Her head bounced off the step and then again as it hit the floor. He took hold of her dress, ripped it open, and unbuckled his belt.

TWO

Paddy Suel held up the Styrofoam cup of tea and said, "You sure you don't want this?"

Dillon shook his head. "No, you go ahead and help yourself. It wasn't that good when it was hot. I don't think the past forty minutes has done anything to improve it."

They'd been in the same spot for over four hours. Parked on Faussagh Avenue in Cabra, just across the street and down a few doors from the Cabra Club, waiting for Riley Dempsey to emerge so they could make an arrest. The club, a two-story brick structure painted black, officially closed at 1:30 am. That had been well over an hour ago, but there were still signs of activity inside.

"I suppose we could make a call, have the local Garda show up, tell the plonkers to shut it down, and grab this wanker on his way home," Suel said. He sipped the tea, grimaced, opened the passenger door, and dumped the tea onto the curb. "Ugh, for once in your life, you were right, more like drinking the piss."

"You'd know more about that than me," Dillon said.

"Wait now, what have we got here?" Suel said as the door to the club opened, and two men staggered out. They took a couple of steps, turned to face one another and chatted for a brief moment before heading off in opposite directions.

"If it's Dempsey, he lost his leather jacket, shaved his head, and put on an eye patch," Dillon said as the two climbed into cars at opposite ends of the block and drove off.

"Oughta phone in the license numbers and get the bastards on a drink-drive. Now what the hell?" Suel said as his cellphone rang. He pulled the phone from his pocket, glanced at the screen, then answered.

"Megan? Everything okay? What's wrong? What? How in the bloody hell? What hospital? No, no, on my way. Well, they'll by god not be stopping the likes of me. Yeah. Yes, soon as I know something. No darling, you'll just be in the way. Get some rest. I know. I know. But try. No, I'm on my way. Yeah. Appreciate the call."

"What's up?" Dillon said.

"My sister, Megan. Some fecker broke into Aideen's house, attacked her, she's in hospital. I'm going to call a squad, have them take me there. You okay to nail Dempsey on your own?"

Dillon turned the key in the ignition and started the engine. "Who the hell knows when a squad can get here. What hospital?"

"You don't—"

As Dillon pulled away from the curb, he turned on the flashing lights. "What hospital?"

"She's in James's."

He took a right and picked up speed heading for Old Cabra Road. Fortunately, at this time of night, there was virtually no traffic. He raced through Stoneybatter and Smithfield, crossed the Liffey, and tore up the hill into the Liberties then sped down James Street to Saint James Hospital.

"You know which building she's in?"

"Megan said she was in surgery, take a left just after the train tracks up here."

The traffic light turned yellow when they were two blocks away, turned red for a brief moment, and back to green as Dillon approached and sailed through, swerving around the corner past a stone building at least a hundred and fifty years old.

"You're going to get us both fecking killed, you crazy bastard," Suel shouted as he grabbed onto the dash with both fists. They sailed around another building, this one only a hundred and twenty years old. "That building on the left, with your man smoking in front of it. That's the ER let me off there."

Dillon screeched to a stop in front of the ER entrance and turned off the car.

"Thanks, Dillon, but you don't have to come in. This could be a long wait."

"I'm coming in just to keep you in line. Otherwise, you're bound to cause problems, so don't even think of trying to stop me," Dillon said.

"I take back some of the things the rest of the section has been saying about you," Suel half-joked, and hurried out of the car.

THREE

It was after five in the morning when they got the word Suel's younger sister, Aideen had been wheeled out of surgical recovery and brought into a room. She'd be one of four women in the room, each separated by a privacy curtain around the bed. Suel asked for her room number and explained he was family. When that didn't seem to work, both he and Dillon flashed their badges.

She was sedated now. Suel was sitting on an orange plastic chair next to her bed. His massive right hand rested on her shoulder as he fingered rosary beads with his left.

Dillon had taken up space out on the bench in the hallway and had just finished leaving a message on DCI McCabe's phone, giving a brief explanation of the situation when Suel stepped out of the room.

"Dillon, she's going to be out for a bit, but I want to be here when she wakes. You should go home and get some sleep."

"You sure? It's no problem for me to stay and—"

"No, now not another word. You've done more than enough. She's liable to be out for hours, and there's no point in the two of us becoming worthless. I'll phone McCabe after nine this morning," Suel said and followed up with a yawn.

"I already left McCabe a message so he'll have that initial information whenever he gets in. Tell me her address. I'll go over there and check some things out, secure the place until we can get a team over to process the site."

"I don't know if they'll send a team over, she wasn't murdered, thank God, and we—"

"You let me worry about getting a team over there. Right now, your top priority, in fact, your only priority, is to be here when she wakes up. Call me if you need anything, anything at all. I'll keep you posted if I learn something."

Suel nodded, wrote down her address in a small notebook he always carried then tore the page out and handed it to Dillon. "Thanks, much appreciated."

They shook hands, Dillon leaned in and gave Suel a hug, and headed down the hall and out to his car. On his drive home, he thought about the attack. Was it a relationship gone bad? A random burglar or rapist? Or was some fool trying to send a message to Paddy Suel? One thing he knew for sure, none of the options would end up positive for whoever was responsible.

He pulled in front of his house, rode up over the curb and parked on the sidewalk. All was quiet as he unlocked the door and stepped inside. Lucifer, his dog, was nowhere to be seen, which meant he was probably upstairs asleep on Dillon's bed.

The wastebasket tipped over with contents scattered across the kitchen floor, suggested Lucifer had been busy. Dillon quietly climbed the stairs to the second floor. He was in the bathroom for a few minutes then tiptoed into the bedroom. Lucifer was asleep on the bed, snuggled onto one of the pillows. Remnants of two bones from the ribs Dillon had eaten for dinner rested on the pillow next to him.

He set his alarm clock for three hours, enough time for a decent catnap. He kicked off his shoes, dropped his coat over the chair, and crawled into bed. After a moment, he reached down by his lower back and pulled out another rib bone. Apparently, Lucifer had stored that one for future reference.

It seemed like only a minute or two later when the alarm woke him. He slowly opened his eyes and looked over to where Lucifer had been ensconced on the pillow, only now he was nowhere to be seen. Never a good sign. He went downstairs and found Lucifer waiting patiently at the front door. He opened the door, and Lucifer hurried outside. Dillon left the door open. He went into the kitchen, filled the food and water dish, and set the coffee maker to start brewing.

Lucifer entered the kitchen, walked around the counter, sat at Dillon's feet, and looked up expectantly.

"Oh, and I suppose you're looking for a biscuit. There's healthy food and fresh water in the bowls."

Lucifer blinked a couple of times and stared up with a mournful look.

"Good Lord, who the hell taught you how to do that?" He pulled the lid off the biscuit jar, reached in, and tossed a biscuit to Lucifer.

The dog caught it in midair and hurried back around the kitchen counter and into the front hallway where he wouldn't have to share. Dillon could hear the sound of the biscuit crunching back in the kitchen.

He walked out of the kitchen with a mug of coffee, stepped over Lucifer finishing the last of the biscuit, and closed the front door. He went upstairs, undressed, and headed into the shower.

FOUR

There was a text message on his cellphone from DCI McCabe when he climbed out of the shower.

'See me when you get in.'

It was after eleven by the time he made it into the office. He went through the security gate, parked in the lot, and took the elevator up to Special Branch. His desk had been the collection point for dirty plates, mugs, and trash in general before his arrival in Dublin. Over the past couple of years, nothing had really changed. Along with two dirty tea mugs, a plate with crumbs and the wrapper from a Yorkie candy bar there was a note on his desk from McCabe,

'See me!'

Dillon did his daily routine of dumping the mugs and the plate into the break room sink before he headed for McCabe's office. The door was open, and he gave a perfunctory knock on the door frame then took a couple of steps into the office.

"You wanted to see me, sir?"

McCabe's head was down, focused on the open file on his desk. His bald head reflected the fluorescent light in the ceiling, giving the appearance of a halo. He looked up at Dillon, closed the file, and said, "Come in, come in. I wanted to get an update on DI Suel. I understand you were with him this morning at the hospital. What's the status of his sister?"

"Couple hours in surgery. She was still sedated when I left around six this morning. Status? Based on what I saw pretty beat up— black eyes, broken nose, swollen jaw. We didn't get a report from anyone in the surgical team, but Suel may have received that by now. She was on an IV when I left, not sure what it was. I'm guessing a sedative. I don't know that she's been raped, but if she has, it wouldn't surprise me."

"And where was Dempsey during all this?"

"We watched him enter the Cabra Club a little after eleven. We waited until almost three for him to leave. It appeared they were still serving after closing. The occasional person stumbled out, none of whom were Dempsey. Suel got the call from his sister right around three, and we raced over to James's. If I might suggest, sir?"

McCabe nodded.

"If you could send a team over to Aideen Suel's home. That's apparently where the assault took place. There's at least the possibility someone is sending a message to DI Suel. No idea at this point who that would be.

It may be nothing related to him, but it was a brutal attack, and it would be nice to have the scene processed before someone with the best of intentions stops in to help clean or cook or do a load of laundry."

McCabe flashed a smile. "Already done, forensics arrived around nine this morning. I want you to head over there as well. You need an address?"

"I've got one."

McCabe nodded, and half said to himself, "Of course you do."

"Anything else, sir?"

"Only that you remind DI Suel that he's not to be involved in any way, shape, or form in this investigation. We find out who's responsible, and we damn well will, I don't want any involvement from Suel that might suggest our work was tainted. Clear?"

"Yes, sir, couldn't agree more."

McCabe flashed another quick smile, suggesting he didn't quite believe Dillon. "Very well, dismissed, off with you now, and I'll want a report at days end."

Dillon left, headed back into the break room, where he grabbed four chocolate covered tea biscuits before he made his way out the door.

FIVE

Aideen Suel lived in Phibsboro, an area on the north side of Dublin. Her home was on Shandon Gardens, a street that overlooked the Royal Canal and was just two blocks off Phibsboro Road. The homes were all two-story stucco structures, five groups of six attached units ran along the length of the street. Each unit had a three-foot-high concrete block wall across the front garden and an iron gate leading into the garden. Most of the units were some version of white or grey. Aideen Suel's unit happened to be pink.

Dillon spotted the unit from down the block, not because it was pink, but because there were two white vehicles parked in front with fluorescent green stripes along the side and the word GARDA on the front, sides, and back of each car along with a set of flashing lights across the top. He pulled into an open space three units down from Aideen's.

The units all had the same floor plan, an enclosed entry, a sitting room, small kitchen and eating area on the first floor, two bedrooms, and a bath on the upper level.

The iron gate leading into Aideen's front garden had seven struts, each with two leaves at the top that were welded into an arch. It had been painted white at some point, but based on the peeling paint and the rust stains on the gate that had been a number of years ago. He walked up to the front stoop and rang the doorbell.

A moment later, a uniformed officer answered the door. She was dressed in dark blue trousers, a light blue long sleeve shirt, and a dark blue protective west with the word GARDA across the back. She wore blue latex gloves on her hands, and despite the uniform and the protective vest, she still presented an attractive figure. As she stepped into the small entryway, Dillon thought she looked familiar, brown hair, dark eyes, and a flashing smile, but he couldn't place her.

"Yes?"

He held his badge out. "US Marshall Jack Dillon assigned to An Garda Síochána."

She looked at Dillon and smiled. "Yes, you're the American, I remember. We met a while back," she said and held out her hand. "Ciara Hogan, we met in the Croker at a hurling match."

He suddenly remembered. "Dublin and Kilkenny," he said.

"Right, and if I recall, things didn't go your way."

"You mean because you had a date?"

She blushed slightly and chuckled. "No, I was referring to the score, Kilkenny won. Oh, I'm sorry, won't you come in, we're just finishing up. Is there a US connection here?" she said as she stepped into the front hall.

"No, but the victim was the sister of someone on our team and—"

"DI Paddy Suel," she said.

"Yes. Obviously, he can't be involved with the investigation, so I drew the short straw."

"Do you know the victim?"

"Only her name, Aideen Suel. I've never been formally introduced." He saw no point in mentioning that he'd been at the hospital in the early morning hours, sat with Paddy until they got the word on her room, and saw her lying sedated in bed because someone had beat the hell out of her.

Officer Hogan had stopped in the front hallway. The walls were painted a shade of orange. The staircase leading up to the second floor was carpeted, and the railing was painted an off-white. A plainclothes officer, light-colored hair, balding, and wearing blue latex gloves was collecting what appeared to be blood samples from the wooden floor. A number of plastic evidence bags were lined up along the far wall. The two bags in front looked like they contained broken glass and a small garment, probably a thong. What looked like blood smears had run down the wall next to the base of the staircase. A good deal of blood was smeared across the hallway floor.

At that point, another uniformed officer came down the staircase carrying a camera. "Everything seems to be in order up there. The bed's made and appears to be untouched. The bathroom is in order. The second bedroom is an office. The computer is still on the desk. All the rooms look untouched. I photographed everything."

"I'm pretty well finished here," the officer kneeling on the hallway floor said. He sealed the plastic bag he held, wrote something across the top, and set it against the wall with the others.

"Any assumptions?" Dillon asked.

"This is Marshall Dillon, a diehard Dub fan," Ciara said.

"How's that working out?" the officer on the stairs said, and all three laughed, clearly not originally from Dublin.

"Depends on the day and the year. What about this place?"

"Like you heard me say, the upstairs appears to be untouched. My guess, somehow, whoever attacked her was let inside. Maybe, someone she knew or at least someone she didn't fear. The neighbor next door heard some noise in the middle of the night, looked out the window and saw a man run out the door and down the street. Apparently, he's the one who phoned it in."

"You talked to him?" Dillon said.

He shook his head no. "DI Walsh did, you can reach him at Mountjoy Garda station. There is one thing, though."

"What's that?"

"Behind you in the sitting room," he said, stepping off the staircase landing and heading toward Dillon with an outstretched hand. "I'm Tommy Gibbons, by the way. You're the one they call Dildo, right?" The comment brought a chuckle from the other two.

"They might call me that behind my back."

"Nice to meet you," Gibbons said and led the way into the sitting room. "We found this here," he said, pointing to the length of ash along the white window sill beneath the front window. The room was painted a soft beige color with a fireplace centered on the far wall. The baseboard and a small piece of wood trim up against the ceiling were painted the same white as the window sill. The room had two windows, one looking out the back and the other looking out to the front garden, the street, and the Royal Canal beyond. Both windows were covered with lace curtains.

Dillon bent down and looked at the ash, and thought he might have picked up the hint of cigarette. "Did you collect a butt from this?"

"Yeah, Noel's got it out there in an evidence bag. We'll test it for DNA. A butt is a good source of saliva, so long as the smoker wasn't sharing. No evidence the victim was a smoker, so keep your fingers crossed. Just a wild guess, maybe putting out the cigarette like that on her window sill is what set things off. They're in here talking, drinking or drugging, that leads to arguing, someone gets pissed and puts their cigarette out on the window sill. Maybe the victim does something, takes a swing at your man—"

"If it was a man."

"Odds are it was, but I take your point. Anyway, that sets the whole thing off."

"Possible, any sign of forced entry?"

"No, none. Your neighbor next door saw a man run from here, peeked out the window and noticed the front door was open. If it weren't for him, there's no telling when she would have been found. All sorts of bad scenarios come to mind."

"You have a name for him, your man next door?"

"Yeah, witness," he said and smiled. "No, we don't, but DI Walsh over at Mountjoy station will have it."

"Anything else?"

"Other than the scene in the hallway, no. We'll have confirmation tomorrow or the day after, but I'm betting on a rape. I still come back to someone she knew, someone she let in. Boyfriend, former boyfriend, neighbor, maybe someone she works with. Odds are she knew the bollocks."

"You going to be here long?" Dillon said.

"Another bit, good hour to get things cataloged and packed up."

"I'm going to step next door, see if your man will talk with me. Which house was it?"

"Gibbons pointed to the wall with the fireplace."

"Thanks, give a yell if I'm still over there when you're ready to leave."

"Good luck," he said as Dillon went out the front door.

SIX

Dillon walked out of the front garden and over to the unit next door. The placement of the exterior windows and the front door were the same as Aideen's, but all similarities ended there. The first thing he noticed was the gate. Just like Aideen's, only it was glossy black and looked to have been freshly painted. A well-tended rose garden ran along either side from the front wall up to the house. A massive pink clematis vine climbed up alongside the front door and across the second floor of the house. The front door was white laminate with a beveled glass panel. Dillon rang the doorbell, and the door to the enclosed entryway opened a moment later.

The man had neatly trimmed white hair and appeared to be in decent shape. Dillon guesstimated his age as maybe late fifties, early sixties. He smiled, flashed white teeth, and gave half a wave before he opened the front door.

"Hi, sorry to bother you. My name is Marshall Jack Dillon." He held out his badge. "I'm assigned to An

Garda Síochána and I wonder if I might ask you a few questions about the events of last night."

"Things are so bad now they had to send an American?" The man held the door open, smiled, and said, "Please, come on in. I was just about to put the kettle on, will you join me in a tea?"

"Yes, that would be wonderful," Dillon lied. He would have preferred a coffee, but he also knew if there were any, it would be instant. "I'm sorry. Your name is?"

"Dugan, Dermot Dugan. Can you tell me how she's doing, the Suel girl?"

"Aideen. Well, she's in James's at the moment. Her brother is there with her. She had some surgery early this morning. She was sedated and in a hospital room. At the moment I don't know much else. From what I could see, I'm guessing a broken nose, maybe a broken or fractured jaw. She may have been sexually assaulted. We'll get a clearer picture once we talk to the hospital, at the moment I'm a bit out of the loop."

"Come on back to the kitchen," Dugan said. He pulled the tea kettle from the back burner of the stove, filled it, and set it on the burner. The kitchen had grey granite countertops and oak cabinets. A window above the sink looked out into the back garden, and double doors led down some steps to a paved patio. The back garden and patio were enclosed by concrete walls, seven feet high and painted white. Another rose garden ran along the walls.

"Lovely kitchen and back garden. How long have you been here?" Dillon said, trying to gain some common ground.

Dugan was filling a plate with tea biscuits. "The wife and I arrived in ninety-two, bought from the original owner, an accountant and his wife. They went into assisted living, and we moved in with three little knuckleheads. Bit of a change."

"It's lovely. Your cabinets are gorgeous."

"Thanks, I was in the business, contracting."

"That explains why it's so nice."

Dugan laughed. "Well, that and the fact there aren't three screaming kids slamming doors and climbing on the countertops. I shut the contracting firm down after the crash in 2008. The wife contracted cancer the same year, gone in six months," Dugan said and shook his head. "Anyway, I'm attached to the place, like I said, raised our lads here, probably have to take me out feet first."

They chatted about nothing in particular until the kettle began to whistle. Dugan turned off the burner and filled both mugs. "Cream or sugar?"

"No, thanks, just black is fine."

"Why don't we grab a seat at the table," Dugan said. He followed Dillon over to the oak table and set down two steaming mugs with tea bags. He reached over to the far side of the kitchen island, grabbed the plate with the biscuits, and sat down opposite Dillon.

Dillon pulled a notebook and pen from his inside coat pocket. "You mind if I make some notes while we chat?"

"I'd be worried if you didn't," Dugan said and grimaced as he slurped from his steaming mug.

"So maybe start at the beginning and tell me what happened last night."

Dugan slurped more tea and reached for a biscuit. "Well, I was in bed, reading. It was maybe one fifteen or so. I heard some noise, voices out front. Sounded like women, you know how they get. Laughing and screeching, oblivious to the hour or their noise. I heard them drive off, and a moment later, Aideen's front door closed."

"No male voice at that point?"

"No, just the women waking everyone on the lane. It's quiet for a minute or two. Then I hear voices, a woman talking loud and then yelling. A male voice was answering once in a while. Tell you the truth, I thought it was the tv."

"And this is coming from Aideen's?"

"No question. The yelling turns to a scream, loud, more like a shriek. That's actually what got me out of bed. I turned the reading light off and opened the blinds. Didn't hear anything else, must have stood there for ten or fifteen minutes, and I'm just about ready to go back to bed when this knacker runs out the door and down the street."

"A male?"

"Yeah."

"Recognize him? Any idea who it was?"

"No idea. I'm pretty sure I've never seen him before. To tell you the truth, I think it's been a while since there's been any man over there. She'd a boyfriend maybe a year ago, but I think he went down to Australia. Haven't seen him since."

"You recall a name?"

"Sean Reilly or Ryan, maybe. Can't be sure on the surname, but the first name was Sean. Seemed a nice enough sort. A hell of a lot better for her than the one before him, that was maybe two years ago, can't recall his name, maybe never knew it. A real prick, if you'll pardon my French."

"And, you eventually went over there."

"Last night? Yeah, I could see the light in the garden. It was obvious the front door was open. I waited to see if she'd close it. After a bit, maybe five minutes or so, I pulled on my jeans, a t-shirt, and went over. Found the poor thing on the floor, in a puddle of blood. Her dress was torn up the middle, torn knickers tossed off to the side. I'd say he had his way with her," Dugan said, not looking at Dillon.

"She didn't move when I called her name. I checked for a pulse to make sure she was breathing. I knew she had a landline in the kitchen so I called 999, told them to send an ambulance, then went back to her, there was a jacket hanging by the front door, and I draped that over her."

"Which way did this guy run?"

He pointed toward the kitchen wall. "Toward Phibsboro Road. But he didn't run far, about four units down the street, the lights came on in a car, and it sped off and around the corner."

"Any idea what kind of vehicle?"

He shook his head. "No, other than it was dark blue, or green or maybe black, all I can tell you is it had tail lights. Course now that I think about it, the left one was only half-lit, right side."

"I'm not following."

"Lot of these newer models, with the boot in the back. There's a light on the boot and another one next to the boot, actually on the rear frame of the car. So both taillights were lit on the right side of the car and just the one on the boot on the left side. Oh, and then the top of the taillight was yellow, sort of a rectangle on the frame and a slash on the boot. Hang on a minute."

Dugan got up, went over to the kitchen island, and came back with an envelope and a pencil. He drew a rough diagram of the tail lights on the back of the envelope and placed an X over the one on the far left. "This is the one that was out."

Dillon looked at it and slipped the envelope into his notebook. "Can you give me an idea of this guy that ran out of Aideen's? Long hair?"

Dugan seemed to think for a moment. "No, but not short, either." He stared in the distance. "Sides trimmed, longer on top but not real long. Dark, yeah dark hair.

When the bollocks ran out of the place, he kept a hand up against the side of his face, like this." Dugan placed his left hand up against his face.

"On the left side of his face? Covering his cheek and nose?"

"Yeah, that's right."

"Anything else you can think of?"

"Don't think he had a beard, can't say if he had a mustache. I waited for the Garda to come. They were here in a few minutes, ambulance service not too long after that. They bundled the poor dear up on a gurney and raced off. She'd a note by the phone with her sister's number."

"Megan?"

"Yeah, that's the one. I didn't know who else to call, so I called her. Told her what had happened and that they were taking her to James's."

"Yeah, I was with her brother when she called him. Anything else you can think of?"

Dugan shook his head. "No, sorry, but it all happened so fast. I wish I'd got a better look at your man or chased the bollocks and at least got his license number. But at the time, middle of the night, I was still half-asleep, it just didn't register."

"Okay, Mr. Dugan, I can't thank you enough for your time. Well, and for going next door last night. No telling how long she would have been there on the floor, or what would have happened if she didn't get to the hospital that quickly."

"You lads just catch this bollocks and get him locked up. Beating a woman, Christ sake, has he no shame?"

"Apparently not." Dillon pulled a card from his pocket. "Please feel free to call me should anything else pop into your mind. It all helps, no matter how small it may seem. And thank you for the tea—"

"You didn't touch a drop."

"Too busy writing down all your information. You've been a big help, Mr. Dugan, thank you."

Dugan saw him to the door. As Dillon stepped out into the front garden, Dugan said, "Just get this bollocks."

"Oh, we will, thank you again, sir."

SEVEN

The two Garda vehicles were still parked out front as Dillon headed toward Aideen's front gate. When he went to open the gate, he noticed what looked like a blood smear along the top of the gate. He stepped back and looked at the sidewalk and, for the first time, noticed drops of blood every four or five feet forming a trail down the sidewalk. He followed the trail down past four units where it stopped in the street. This dovetailed nicely with Dugan's description of the guy running out the door and down the sidewalk to his car.

He walked back to Aideen's and pushed the gate open with his foot. He tried the doorknob, but the door was locked, and he rang the doorbell. Tommy Gibbons answered the door a moment later.

"That was fast," Gibbons said.

"Not much to it, I'll check with your man DI Walsh in just a bit. Say, I noticed some blood on the front gate and then drops going down the sidewalk."

"Really? Hold on just a moment," Gibbons said then walked down the hall to the kitchen door. "Noel, it's the American. Said there's blood on the front gate and out on the footpath. Hand me my camera. I'll get some shots, and you should see if you can get a sample."

Gibbons walked back out with his camera, Noel followed a few steps behind, carrying his kit. "How in the bloody hell did we miss it?" he said, following Dillon out the front door.

"I'd say the peeling paint and the rust on the gate, it sort of blends in. If it makes you feel any better, I missed it twice. Once coming in and then again heading out and going next door. It fits perfectly with the description I got from the neighbor. He said he saw the guy running out of here with his hand over his face like this." Dillon placed his left hand on his face covering his cheek and nose the way Dugan had done.

"That might explain the broken wine glass, the shattered end of the stem was bloody. Maybe she was able to slash your man. Hopefully, I collected some of his samples."

Dillon stood next to the gate and pointed to the blood.

Noel set his kit on the ground and bent over, looking at the blood from a number of angles. "Tommy, get some shots of this. It's perfect. God bless peeling paint. I think I can probably lift the entire sample. Nice eye, Dillon," he said, then opened the lid on the kit and pulled on a pair of latex gloves.

Gibbons began photographing the gate, taking at least a half dozen pictures from different angles.

"There's a trail of blood running down the sidewalk to where he got in his car."

Gibbons stepped onto the sidewalk, followed the trail of drops, then began photographing the entire trail and then each drop.

Noel slipped a razor blade beneath the peeling paint along the top of the gate and, with a pair of tweezers, easily lifted the paint with the entire bloody smear. He placed the paint strip in an evidence bag, labeled it, walked over to one of the cars, and raised the lid of the boot.

"How soon do you think you'll be able to run that sample?"

"If we rush it, and we will, three maybe four weeks."

Dillon was prepared to hear three or four months, so he smiled, "Keep me posted. You got a number for your man Walsh?"

Noel pulled out his cellphone, read a number off to Dillon, who input it on his cell at the same time. He put the phone up to his ear, smiled, and nodded thanks to Noel. He listened to the phone ring as he headed to his car.

EIGHT

The Mountjoy Garda station, which covered Phibsboro, was housed in a three-story red brick building with a slate roof and four large chimneys topped with clay pots. It was located on North Circular Road and stood just outside of Mountjoy prison. The building was built in 1880, and Dillon made a note of the worn granite steps and the iron handrail leading up to the main entrance.

Inside he approached a desk that reminded him more of a judge's bench in a courtroom. The sergeant working the desk looked down at Dillon, studied him for a long moment then said, "What can I do for you?" Making it sound more like an unwelcome interruption than an offer of assistance.

"US Marshal Jack Dillon, here to see DI Brendan Walsh."

The sergeant studied Dillon for another long moment, then pushed a couple of buttons on an antique phone and placed the receiver to his ear. The phone cord was knotted in several places.

"Yeah, your American is down here in the lobby. All right, I'll let him know," the sergeant said and hung up. He made a point of folding his hands together, leaning forward and looking back down at Dillon. "He's just finishing up. Should be down shortly. You can take a seat over on the wall," he said, nodding in the general direction of an antique wooden bench set below a large window.

Dillon smiled, headed over to the bench and sat down. Over the course of the next ten minutes, he adjusted positions uncountable times, never quite finding one that was comfortable. Eventually, a dark-haired man with glasses, wearing a black suit and a striped tie, walked into the lobby and yelled, "Marshal Dillon?"

Other than the desk sergeant, Dillon was the only individual in the lobby. He hurried off the uncomfortable bench and took a half-dozen steps as the blood flowed back into his lower body. "DI Walsh?" he said, holding out his hand.

"Brendan Walsh," the man said. He was maybe an inch or two shorter than Dillon and smiled as they shook hands.

"Jack Dillon, thanks for making the time."

"Come on up to division," Walsh said and headed for a staircase. Much like the granite steps leading up to the building, the stone staircase was worn from almost a hundred and forty years of people treading up and down the thing. Once up on the third floor, they walked down a hallway with oak wainscoting that looked to be original to the structure and in through a door with a brass plaque labeled Homicide.

With the exception of the oak trim and the twelve-foot ceilings, the room was similar to dozens of unit offices Dillon had been in. Desks, computers, people on phones, someone at the copy machine, coffee and tea mugs, stacks of files, in short, organized chaos.

Walsh headed for a desk in a far corner, which suggested to Dillon he was somewhat senior and had been able to claim a space away from the high traffic areas. Other than a stack of files and blue coffee mug with the Dublin coat-of-arms of three burning castles, his desk was clear. He pointed to a chair alongside the desk, not as a command, but more in a polite 'help yourself' sort of way.

"Talk you into a coffee? I can't attest to the quality, but it's better than the tea."

"If you're going to have one, yeah, otherwise, don't worry."

"Back in a moment," Walsh said and hurried around a corner. He returned in little more than a minute and said, "Forgot to ask, you take milk or sugar?"

"Just black," Dillon said, taking a mug from Walsh and setting it on the desk.

Walsh set his Dublin mug down, pulled a chair back, and settled in. He took a sip of coffee, grimaced, set the cup down, and faced Dillon. "I don't want to beat this too hard, but right off the top, I know you happen to be close with Paddy Suel. Know the two of you were at the hospital this morning. And, unless I'm wrong, Suel's still there. I don't have a problem with any of that. I get it. Believe me, I'd be the same. God forbid this ever happens to a member of my family. Here's the thing," he pasted on a smile meant to look like it was pasted on. "This is my damn case. I know you're in special branch and all that, but this is my case. The assault occurred in our jurisdiction, and I don't want either one of you's gettin' in the way. Clear?"

Dillon brushed some imaginary dust off his trouser leg and looked up at Walsh for a long moment. "Couldn't have said it better. And I'm in full agreement. The only reason I was at the crime scene this morning was to allow Suel the opportunity to stay away from the investigation. DCI McCabe has already said as much. I intend to follow that directive, and I'll make sure DI Suel does not get involved in your investigation."

Walsh had a questioning look on his face. "So why in the hell are you here?"

"Two reasons. First, to let you know neither Suel nor I have any intention of getting involved, and second, having said that, I did have a brief chat with Dermot Dugan."

"Your man next door."

"Yeah. I just wanted to compare notes. See if I may have picked anything up that he neglected to tell you. And then to bring you up to date on the forensic team."

"So you're not going to get involved, but you interrogated Dugan. Listen, Dillon, I meant what I said. This is my case. I don't want you or Suel getting in my way."

Dillon raised his hands as if in surrender. "Not in your way, won't be in the way. Didn't really interrogate, just chatted for a few minutes. That said, you must already know about the perp being slashed. And if you know that, you know about the vehicle. So I guess I made the trip for nothing. Keep me posted. Hope you get this bastard soon. Believe me, I've got my own caseload, so I'll get back to working that. Sorry to take up—"

"Hold on a minute. Just hold on. What are you talking about this bollocks being slashed?"

Dillon told him about the blood smear on the gate and the drops of blood leading to the car and that the man ran out of Aideen's with his hand covering his cheek and nose. How the forensic team thought the perp might have been slashed with the broken wine glass.

"And they got a sample off the gate?"

"Yeah, pulled a piece of paint off about two inches long and bagged it. It was covered with blood, so they should be able to run tests. I left before they gathered any samples off the sidewalk. What's the photographer's name?"

"Tommy Gibbons."

"Yeah, he was just beginning to photograph the trail when I left."

"And the car?"

"Taillight was out, distinctive taillight." He drew Walsh a version of what Dermot Dugan had drawn for him. "Based on Dugan's description, I'm thinking it might be a pricey sort of vehicle."

Walsh nodded, then said, "Umm, I may have been a little hasty in my judgement. I hope you understand, the sister of a member on the force, we want to get this bastard and we will. But if—"

Dillon cut him off and said, "Believe me, been there, said essentially the same thing. You have to, otherwise with a family member involved, the investigation heads south immediately It's almost a given."

Walsh smiled, this time, a sincere smile. "Thanks. Tell you what. I'll head down to Phibsboro center. They've got cameras covering the intersection. Good possibility we might spot the vehicle on security tape. Especially with this taillight tip. Thanks, your man Dugan didn't mention that."

"He probably just had more time to process information, you know how that goes. Thank you, appreciate the offer, but like I said, I got my own caseload, which continues to grow. But, if it's not too much trouble, let me know if you get something. I'd just like to keep Suel up to date. Let him know things are progressing." Dillon stood and said, "Nice to meet you, Brendan. If I can be of any help, just let me know." He tossed his card on the desk, shook hands, and left.

NINE

The parking ramp at St. James Hospital was full and had a line of cars waiting to enter. Dillon drove back around the block past the hundred and fifty and hundred and twenty-year-old buildings. He pulled to the curb in front of Aideen's building and parked. He took a sheet of paper from his glove compartment with the logo of An Garda Síochána printed on it and below that the words, 'OFFICIAL BUSINESS.' He placed the sheet on the dash, then climbed out and hurried into the building, listening for the chirp indicating the car doors were locked.

Dillon stood outside Aideen's room and studied her and her brother for a minute. The curtain around her bed had been pulled back. Paddy Suel was now seated in a green leather upholstered chair he'd apparently commandeered from somewhere, and he was sipping from a white Styrofoam cup. Dillon figured it was probably tea.

Aideen's bed was raised, her eyes were open, and she was occasionally saying something in response to whatever Suel said. She looked like she'd been run over by a bus, twice. Her eyes were black and swollen. The left eye appeared to be almost swollen shut. The left side of her jawline was bruised and swollen, and her mouth looked like she'd been hit with a baseball bat. It was impossible to determine the condition of her nose because there was a large green splint taped to her forehead and across her face that covered her nose. Her hair was pulled back, and her left ear was covered with a gauze bandage. Her right arm appeared to be in a sling, and the left arm, what he could see of it, was black and blue. Her left hand was wrapped in gauze, running from her fingertips up over her wrist.

"So, Aideen," Dillon said as he entered the room. "This mean you're not going to the dance with me tonight?"

Suel didn't smile.

"Don't make me laugh, Dildo. It fecking hurts," she said, then smiled ever so slightly.

"Listen, sweetheart. We're lucky you're here and not in some cooler with a toe tag. You were—"

"Ya bollocks, this is your idea of making things better? What the feck are ye goin' on about?" Suel said.

"Stop it, Paddy. He's here to make the likes of me better, not you, you miserable gobshite. It's good to see you Marshal, and thanks for interrupting my brother's latest lecture. I've only heard it about a thousand times today."

"And you'll hear it a thousand more times until you start to cop on. Strutting about like some kind of slapper just looking to get—"

"All right, you two, enough of the happy family routine, knock it off," Dillon said.

"Just want to say thanks for being here with Paddy when they brought me in last night. No telling what he would have told the staff to do left to his own devices."

"Just want what's best for you, Aideen," Suel said.

"Well, give it a rest, will ya's. Christ sake, I've heard enough to last me a lifetime."

"Oh-kay," Dillon said attempting to get both of them to calm down. "So, how's the food in this place?"

Suel gave a little chuckle as Aideen said, "I wouldn't know. They got me sipping through a straw till the jaw heals up." She pointed to a tall Styrofoam cup with a plastic straw inserted in the top.

"Broken jaw?"

"Not broken enough, she's still able to give me the lip."

"And you damn well deserve it, you fecking gobshite."

"Oh, isn't that just the business. I've been here for damn near the past twelve hours and you—"

"Okay, enough, the two of you," Dillon said, then reached in his pocket and pulled out a ten euro note. "Go on down to the cafeteria and get me a coffee, decaf, and something to sweeten you up. I'll stay here and lecture Aideen while you're gone." He winked at Aideen as Suel slowly climbed out of his chair, stretched, groaned, snatched the ten euro note for Dillon's hand, and headed out the door.

Dillon waited a long moment then said, "He was really worried Aideen, had me racing across town to get here. He was gonna arrest everyone in the ER who wasn't giving him an answer."

"I know, I know. But for Christ's sake, take a look would you. It wasn't much of a picnic for the likes of me either, you know."

"What the hell happened?"

She slowly turned and looked out the window. "I was a stupid cow a few weeks back, and this is the thanks I get." She looked at Dillon. "Hey, I know, I made a mistake, a big mistake. Okay. I get it. So can we all just leave it alone?"

"Aideen, whoever did this, damn near killed you. In fact, if it weren't for your neighbor Dermot Dugan running over, you might be dead. Now, I don't know what you and Paddy have talked about, but this is our business. It's the sort of thing we have to deal with day in, and day out, and have for years. So let me just tell you something, if you think this is the end, you're wrong. The guy or guys who did this are laughing right now. Bragging. And they'll be back again. You know why? Let me tell you. They'll be back because there are no consequences. You don't tell your brother who did this or give a description, this isn't over, honey. Hell, it's just the beginning."

"You've just become this fuck's official punching bag. Every time he has a bad day, he's gonna show up at your door and take it out on you. And then, eventually, after you've been beaten up enough times that you look like shit and you've turned into a drunk or a druggy, then the only fun thing left for him to do is to kill you. If you're lucky, he'll drag your body up to the Dublin mountains and leave you in a ditch somewhere no one will find you."

A tear ran down from the eye that wasn't swollen closed.

"I'll, I'll leave Dublin, I'll go somewhere. Maybe to Australia."

"And he'll find you. He'll look for you, and one of your girlfriends will tell a friend who will tell a friend, and he'll know, and then he'll find you and kill you."

"Stop it. Stop it. You're sounding just like Paddy. You don't know. You don't—"

"Actually darling, the bad news is, we do know. Cause we see it all the time. You don't know, or more correctly, you don't want to know because you don't think it can get any worse. But your brother and I, we know it can. Right now you're the victim, don't become the corpse. You can stop this in its tracks. I know, and Paddy knows that you know who did this. You need to tell us before this gets any worse."

"If I tell you, then they'll do the same thing to you and Paddy. I'm not protecting the bastard that did this to me. I'm protecting you two."

TEN

Dillon wasn't back in the office two minutes when McCabe stepped out of his office door and called, "Marshal, a word please."

Dillon set down the three plates and the tea mug that had collected on his desk and hurried into McCabe's office.

"Take a seat, Marshal," McCabe said as he flashed a quick smile and closed the file on his desk. "First, give me an update on the Suel situation."

"Well, his sister is alive, more black and blue than not. Based on the evidence forensics recovered and what her neighbor told me, she was raped, but we haven't received a medical confirmation. She has three broken fingers, a fractured jaw, a temporary nose splint until the swelling goes down and they can get in there and do some repair work. Her right arm is in a sling. Her left eye is swollen shut. I don't know this, but she probably has a concussion, and just to round things off, she's at least as stubborn as her brother."

"How's he doing?"

"Frustrated, upset, which is about what's to be expected. I'd say she knows who did this, but she won't name the perpetrator. She's not going to press charges, or at least told us as much."

"And you and DI Suel explained things to her?"

Dillon nodded. "Yes sir, independently and together. She's a Suel, nothing if not stubborn. We both explained the scenario to her. This guy will be back for more and every time something goes wrong in his life, she's going to pay the price."

McCabe shook his head. "Damnit, what does it take. They think if they just remain quiet, it'll go away. All right, forensics?"

"They were there, got some blood samples, fingerprints from a broken glass. They're processing the evidence. It'll be three or four weeks before we have results and that's with a rush put on it. But, if she doesn't press charges—"

"We'll hold off on alerting them to that decision. After some time and reflection sometimes the victim comes around," McCabe said shaking his head.

Dillon shook his head knowing that particular scenario was only about five percent of the time. More often than not when the victim knew the perpetrator they arrived at the conclusion the beating was somehow their fault for setting him off in the first place, and so began the cycle that all too often eventually ended in someone's death.

"I did talk to the neighbor, a retired contractor by the name of Dugan. He saw the perp run out of the house though he wasn't able to identify him. He did give me a description of the taillights on the vehicle he drove off in, one of the taillights was out. Based on the description I'm guessing it's a pricey thing."

McCabe gave a long sigh, "All right, follow up on it. Oh," he said pulling a phone message from the top of a pile at the edge of his desk. "Had a brief chat with a friend of yours, Eric Bergman with the American embassy."

"Everything okay?"

"Depends on your point of view. Missing American student." McCabe said as he handed the phone message across the desk to Dillon. "Give him a call."

"We get at least one of these a month. It'll be some young girl. She'll either be in France, Italy or listening to session music in some pub after falling in love with a fiddle player."

"Hopefully that's all it is."

"Anything else, sir?"

McCabe shook his head, dismissed Dillon with a wave of his hand and reopened the file he'd been looking at earlier.

ELEVEN

Dillon went back to his desk and hauled the plates and now two tea mugs into the break room where he dumped everything into the sink. Once back at his desk he glanced at the number and phoned Eric Bergman at the US embassy. The number was his cellphone, and Bergman answered on the third ring.

"Bergman."

"Eric, Jack Dillon, returning a call you left with DCI McCabe."

"Just playing by the rules, Jack. I phoned McCabe and asked him to have you call me."

"Yeah, he mentioned a missing student. Amazing, first one this month. I'm guessing female. Where is she going to school?"

"She's at Trinity. Actually, we were contacted by the school. Roommates reported her missing. I've got a couple of pages of information. You free for an early dinner?"

Dillon thought about that for a moment and said, "Yeah, I could do that. Fallon and Byrne sound okay? Say half-past-five."

"Perfect, and I think it's my turn to buy."

"I'm sure it is and I'm kicking myself, should have suggested some pricey joint."

"Too late, my man, see you in a couple of hours."

Dillon hung up the phone and went online. He took out the sketch Dermot Dugan had made of the taillights. It took the better part of an hour but he found an exact match on a 2016 BMW M3 LCI. The vehicle was available in two dark colors, tanzanite blue and Azurite black. Retail price, depending, ran between fifty-seven and sixty-nine thousand euros for the 2018 model. Not exactly cheap, but certainly not the most expensive vehicle out there. He made some quick notes then headed into town. He took the long route, driving through Phibsboro. He pulled onto Shandon Gardens and parked in front of Aideen's home. It was still early enough in the day that most employed people would be at work. There was an older model car parked in front of the house next door. He wrote down the license number to check later, and guessed it probably belonged to Dermot Dugan. Up the street three young girls, looking to be maybe eleven or twelve, in grey school sweaters with plaid uniform skirts were jumping rope. On the far side of the canal a couple walked along the path as three ducks swam in their direction, no doubt hoping for food.

Crime scenes can be held for twenty-four hours and then receive a further forty-eight hour extension once an application has been made to the district court. That wasn't done in this instance and the house was available for Aideen to reenter whenever she wanted to. Dillon walked to the front door just to make sure the door was locked. It was. Other than the drops of blood every four or five feet along the sidewalk you'd never know a serious assault had taken place here early in the morning. It was just a nice quiet neighborhood, enough off the beaten path so you wouldn't drive through unless you were going to a specific destination.

Dillon pulled his phone out and pressed the number from a recent call.

"Mountjoy Garda station, how may I direct your call?" the woman answered and he immediately thought of Ciara Hogan, the officer who'd let him into Aideen's home earlier that morning.

"Umm, DI Brendan Walsh, please."

"One moment while I connect you."

Dillon listened to four rings then was dumped into a message center.

"You've reached DI Brendan Walsh at Mountjoy Garda Station. Please leave your name and number and I'll return your call as soon as possible."

Dillon left his name and number and then called the station again.

"Mountjoy Garda Station, how may I direct your call?" the same woman from a minute or two earlier answered.

"Ciara Hogan, please," he said trying to put on an Irish accent and at the same time lowering his voice.

"One moment while I connect you."

After another four rings he was dumped into her voice mail and immediately forgot what he was going to say. "Oh yeah, umm, Ciara, ahh Jack Dillon here, US Marshal. We met this morning at the scene on Shandon Gardens. Just touching base. If you could give me a call I would appreciate it." He disconnected then felt like kicking himself for making the call let alone sounding like such an idiot.

TWELVE

Fallon and Byrne was a trendy gourmet grocery store and food hall carrying all sorts of unique items and hundreds of wines. It had a fancy restaurant on the second floor and a trendy, less formal menu in the basement. Eric Bergman was waiting at a table sipping a glass of red wine when Dillon came down the basement stairs. The table was actually a large wine barrel and he gave Dillon a wave to catch his attention.

"Hi Eric, been a while. How are things?" Dillon said as they shook hands.

"You know the gig, same day different shit. How 'bout you?"

Dillon nodded. "Same, only even shittier," he said.

A waitress came over, smiled. "Something to drink sir?"

"I'll have whatever he's having," Dillon said.

Bergman raised his glass slightly and said, "A Pinot."

Dillon pulled out a stool and sat down. "Shall we get the business over first?"

Bergman pulled three pages stapled together from his inside coat pocket and handed it to Dillon. "Madeline Keller, age twenty, from Schleswig, Iowa. Her passport image is on the back page."

Dillon flipped to the back page, the image had been enlarged which made it even more bleary, but he still got a fairly decent sense of her. She had dark, shoulder length hair. Dark eyes, and what looked like a small mole just to the left of her mouth. The mole was mentioned in the two sentence listing of identifying characteristics along with a butterfly tattoo on the small of her back. He would have rated her as attractive. The sort of young woman you'd watch for a moment or two as she walked past.

"How long has she been missing?"

"Four days now," Bergman said which caused Dillon to look up. "She lives in a dormitory on campus with three roommates. They notified the school within twenty-four hours, the school, in its wisdom, waited another three days before they decided they might have a problem on their hands."

"Any circumstances that might point us in a direction."

"Broke up with a boyfriend, Colin Cominsky, about two weeks ago. The kid's from Belfast and has supposedly been up there for over a week. Father is a minister in Belfast, Church of Ireland, it's all in that report."

"You contact them?"

"Not yet. Thought there might be a little more urgency if the call came from you," Bergman said.

Dillon turned to the second page in the report listing a phone number and an address on Maryville Park in Belfast. Dillon was vaguely familiar with the area, referred to as lower Malone Road.

"Thanks, I'll check it out," Dillon said. "Most of these situations, they're with a new significant other or they get a wild hair and head off on their own to see the Eiffel Tower or Rome or something and didn't want their parents to know."

"Yeah, but that description doesn't ring true here. The roommates say they were all over in the Temple Bar area. The roommates want to head back to the dorm and Madeline decides to stay longer. Listening to some band at the Quays. You know the place?"

Dillon shrugged. "Yeah, music all day and into the night, place is jammed with tourists. Not exactly my choice, but big with the visitors. These roommates say anything, like she was with someone or there were others in the group or something? The Quays isn't all that far away, it's almost within sight of Trinity."

"Not aware of anyone else in the group, but to be honest, I only gave this a perfunctory look and determined it was out of my league. I'll email a copy of the full report over to you, it'll be waiting on your desk in the morning. We've got a congressional tour coming over in a few days to look at trade and I'm up to my eyeballs."

"A Congressional tour, talk about criminals," Dillon said and smiled.

"Don't get me started."

The waitress arrived with Dillon's wine. "Are you ready to order, gentlemen?"

"Haven't even looked at the menu," Bergman said.

"Just give me a wave whenever you're ready, enjoy the wine."

"Here's to you, Eric," Dillon said raising his glass.

"And you, good luck on that," Bergman said nodding at the sheaf of papers and clinking his glass against Dillon's. "I don't like the feel of this one."

THIRTEEN

Once they'd finished dinner Dillon walked two blocks to his car and drove home. He let Lucifer out, filled his food and water dish. Picked up everything from the kitchen wastebasket Lucifer had knocked over then took an orange tennis ball out into the front garden and tossed the ball for a good thirty minutes until Lucifer grew tired and laid down on the grass. They headed back in the house, Dillon pulled a dog biscuit from the cookie jar, tossed it to Lucifer then closed the door behind him and drove over to James's hospital. He parked in the parking ramp, which, at this hour of the evening was more empty than not and headed up to Aideen's room.

The curtains around three of the beds were pulled back. Two of the women appeared to be in their mid-forties. They were sitting cross legged on their beds, directly opposite one another, and chatting nonstop. Dillon pegged the third woman, directly across from Aideen, as maybe sixty. She had a cellphone up against her ear and was in the process of explaining that she had no idea when she would be released. The curtain surrounding

Aideen's bed was closed, sealing her off from the rest of the room.

Dillon nodded at the woman on the cellphone then cautiously peeked around Aideen's curtain. She was in bed, the bed was raised, and she had a frustrated look on her battered face as she stared at a distant corner of the curtain. Her brother was sitting in the green leather upholstered chair staring at the opposite corner of the room. Neither one said a word and the air felt heavy with tension.

"Oh, sorry, am I interrupting?"

Suel glared.

Aideen smiled and said, "Oh please, tell me you're going to take him home. It's like I don't have a bad enough headache, he's determined to add to it."

"I told you before, I'm not leaving until you tell me who did this. And if you don't tell me you're going to end up in traction and you can just think about what a stupid slapper you are while you lay here for the next month or two."

"Oh, so I see we're all getting along just fine," Dillon said.

They both glared at him and the tension seemed to increase.

"Paddy, come out in the hall with me for a minute."

"I'll be staying right here until this—"

"There, that helps, that's going to make me get better. I've been asking you to leave for the last four hours and you won't listen to me. Now I'm telling you, you stupid bollocks. Get the hell out." A tear ran down the right side of her cheek, a single tear, but only because her left eye was swollen shut.

"Paddy, step out in the hall with me, come on. I talked with McCabe and forensics."

The mention of forensics seemed to get Suel's attention and he groaned as he slowly stood from the chair. "Don't go anywhere," he said and pulled the curtain back, stepped out next to Dillon and yanked the curtain closed. The other three women in the room immediately grew quiet and stared as Dillon and Suel headed out into the hallway.

FOURTEEN

Suel said, "God save me, but I'm ready to strangle her. Not so much as a hint and I know she fecking knows the bastard that did this. She thinks she's keeping the world safe by not telling me, for Christ's sake," he shouted that last bit just loud enough that two nurses down the hall turned and stared for a long moment.

"Paddy, I understand you're upset, I'd want to kill if I were you. But, right now, that isn't helping. You keep this up and the hospital is going to restrict you from seeing her."

"Did you even hear what I just said? I said she fecking knows who in the hell did this and she's not telling. She's protecting the bastard, like that's going to help." His voice was raised and his face had taken on a deeper shade of red.

"Paddy, I'm not kidding you. Now, get ahold of yourself, and keep your voice down or they are going to call security and have you thrown out."

"I'd like to see the bollocks try."

"You need to go home, man."

"Were you even listening, I'm not leaving until I find out who in the hell did this and then—"

"And then what? You going to put him in the hospital? Kill him? Yeah, that'll help. Calm the hell down and listen to me. You get personally involved, and all you're going to do is screw up the investigation."

"They're not going to investigate, you stupid bastard. They'll write a damn report and it'll be out in a file and forgotten about. They probably haven't even cleared the initial—"

"Listen to yourself, you're crazy and you don't know what in the hell you're talking about. I was there at Aideen's. McCabe called a forensics team in and they were working the site this morning, taking photographs, gathering fingerprints, and blood samples. Mountjoy station has someone on it, DI Brendan Walsh. He's already interviewed neighbors and has a possible lead on a vehicle and the assailant. This is not going to be swept under the carpet. It's an assault that will be pursued and we'll get the bastard, provided you stay the hell away. You know I'm right here, Paddy, you've seen it yourself. Good people, with the best of intentions, get involved, compromise the situation, and end up ruining the investigation."

"She knows who the hell did this."

"Yeah, and if she tells you the only thing that's going to happen is you'll end up being charged with murder. You want to get this bastard? Go home and get some sleep and let us do our damn job. You look like shit, you've been up for almost forty-eight hours and you are not helping."

"There really was a forensics team?"

"Yeah. Three of them going over the place from top to bottom. Tommy Gibbons, Ciara Hogan and Noel something, but I didn't catch his last name."

"Probably Noel Haggerty, balding, sandy colored hair?"

"Yeah, sounds like him. They were gathering evidence, getting fingerprints, blood samples, they found a cigarette butt. It looks like someone put it out on the window sill in the sitting room. They got the butt, they'll do a DNA search. Looks like she might have slashed the guy with a broken wine glass. So the investigation, and there is one, is moving. The best way you can help is to go home, get some rest and come into the office tomorrow and get back on the cases we were working. We've got a missing student at Trinity we've got to get on, we still have to bring in Riley Dempsey, and I could sure use your help. Now, you need a ride home?"

Suel seemed to think about that for a long moment then shook his head. "No, I'll just grab a taxi."

"You sure? I'd be happy to give you a lift and—"

"What part of I'll take a taxi don't you understand?"

"Okay, good, just a word of caution. Don't even think about going to Aideen's place. The neighbors have all been interviewed, they see someone lurking around or going inside and they're going to call the Garda, you'll get nailed, and there goes the investigation. So please, just stay the hell away."

"You know, Dillon, sometimes you're a royal pain in the ass," Suel said and started to walk away. Then he turned, flashed a smile and said, "But thanks."

"You'd do the same for me, Paddy. Straight home now."

"I heard you the first damn time, ya bollocks. Good night," Suel said and headed down the hall. As he walked away he gave a wave without turning around.

FIFTEEN

D illon watched until Suel disappeared around the corner then headed back into the room. The conversation, now all three women talking to one another, came to an immediate halt. He pulled the curtain back and stepped in next to Aideen's bed.

She looked up, gave a disgusted sigh and after a long moment said, "So where's me pain in the hole brother?"

"He's grabbing a taxi and is going home."

"Bollocks will probably go out and get jarred at his local."

"Hey, Aideen, I know he can be a pain sometimes, but he's worried about you, and he's just looking out for—"

"He can just stay the hell away is what he can do. I didn't ask him to get involved."

"And he's not going to get involved."

"Says you. You've no idea how crazy he can get. He's going to insert himself and—"

"Stop it, Aideen. He's upset, and if you want the truth, he's furious with himself because he wasn't there to protect you."

"Protect me? I don't need that wanker's protection. I can take care of meself, and if you think for a moment he is in any way making me feel better you can just feck off with the likes of him, is what ye can do." She sort of adjusted her shoulders against the pillow and went back to staring in the corner.

Dillon was beginning to understand Suel's state of mind a little better. "Let me explain something to you, Aideen," he said in a calm, soft voice.

"Please don't bother, I'm sure I've already heard it from my fat head brother. And believe me, I'm painfully aware of what happened," her voice began to crack and more tears rolled down the right side of her cheek. "Are you so stupid you don't get it? I'm protecting Paddy, and you. Sure, I'll recover and the bastard will hopefully stay the hell away, but he'd like nothing better than to kill Paddy and the likes of you, too, Dillon. You've no idea what you're getting into. So for your own sake, just let it all go away. Please?"

"Aideen, listen to me," Dillon sat down on the edge of the hospital bed and gently placed a hand over Aideen's. "People like your brother and me, we deal with this sort of thing day after day. As terrible as it is for you, and believe me, it's terrible. But we know how this works and we've seen it a thousand times. We know that you know who did this. Let me tell you what's going to happen. He's going to come to you at some stage and say he's sorry. He'll send you flowers, maybe take you to dinner or buy you a new tv. Then he's going to say you shouldn't have made him do it. He's going to convince you it was really your fault. Your fault because of something you did that made him mad. He's going to promise it was the first and last time. And then, it's going to happen again."

"No, you don't know," she said and started sobbing.

"Yeah, actually we do. We deal with this shit all the time. And let me tell you something else. We've dealt with tougher people and we're still here to tell the story. You think you're protecting Paddy? He's been protecting you all these years."

She gave him a questioning look with her right eye.

"Yeah, that's right. You and everyone who thinks your brother is a fun guy, just an easy going, happy go lucky 'Mr. Party' sort of guy? You don't know the half of it. You don't know the sort of shit he's had to deal with. The lives he's saved and the lives he couldn't save. You know why? Because he didn't tell you. Didn't want to scare you. Didn't want to let you into the hell that is his life every single day. Wait," Dillon said in response to her looking like she was about to say something. "Don't say a word. I'm leaving in fifteen seconds and you can just think about everything. But as sure as I'm sitting here on your hospital bed I know whoever did this is going to come back. And, maybe not right away, but he will do this again. As beat up and busted up as you are, Aideen, you got off easy. And you, slashing his face, he's gonna pay you back, big time."

"How did you—?"

"Like I said, we deal with this all the time. Now you just rest up and you better think about how lucky you were, this time. You have a nice night."

SIXTEEN

A massive hand shook Dillon's shoulder and a rough voice said, "You stupid plonker. Were you here all night?"

Dillon blinked his eyes open and looked up at a clean shaven Paddy Suel. "Yeah, 'course they kicked me out of the room." He was stretched out on a bench in the corridor just outside of Aideen's room.

"Who can blame them?" Suel said. "All right, I'm back in five minutes with the coffee. Try and make yourself somewhat presentable in the meantime."

Dillon sat up, took the cushion he'd borrowed from a chair in the waiting room and handed it to Suel. "Might as well return this to its rightful owner." He cracked his neck back and forth and listened to it snap, crackle and pop.

"Jesus, but you're a piece of work," Suel said. He grabbed the cushion and headed down the hall. He was back ten minutes later with a steaming cup of coffee and a white paper bag filled with pastries. At the far end of the hall a woman rolled a cart stacked with food trays next to the nurses desk.

Dillon took a noisy sip of coffee, grimaced more from the heat than the taste and said, "You're looking like you're back up to almost fifty percent."

Suel raised his tea in a partial toast and said, "That put's me about forty-nine percent ahead of you. Hey, thanks for staying here, Jack. You didn't have to do that."

"Yeah, I did. If something happened to her I'd never be able to forgive myself. With all due respect, you were at the end of your rope on a number of different levels last night and you needed to get the hell out of here."

"You talk to her at all?"

"Little bit. She's been through a lot, Paddy. Anything like this ever happen to her before?"

"Not that I know."

"It's gonna take some time. I was probably a hell of a lot more understanding than you, but basically said this is just the first incident and she needs to think about that. Told her we were aware she slashed his face. Didn't tell her about the cigarette butt being put out on the window sill in the sitting room."

"So we're just supposed to sit here and wait."

"Sort of."

"Sort of? What the hell does that mean?" Suel said and slurped more coffee.

"It means I think we should tell the hospital they need to hold her for three or four more days. Give her time to think about it. Give forensics a chance to rush things through. In the meantime, we investigate the missing Trinity student and see if we can't drop a net over our friend Riley Dempsey."

"Let me go in and check on her," Suel said getting up.

"Be nice, Paddy, you get into it with her, it's just gonna drag everything out that much longer. I'm going down to the nurses station and see who we talk to so they can keep her here for a few more days."

SEVENTEEN

DCI McCabe asked, "Are they're going to keep her there?" He was seated behind his desk, three stacks of files, each about eight inches high rested on the outer edge of the desk acting like a wall, keeping Dillon and Suel, both seated in the chairs in front of the desk, from getting any closer to him.

Dillon glanced over and noticed that Suel was shaking his right knee up and down. Nervous energy.

"Doctor said they would keep her for another three days. Just as well, I know what she's like," Suel said. "She goes home, she'll be scrubbing and cleaning. This way she's got nothing to do but take it easy and recover in a safe environment."

"Security?" McCabe asked.

"We'll alternate late nights outside the room, Terry O'Shea is in charge of security at St. James, he promised to have someone do a pass by on a regular basis. We've alerted the nurses station, anyone visiting is supposed to check in with them. Other than my sister, Megan and the two of us, I can't see anyone visiting. Not the sort of hospital stay you'd want to advertise to friends."

"You satisfied with that?"

"I think it's the best we can do. Hope she'll calm down and either give us a name or the forensics search identifies the bastard," Suel said, his right knee had picked up speed.

McCabe nodded. "Our friend Riley Dempsey. What's the word?"

"Not much," Dillon said. "We're in touch with the woman who put us at the Cabra Club, hoping she might be able to give us another line. We'll get him. The other thing is this missing student, Madeline Keller. Come this evening she'll have been missing for five days. We've got an interview at Pearse Street Garda station later this morning with her roommates. Once that's completed, we're going up to Belfast to interview the boyfriend."

"Former boyfriend," Suel said.

"What the hell is he doing up in Belfast?" MaCabe said.

"He supposedly left Trinity after they broke up. He's from Belfast and is back home now with his parents. They agreed to let us talk to him, but only up there in Belfast. They don't want him coming back down here. The father plans on being in the room. I wish that wasn't the case, but I can understand his concern."

McCabe turned his chair about 90 degrees and nodded. "Mmm-mmm, can't say that I can blame him. The boy was a student?"

"Yeah, at Trinity, the kid's twenty, just a year older than the Keller girl. Claims to have broken up with her before she went missing. We'll see," Dillon said.

"You'll be back tonight?"

"Hopefully by late afternoon," Suel said.

McCabe exhaled loudly, rolled his chair up against the desk and reached for one of the stacks of files. "All right, best get going. We'll touch base in the morning."

EIGHTEEN

Dillon and Suel hurried out of the office. Suel drove them over to Pearce Street Garda Station, just across from Trinity College. The drive took three or four times longer than it used to. With the new Luas Line now running up and down O'Connell Street, they had to drive over to the Samuel Beckett Bridge to cross the Liffey. Once across the river, they drove up Cardiff Lane which two blocks later became Macken Street. They took a right onto Pearse Street past the Starry Night Chinese and Thai takeaway and over to Trinity College, almost within sight of the O'Connell Street Bridge. The Pearce Street Garda Station stood just across from Trinity College dormitories.

The Garda Station was built in 1915 and was originally known as the Great Brunswick Police Station. A three story granite structure with a slate roof and an archway entrance that features two carved heads of Dublin Metropolitan Police as they were known in 1915, wearing custodian helmets.

Suel backed into a parking place in front of the station. He turned the car off and placed an official looking notice on the dash with the An Garda Síochána logo in bold blue letters below the logo with the words, **'OFFICIAL BUSINESS'.**

"I always worry about using this thing," Suel said. "Like maybe we're just inviting some knacker to slit our tires or spray paint something dreadful on the side of the car."

"We're parked twenty feet from the front door of the station on a busy street. Has it ever happened?"

"Not yet, at least not here, but sooner or later it no doubt will," Suel said and opened the door. As they walked into the building he pressed the button on the ignition key, the horn honked, the lights flashed and the locks made an audible sound.

Suel had set it up with someone he knew and twenty minutes later they were waiting in a conference room on the second floor sipping tea. The windows in the room looked out onto Pearce Street. On the far side of the street was a five foot high block wall with a six foot wrought iron fence mounted on top. As they chatted they both kept an eye out for three girls heading toward the station. They had a paper plate of chocolate chip cookies set in the middle of the table, neither one was eating.

"I'll bet that's them waiting to cross," Dillon said and nodded at a half dozen girls, holding hands and standing opposite the Garda Station.

"I thought there were only three?"

Watch," Dillon said. As the traffic began to clear, the girls quickly hugged one another. Three of them hurried across Pearce Street toward the front door of the station and disappeared from view. The girls remaining on the far side of the street called out something, waved, then stood for a few seconds until one of them shook her head, and said something. They turned as one and headed back toward the college entrance.

Five minutes later Dillon and Suel could hear them coming down the hallway. A uniformed sergeant, Suel's friend, opened the door and ushered the three roommates in with a wave of his hand. Two dark haired girls and one blonde. Their hair was shoulder length and they were dressed conservatively in sweaters and slacks. Like all young women their age their makeup looked perfect.

"Thanks, Tommy," Suel said.

"Take all the time you need, Detective."

They had decided Dillon would do most of the talking, hopefully the American accent would help to calm them. "Ladies, thanks for joining us. Please grab a seat. Would any of you girls like a tea or a coffee?"

"No, thank you," they said almost as one.

Dillon slid the paper plate of chocolate chip cookies toward them. "Please, feel free to help yourself," he said as the girls sat down. One of the girls looked like she had been crying, another looked like she was about to cry, and the blonde girl was biting her lower lip. They all appeared stressed and nervous.

He pushed the button on the recording device and said, "Okay, we're going to tape this conversation so we can replay it to see if there is anything we missed. We're just talking here, this isn't a formal interview. We're just trying to learn as much as possible about Madeline and the night she disappeared."

The girls nodded as one.

"My name is Jack Dillon. I'm a US Marshal assigned to An Garda Síochána. This," he said pointing to Suel, "is Detective Inspector Paddy Suel with An Garda Síochána. We've been designated to help find Madeline Keller. We thought it might be best to talk to the three of you first since, as far as we know, you were the last ones to be with her and you probably are more familiar with her than just about anyone else."

"Now, who is Maggie White?"

"That's me," the dark haired girl who looked like she'd been crying said.

"Okay, and Maureen McGrane?"

The girl who looked about to cry sort of raised her right hand but didn't say anything. She quickly put her hand down, grabbed her left hand and hung on tightly.

"And you're Emily Fischer?" Dillon said to the blonde girl.

"Yes, sir."

"I want to let you know, you are not in any trouble. We just want to get whatever information you might have so that we can find Madeline. We may be asking you the same questions a few times, just to make sure we understand, so please, be patient with us," Dillon said and smiled.

"Is Maddy going to be all right?" This from Maureen.

"We're going to do our best to make sure she is."

They asked the girls questions. How they met? How long had they been in Dublin? The usual sorts of questions followed by the usual sorts of answers. As they talked the chocolate chip cookies gradually began to disappear. Unfortunately, nothing unique came from the conversations. All three girls, along with Madeline, were studying Global Business, working toward a Bachelor's degree in Business Studies. They did not know one another prior to arriving at Trinity and were randomly chosen from the group of American students to share one of the student housing units accommodating four students.

Her roommates called Madeline, Maddy. The night she disappeared she was wearing blue jeans and a silk tank top with spaghetti straps, either white or grey, they weren't sure which. She had on white Nike shoes, with a pink Nike swoosh logo on either side of the shoe. She carried a denim purse with red lining. They all identified her in the passport picture Dillon had printed off and confirmed that she had a butterfly tattoo on the small of her back although they couldn't agree on whether the butterfly wings were orange or yellow.

They left her at the Quays Pub following a discussion. The three girls wanted to return to the dormitory, Madeline had changed her mind and decided to remain at the Quays. Yes, they'd been drinking, but all three insisted no one was intoxicated. They were drinking half pints of Guinness, and they agreed Madeline had two half pint glasses over the course of nearly three hours. They were adamant that an argument had not ensued over staying or leaving. It wasn't the first time they'd gone out together and returned to their rooms separately. They had attempted to call Madeline over the last four or five days and had at first been dumped into her voice mail. The last three days they'd received the message the cell was not in service, suggesting a dead battery.

All three pulled out their cellphones and showed various pictures of Madeline. Dillon had them send the images to his official email address.

Two of the pictures also included her former boyfriend, Colin Cominsky. A ginger haired young man with a neatly trimmed beard. The night she disappeared, Madeline had informed the girls she had ended her relationship with Cominsky. They apparently had broken up a few days earlier after he had left Trinity the week before. She had alluded to Cominsky's being involved in an affair with another girl, although she didn't go into detail. She did not tell them the girl's name and they didn't know if she was a student at Trinity. Other than the additional photos and the news of an affair leading to the breakup, they didn't learn much. They took the girls cellphone numbers, handed out their business cards to each of the girls and hurried over to Connolly Station, making the train to Belfast Central Station with two minutes to spare.

NINETEEN

As the train pulled out of Connolly Station Suel folded a copy of the Irish Times on his lap, and asked, "Any thoughts?"

"About the girls? I'd say this disappearance is probably all they've talked about for the better part of the week. The fact that they were escorted to Pearce Street by friends suggests the situation has been all consuming. The boyfriend's affair with another girl is interesting, but I don't get why that would cause this Cominsky kid to go back home. You think Madeline may have threatened him? Maybe she was going to confront the girl?"

"Possible, a girl that age, or the lad for that matter."

"How about this? Maybe he was playing both of them. Somehow Madeline finds out, breaks up with him, threatens him, tells him she's going to contact the other girl, and he decides he can't let that happen."

"Or maybe she hopped on a ferry and is taking her picture in front of the Eiffel Tower right now with some handsome French lad and she's going to send him the photo," Suel said.

Dillon felt his cellphone vibrating and pulled it out of his pocket. Eric Bergman. "Hang on, maybe this is something," he said to Suel. "Hello, Eric."

"Hi, Jack. You free to talk?"

"Yeah, I'm on the train with Paddy Suel, we're heading up to Belfast. We're conducting an informal interview with Colin Cominsky, the former boyfriend of Madeline Keller."

"How former?"

"Sounds like maybe a week or so before she disappeared. We spoke with her three roommates this morning."

"And?"

"And not much, at least at this stage. We got a description of the clothes she was wearing, learned a little about a romantic break up. We already had the appointment with the boyfriend scheduled so it's a little added information. You calling just to check in or did you have something?"

"Little of both, Jack. We got word Mr. and Mrs. Keller will be on a flight arriving early tomorrow morning. They'll be staying at the Westin Hotel."

"Right near Trinity."

"Yeah. I haven't spoken with them. Obviously, they're going to be distraught. Would you be able to give them some semblance of a briefing, let them know we're doing everything we can?"

Dillon exhaled into the phone, he understood the situation. For God's sake, their daughter had gone missing, not to mention missing in a foreign country. It was just that he didn't have anything to really tell them. "I can meet with them, Eric, but I don't know how much I'll have to tell them. About all we know so far is that she's missing."

"Yeah, I get that. I guess this is more a case of a little hand holding."

"How does late afternoon sound? Give them a chance to rest up after the flight and—"

"Actually, I was thinking more like right at the airport."

"The airport?"

"Look, their daughter is missing and they're flying halfway around the world to see what's happened. You really think they're going to want to take a nap and have a leisurely lunch before they meet with us?"

"Eric, we got jack shit to tell them."

"I'm going to meet them at the airport, if you could be there, give 'em even ten or fifteen minutes and just let them know you're doing everything possible. Can you do that?"

"Yeah, I can, where and when?" Dillon said, resigned to the request.

"Thanks, I'll owe you. Let's say half past eight, the Garda offices in Terminal Two. I'll have someone on standby to rush them off to their hotel after twenty minutes."

"Okay, after that I'm going to head to Trinity and go through the girl's room. Probably don't mention that to them."

"You looking for anything in particular, Jack?"

"Yeah, a signed letter telling us not to worry, she just went to Paris. No, nothing's standing out, more a case of just due diligence, checking the box off."

"Okay, see you at the airport tomorrow, and Jack, thanks, much appreciated."

"See you tomorrow."

"Problem?" Suel said.

Dillon shook his head. "No, just an unpleasant undertaking. The girl's parents are flying in tomorrow morning and, unless something changes, I'm going to have to tell them we're pursuing every available lead and we got shit."

"Want me to go with you?"

"I got a better idea. While I'm at the airport, why don't you pay an early morning visit to Trinity and go through the girl's room. I'll catch up with you once I talk with the parents."

"You looking for anything in particular?"

"Like I told Bergman, just a signed letter telling us not to worry, she's in Paris."

A voice came over the loud speaker announcing they would be pulling into Belfast Central in fifteen minutes. Suel flashed a quick smile, pulled out his phone and hit a speed dial number. "Inspector Ronnie Maxwell, please. Paddy Suel. Yes, I'll hold." He looked over at

Dillon and raised the phone away from his mouth. "Friend in the Seirbhís Póilíneachta Thuaisceart Éireann."

"What the hell are you talking about? You know damn well I can't speak Irish except to ask for a pint."

"PSNI, just giving him a heads up we're here unofficially. Any problem develops down the road we can demonstrate we contacted them. Not to worry, I've done the same for him a time or two. Couple years back I—. Ronnie, Paddy Suel. Yeah, right. Say, just wanted to touch base. I'll be in Belfast later today talking to a lad informally. No, nothing like that. Missing student at Trinity College. An American student. We interviewed her roommates, the lad's name came up. Just going through the motions. To be honest we've nothing to go on, and anything he can tell us would help. No, thanks for the offer. What? No, nothing like that. I'll be talking to him in his parents' home. Lad's a college student, good grades. Oh, that's nice of you, but this is going to be short and sweet, hope to be on the four o'clock back down to Dublin. Oh, grand. Some other time then, I think it's your turn to buy. What? Well then forget the offer," he laughed and disconnected.

"Everything okay?" Dillon said.

"Yeah, except it's my turn to buy. I doubt we'll need it, but I wanted to be on record that we touched base. If a problem arises, he'll provide cover. If your lad happens to confess when we walk in the door we can call Ronnie and he'll step in for us."

"And you worked with him before?"

"We worked together on a series of cross border bank robberies maybe six or seven years ago. Group of four plonkers coming down from Armagh and robbing businesses in Monaghan. Small towns like Glaslough, Mullan and Carrickroe. We finally got them, caught them in the act in Emyvale, they were in the process of robbing a credit union. Ronnie Maxwell had them under surveillance, followed them on a back road right up to the border. We nailed all four of the bollocks, not a shot fired, no one hurt. Due in large part to Ronnie working with us. We've been friends ever since. You'd like him, Dillon, he even buys the occasional pint."

TWENTY

They arrived at Belfast Central Station right on time, twenty minutes before two. Then taxied to the Lower Malone Road neighborhood in Belfast.

Along the way Suel asked, "Anything in mind on how you want to play this?"

Dillon shook his head. "Play it by ear, again let me do the talking, at least until we get a feel. The father's going to be in there. Just from the brief conversation with him on the phone, I got the impression it's been an awful long time since he made a mistake. Apparently he's an ordained minister, so he's used to pointing the finger at others, telling them they're sinners and should repent."

"Here we are, 92 Maryville Road," the taxi driver said in a hard northern accent. He pushed a button on a small box attached to the dash and a red digital readout of the charge flashed, £23.90.

Suel pulled out two pound sterling notes from his wallet, a twenty and a five. He grabbed the receipt and said, "Keep the change," as he climbed out of the back seat.

Dillon tossed a five Euro note into the front passenger seat.

"Thanks, Yank," the driver said and smiled.

"You give that bollocks more?" Suel said as he watched the taxi travel down the road.

"Somehow, I didn't think one pound was a very generous tip."

"Damn near twenty-five pounds for not even a twenty minute ride. I'm keeping the receipt."

Suel turned and stared at the century old house in front of them, easily three times the size of their homes. The house was a three story brick structure with a black slate roof, an elegant front entrance, and buff colored stone trim around all the windows. Two large chimneys stood on either end of the house and three steps led up to a semi-round stone porch. A large oak tree shaded the better half of the front garden. A black, wrought iron fence, that appeared to be original to the house and maybe six feet high, ran along the front sidewalk.

"Nice to see how the other half lives," Suel said. "The man's supposed to be a minister, so much for the vow of poverty."

The iron gate squeaked as they opened it. They climbed the front steps, and when Dillon rang the doorbell they could hear it chiming inside. The front door appeared to be quarter sawn oak and maybe a hundred years old. After a moment a woman, perhaps late forties or early fifties, opened the door. She was dressed in a plain black dress with a white apron, she clasped her hands together, flashed a smile for a half second and said, "May I help you?"

"Yes, we've an appointment to speak with Colin Cominsky and his father, Ian. I'm US Marshal Jack Dillon."

"DI Paddy Suel," Suel added.

Another nanosecond smile. "Yes, of course, the gentlemen from the south. Please come in. They're all waiting in the library."

As she turned to walk across the entryway Suel glanced at Dillon and mouthed, 'All?'

Dillon simply shrugged.

The polished oak floor creaked as they passed the carved staircase. A framed oil painting of a balding white haired man in a black robe holding what appeared to be a Bible hung on the wall halfway up the staircase. Suel shot a look at Dillon and rolled his eyes. They walked past the entrance to a large sitting room with a sliding door embedded in the wall, farther down the hall a similar entrance led into an elegant dining room and beyond that was an eight paneled oak door, closed.

The woman knocked on the door, then took hold of the antique brass doorknob and opened the door.

Three individuals were in the room seated around a massive antique desk. A young, ginger haired man with a beard, presumably Colin, half nodded and swallowed nervously. Seated next to Colin was a man in an expensive looking grey suit, a red tie, and a starched white shirt. His head was tilted at a slight angle and his eyes moved over Dillon and Suel, as if taking in details.

Behind the massive desk sat a balding man with shoulder length white hair. The same man in the painting on the staircase wall. He was dressed all in black, with the exception of a white clerical collar. He focused in on Dillon and Suel through gold frame wire rim glasses, but he wasn't studying, he was glaring.

"Gentlemen, please come in, come in," the man in the grey suit said as he rose from his chair and stepped towards them with an extended hand. "Nice to meet you both, I'm Cal."

"Paddy Suel, pleased to make your acquaintance." Suel said and shook his hand.

"And you must be the American, Dillon is it?"

"Yes, Jack Dillon nice to meet you."

"This is Reverend Cominsky," Cal said extending a hand in the general direction of the man seated behind the desk. "And, his son, Colin."

Colin nodded nervously and in a soft voice said, "Pleased to meet you." The reverend continued to glare.

"I'm wondering, Ian, if we all wouldn't be more comfortable sitting over here. Gentlemen," he said directing Dillon and Suel over to a brown leather couch. Two wingback chairs were arranged opposite the couch with an antique coffee table positioned in the center. A Bible with a worn black leather cover sat on the edge of the coffee table and beneath the Bible, a manila file folder. The table had a one inch slab of marble on the top and brass ornamentation around carved legs.

"That only suits for the purpose of—" Ian began to say, but Cal cut him off.

"I think we'll all be more comfortable over there. Colin, if you'd be so kind as to bring your chair over."

Colin immediately stood and carried his client chair from in front of the desk over toward the coffee table, placing it between the two wingbacks and opposite the couch.

"Gentlemen, please," Cal said indicating the couch. "Ian, are you thinking of joining us?"

Dillon and Suel stepped over and sat down. Suel flashed a quick glance as they sat down and sank into the couch, to the point where their legs were almost even with their chest. Ian and Cal settled into the wingback chairs, easily three inches higher.

"Before we begin, let us ask for Christ's blessing," Ian said. He, Cal and Colin bowed their head, Dillon did the same. Suel exhaled just loud enough for Dillon to hear. "May the God of Jacob protect us. May he send us help from his Temple and give us aid from Mount Zion. May he accept all our offerings and be pleased with all our sacrifices. May he give you what you desire and make all our plans succeed. Then we will shout for joy over our victory and celebrate our triumph by praising our God. Amen."

Once everyone raised their head. Suel waited a second or two before he made the sign of the cross, causing Ian's face to grow three shades redder.

Cal quickly jumped in. "So, gentlemen, you have some questions. How may we be of assistance?"

TWENTY-ONE

D illon asked, "Colin, what can you tell us about your relationship with Madeline Keller?"

"Well—"

"They were simply college friends," his father interjected.

"Colin?" Dillon said.

"We met a couple of days before classes started. I'd taken classes over the summer term, biology and a third year chemistry class. Once those were completed, it was just two weeks before the new term began, so I decided to remain on campus."

"You were in one of the dormitories?"

"Yes, I was in the Pearse Street dorm."

"Roommates?"

"No, sir. I had an ensuite single room."

"And you met Madeline Keller?"

"It's a college, for God's sake, he met a lot of people, and a lot of people met this Keller girl," his father said.

"Why don't we let Colin tell us?" Cal said and nodded at Colin to continue.

"Okay. So, international students arrive two weeks in advance of the term. Just as I finished my summer classes they were beginning to come in. The school hosts tours to get them acquainted with Dublin. You know, where things are on and off campus, transportation, tourist sites like the GPO, Stephens Green, National Art Museum, Dublin Castle, that sort of thing. In the evenings the school had a social hour and that's where I met her."

"It sounds like it could be a lot of fun, great opportunity to meet people from all over."

Colin nodded. "Yeah, Trinity encourages the upper class students to attend the social hours. You know, just to help the international kids get more acquainted and involved so they don't become isolated."

"Was her room in the same dorm as yours?"

"Madeline's room? No. She's in Goldsmith Hall, four or five to a room."

Dillon made note of the fact Colin used the present tense. "And you had a private room?"

"Conducive to study and the grades Colin obtains," his father said.

Cal shot Ian another look.

"So you met at one of the social hours?"

"He just finished telling you, if you'd listened," Ian said.

"Ian, you're only making this interview run longer and in the process inadvertently casting dispersions on Colin. It would be best if you remained quiet, please. If you continue to interrupt and interject I'm going to insist that you leave the room." Cal said, raising his voice. "Pardon me, please continue Mr. Dillon."

Ian sat back in his chair, red faced, chest heaving as though he'd just run a race.

"You were telling us you met at one of the social hours," Suel said, and smiled. Ian's face grew even redder still.

"Yes, sir. It was a pleasant evening and this particular social hour was held out on Fellows' Square, just in front of the Lecky Library, if you know where that is."

Suel nodded as if to say, of course, everyone knew where the Lecky Library was. "Lot of people at that social hour?"

Colin looked up to his left, thinking. "Mmm-mmm no more than other nights, but they were always well attended. People throwing frisbees on the green, the school always had tables set up, sweets and something to drink." He glanced at his father. "No alcohol, just tea, coffee, some sparkling water. There were maybe a hundred and fifty, two hundred foreign students and about a hundred or so of us upper class students."

"Wow, all those people and you were able to pull her out of a crowd, pretty good," Suel said.

"Actually, nothing like that. I was talking to some mates, when some plonker missed the frisbee he was supposed to catch and it hit Madeline, surprised her, and her tea spilled onto my back. I thought it was funny, but she was mortified which made it even funnier. No big deal. So then, as things are winding down she comes up to me and said she and a gang were going into Temple Bar and did I want to come? I figured why not, no classes the next day so I told her I'd go change my shirt and catch up with the likes of them. We ended up chatting the rest of the night away and I walked her back to her dorm room at the end of the night." He looked over at his father. "She and her roommates, so I walked the four of 'em home. The next morning at breakfast she sat down at my table."

"You must have thought she was a nice girl, if you talked to her over the course of the evening and walked her home," Dillon said.

"Yeah, she's very nice," Colin replied and Dillon again made note of the present tense.

They continued, Dillon and Suel, asking general questions, getting a sense of the relationship between the two students. After the better part of an hour, they had a pretty good idea of the two.

"So, from everything you've said, things seemed to be going very well for you and for Madeline. Why'd you leave Trinity?" Dillon asked.

"Two reasons, I'd a girlfriend here in Belfast, Dawn Davies, and six weeks into the term I received a letter from Queen's University here in Belfast. I'd been accepted into their medical program."

"So you want to be a doctor?"

Colin nodded.

"And your girlfriend, Dawn?"

"Dawn Davies, yes, I see her every day," Colin said and smiled. "As a matter of fact, I usually visit her just about now. Would you like to come with?"

"All right, that's just about—"

"Ian, it's fine, now not another word. Gentlemen, I was going to drive Colin over to see Dawn. If you'd care to join us you're more than welcome. If you have no further business and you're satisfied, I would be happy to drop you at Belfast Central afterward. Provided we've answered all your questions."

Dillon looked at Suel who gave a slight nod.

TWENTY-TWO

Almost Everyone smiled. Dillon and Suel received a frosty goodbye from Reverend Ian Cominsky who never bothered to rise from his chair. Colin pulled the manila file from beneath the Bible on the coffee table. They walked out to the street with Cal and Colin leading the way and climbed in the back of Cal's four door Mercedes, a dark green Maybach S-class. It wasn't that long a drive and Dillon and Suel kept up the conversation with Colin. The tension had definitely diminished since they left the reverend back in the library, fuming.

Off to the right, Dillon saw a two story house of dressed stone. It appeared to be about two hundred years old standing more or less by itself behind a long wrought iron fence. He was about to ask what it was when they took a right and drove in through the gates of the Belfast City Cemetery and past the house.

"Where are we going? I thought we were going to meet Dawn Davies," Suel said.

"We are," Cal said glancing at Dillon and Suel in the rearview mirror.

"She died about three weeks ago, ovarian cancer," Colin said. "It's been crazy ever since. They'd given her another year back in July, but she just slipped away in the middle of the night. We'd known one another since we were kids. I always told her she was my first love. She died, and two days later I got the letter from Queen's, telling me I'd been accepted. I'm making it my life's goal to find a cure for ovarian cancer so other people don't have to go through this."

"Did you tell Madeline this?" Suel asked.

"She didn't really give me the chance. She just focused in on Dawn's name and became more and more upset. When she started shouting, I just left. I was pressed for time, and she wouldn't answer my phone calls. Her roommates said she didn't want to talk to me. I figured I would just let her calm down and after a couple of weeks contact her. Now this bit of shite, she's missing."

The tombstones were black and white marble, positioned about four inches apart for as far as they could see. Further along on a rise, there looked to be a number of memorials. Cal stopped the car, Colin got out and Dillon and Suel followed.

Colin wove his way through a maze of headstones and memorials and stopped at a fresh grave. There was no grass, just earth obviously filled in recently, mounded slightly and covered with peat moss. There were three areas where it looked like something had dug in the dirt, possibly dogs. Colin looked frustrated at the digging and used his foot to kick the soil back onto the mound then gently tamped it down. He straightened a simple wooden cross that had been painted white and inserted in the dirt.

"I made this. It's just a temporary thing, you know, until they get the headstone. People and their stupid dogs. They let them run off the leash in the cemetery, even though they're not supposed to. The things just make a mess. We have to wait a couple more weeks until the soil settles before they can put the headstone in. I want to be here for that." Colin said and shook his head. "She was always kind to everyone, especially me. She was my best friend. It's just such a waste."

He bowed his head and appeared to say a short prayer then looked up and smiled. "Anything else you guys need to know? Sorry about my father interrupting, he's always been like that, and after a while you just learn to deal with it."

Dillon looked at Suel and shook his head.

Once they were in the car and headed toward Belfast Central, Cal said, "Colin, why don't you hand them that file."

Colin passed the manila file back to Dillon, and he opened it. The file held an envelope of kraft paper, large enough to hold documents with a string on the flap wrapped around a red cardboard button.

"I took the liberty to copy Colin's termination letter to Trinity College, his acceptance letter from Queen's University, the name and address of the pub he was in up here in Belfast the night the Keller girl went missing, the

Empire Pub. I've included sworn statements from the three mates he was with, all attesting to his activities and whereabouts on that evening. I've included their addresses and phone numbers should you wish to contact them. A fourth lad, Darren Otis left early, I've listed his name in the file, but did not request a statement. I've also taken the liberty of including my card. Should you have any questions, we would appreciate it if you went through me," Cal said as he pulled to the curb in front of Belfast Central. "Thank you, gentlemen. It's been a pleasure. If you hurry you can make your train."

Dillon didn't know what to say, so he said, "Thank you, both. Cal, it was nice to meet you. Colin, wishing you all success in med school and your endeavor. It's been interesting."

He and Suel climbed out of the car then stood on the sidewalk and watched until the car disappeared.

Suel shook his head and said, "What the feck?"

"I'd say your man was more than ready for us," Dillon said.

TWENTY-THREE

Suel took a final sip from his whiskey glass and asked, "You don't think it was a setup?" They had seated themselves in the club car before the train had even left Belfast Central.

"I think they were obviously prepared to meet with us. I'd say Cal probably coached Colin. As a matter of fact, I'm not so sure the right reverend wasn't putting on an act as well. Cal probably coached him, too." Dillon looked at the business card that had been included in the file. It read, 'Calvert Cominsky'. Cal was most likely the reverend's younger brother and a barrister with one of the more prestigious law firms in the entire UK.

"Coached the reverend? What? To act like a right bollocks? He certainly didn't need any coaching there, he's got that act down pat," Suel said and started punching keys on his cellphone.

"He's included names, addresses and phone numbers from three individuals, not to mention their sworn statements that the kid was up in Belfast the night Madeline disappeared. Shuts everything down nice and tight."

"Jesus, a hundred and thirty seven thousand euros. Amazing," Suel said looking up from his cellphone shaking his head.

"What are you talking about?"

"Your man's car, that Mercedes Maybach. The damn things run a hundred and thirty-seven thousand euros. For God's sake, I only paid sixty for my entire house just eighteen years ago."

"Yeah, and you haven't updated anything since."

"All I'm saying," Suel said, hitting the file envelope with a flip of his hand. "It sure seems to be wrapped up and air tight on their end. Plus the request that we contact him first from here on in, should we want to talk to your lad. Good Lord, no one has even been charged. Be prepared for a registered letter to arrive in the next twenty-four hours stating that exact fact, that we contact him first."

"What do you think of the way the kid answered the questions?"

"Well, if he ever went off script I can't recall when. He was coached, he obviously practiced, and in the end he did a credible job. Maybe just a little too credible for my tastes."

"What are you saying?"

"The girl in the cemetery, this Dawn Davies, she was supposed to have died three weeks ago, right?"

Dillon nodded.

"I went back and checked while they drove us to the station, and up until today, I can't find an obit for the girl anywhere. I've checked the Belfast Telegraph and the Irish News, nothing," Suel said and held his phone up to Dillon. The screen displayed a search for the Dawn Davies obituary with a reply stating no information was available and offering a half dozen alternative spellings. None of the suggested spellings came even remotely close to the spelling Suel had copied from the file Calvert Cominsky had provided.

"So you're thinking we were played?"

"I'm thinking there's a chance. I'm also thinking your man Calvert is nobody's fool. So where does that leave us?"

"I guess it leaves me making phone calls to Belfast City Cemetery tomorrow morning to find out exactly who is buried in that plot. There is the chance the family, or whoever the survivors are, simply didn't want to spend the money. On the other hand . . ."

"On the other hand, before I go through the Keller girl's dorm room I've got to run over and deal with Aideen at James's."

"I thought she wasn't getting out for another few days?"

"That doesn't mean I can ignore her, she's my sister, for God's sake."

"Given that attitude I'm sure she'll be looking forward to your arrival."

"I want to check her home, too. Just to make sure it's locked up nice and secure."

"Just check the locks, Paddy. Don't be going in there until I catch up with you. We'll go in together and maybe see what we can find. Maybe check in with Aideen first thing, that way if we come across anything in Madeline's room we can jump on it."

"That was my plan, all along. And you're meeting with the American parents?"

"Yeah, at the airport, Terminal Two Garda office at 8:30. I didn't think it was possible, but I feel like now we've got even less to tell them than before we went to Belfast."

TWENTY-FOUR

They climbed into Suel's car parked a block away from Connelly Station. Suel drove up Drumcondra before either of them spoke.

"Once I finish up at the airport with the Keller's I'll give you a call. I'm curious to see the dorm room, shouldn't be much past nine. Will that give you enough time with your sister?"

"You're worried about the likes of her? What about me? She's me driven demented with the ranting and raving," Suel said as he turned off Drumcondra and headed down Griffith Avenue.

"I want to pay special attention to anything that might suggest Colin Cominsky."

"Oh, really? Now, why would that be?" Suel said. "If there's a laptop or a phone we'll be grabbing them, plus the usual, medications, letters, possible photos."

"Let's remember to leave it looking nice. The parents will most likely be there sometime tomorrow."

"Don't I always," Suel said. He passed by DCU, Dublin City University, then took a left off Ballymun Road at the Eurospar. He drove down St. Pappin's Road, took the second left onto Dean Swift Road and pulled to a stop in front of Dillon's. "I wished we'd gotten more up there in Belfast," Suel said.

"I wish we'd gotten something, anything," Dillon said then slapped the file envelope from Calvert Cominsky across Suel's arm. "Guess this will just have to do at least for the time being. See you in the morning and thanks for the lift."

"Thanks for the warning," Suel laughed then drove off down the street and around the corner.

Dillon unlocked the front door, and carefully stepped inside. He turned on the hallway light expecting to find a deposit from his dog, Lucifer, but the hallway was clean. He walked into the kitchen, set the wastebasket upright, picked up the paper napkins, paper towels, the egg carton, a plastic bag that had held sausage, bits and pieces of two takeout Styrofoam trays along with a small pizza box and put them back in the wastebasket. He walked back out in the hallway and called up the staircase, "Lucifer. Oh Lucifer, come on outside."

He didn't hear a reaction.

He walked back into the kitchen, took the lid off the cookie jar that held the dog biscuits, pulled a biscuit out then clinked the top on the cookie jar a few times. He heard Lucifer jump off the bed upstairs and land on the bedroom floor.

"Lucifer. Come on down for a biscuit," he called and the dog suddenly appeared at the top of the stairs, took one look at Dillon holding the dog biscuit and hurried down the stairs. Dillon opened the front door and tossed the biscuit out into the garden. Lucifer shot past him, leapt off the front stoop and grabbed the biscuit on the first bounce.

Dillon closed the door, walked into the kitchen and opened the refrigerator. Dinner choices appeared to be a half-eaten pizza, leftover chow mein, or a piece of lasagna that he couldn't quite recall when he'd put it in the refrigerator. He decided on the pizza, placed the three pieces in the microwave, and called Lucifer in from the front garden.

He filled Lucifer's food and water dish, placed the pizza on the kitchen counter, opened the file envelope from Calvert Cominsky and proceeded to eat and read. He was in bed before eleven and slept the night through until his alarm went off just before six the following morning.

He let Lucifer out the front door, sipped a cup of coffee and did an internet search on Calvert Cominsky, coming up with nothing but glowing reports on the internet.

He let Lucifer back inside then climbed in his car and headed out to Dublin Airport dreading the meeting that was about to take place.

TWENTY-FIVE

Dillon arrived at Dublin airport's Terminal Two Garda Station twenty minutes early, only to find Eric Bergman and the Keller's already waiting for him in the conference room.

He watched them through the window for a long moment, a distraught couple holding each other's hand as Bergman appeared to be doing his best to calmly explain the little they knew thus far. Unfortunately, Dillon had nothing more to offer. He knocked on the door and stepped in.

"Oh, perfect timing, here he is now," Bergman said as a wave of relief washed over his face. "Marshal Dillon, these are Madeline's parents, Lois and Arthur Keller. They've just arrived."

Madeline's father rose to his feet and shook hands with Dillon. He was a stout man, not fat, but solid, possibly from labor. His hand was as hard as a brick, although he gave a gentle squeeze to Dillon. He had blonde hair, greying a bit, but not thinning, and neatly combed back. His eyes were blue and his skin was tanned. Dillon figured he might work construction or, coming from Iowa, possibly he was a farmer.

Madeline's mother didn't stand. She held on tightly to her husband's left hand with both of hers. Her brown eyes were red rimmed and Dillon noticed the crumpled tissues on the table in front of her. Her clothes had the appearance of having been worn for the last few days. Her brown hair hung limply and needed a wash, she wore no makeup. When introduced by Bergman she only blinked at Dillon and gave a slight nod. Given her appearance, it was quite possible she had been medicated.

"Please, have a seat, Marshal," Bergman said, and all three men sat down.

Dillon didn't ask how their flight was or wait for a question, instead he went right into the heart of the matter. "As you probably know, my partner and I traveled to Belfast yesterday to speak with Colin Cominsky, a boy who met Madeline when she arrived at Trinity. We were in Belfast because that's where Colin's parents live. It's where he was raised."

"But why is he up there if school is in session here?" Arthur said.

"That was one of the many questions we had. Colin was a chemistry and biology major at Trinity. He had a friend in Belfast, a girl named Dawn Davies, they've—"

"Oh, no, no. Madeline was taken advantage—" Lois sobbed. She let go of Arthur's hand and brought both hands up to her mouth.

"No, that does not seem to be the case. The Davies girl and Colin have been friends since they were small children. She was a couple of years older than Colin. She was diagnosed with ovarian cancer two and a half years ago. She was undergoing treatment and had recently been given another year to live. Unfortunately, she passed away in her sleep just a few weeks ago."

A tear ran down Lois Keller's face.

"A month or so prior to her passing, Colin had applied to Queen's University in Belfast for their premed program. He told us he was dedicating himself to finding a cure for ovarian cancer. He received his acceptance two days after Dawn Davies passed away. From our initial investigation, it appears they, Dawn and Colin, had a best friend platonic relationship. We received documentation from Colin's attorney corroborating the application and acceptance to Queen's University along with Colin's letter withdrawing from Trinity."

"But he could have come back—"

"On the night Madeline went missing, he was with three individuals who have provided sworn statements that they were together for the entire evening in Belfast. We've not interviewed these individuals as of yet, we will, in the next day or two. But that is where we stand at this moment as far as Colin Cominsky is concerned."

"Additionally, we've given preliminary interviews to Madeline's roommates. They corroborated the fact that Madeline was with them listening to music at a pub in the Temple Bar district called the Quays. The area is very close to Trinity college. The Quays is a popular tourist destination and has security on the premises. All of the girls stated that they wished to return to their dorm rooms and Madeline opted to stay. They informed Trinity College that Madeline was missing and, eventually, the school informed us."

"Where do you go from here? What other leads do you have?" Arthur Keller said.

"At this stage we're going to double check the Belfast information we received. We'll be meeting with people at Trinity later this morning. We're looking into a couple of other possibilities, but nothing remotely concrete at this point."

"We want to be there when you talk to the people at Trinity," Lois said.

Arthur got a surprised look on his face.

"That's not an option," Dillon said. "We'll want to—"

"Not an option? What, in God's name, is wrong with you? It happens to be our daughter you'll be discussing. We need to be there."

"I'm sorry, but your presence would only curtail the investigation. We'll want to speak with a number of people, much of it background information that—"

"Background information. She's been missing for the better part of a week. What other sort of background information could you possibly need? You come in here and—"

"Lois," Arthur said. "They're doing everything they can. He's right, our being there will only slow things down."

"But we need to know what's happening. We need to—"

"We need to let them do their job, Lois. When they have something they'll let us know. Marshal, I appreciate you taking the time from your investigation to bring us up to date. Please, don't let us hold you up from getting back to work."

"But we need—"

"No, Lois, we need to let them get on with it. Thank you, Marshal."

"Thanks, Jack," Bergman said. "You learn anything you'll keep us posted?"

"Yeah," Dillon said. "Mrs. Keller, we'll find Madeline."

She didn't acknowledge Dillon's statement, but just sat slumped in the chair looking beyond exhausted as a steady stream of tears ran down her cheeks.

TWENTY-SIX

Dillon phoned Suel as he left the airport. Suel answered on the second ring. "Did you survive?"

"Barely, a distraught mother and father looking for answers and I didn't have any. I got there twenty minutes early and they were already waiting for me. Poor Bergman looked exhausted. Not the best way to start your day. What about you?"

"I'll be at Trinity in another five minutes."

"How was Aideen?"

"Bitching about everything, she's bored, the television's no good, doesn't like her roommates, the food is terrible. Now that I think about it, I'd say she's getting back to her old cantankerous self. Swelling's gone down, they're supposed to fit her with a new nose splint later today, that's about the extent of her excitement."

"Any word on who attacked her?"

"From her, no. And before you go there, no, I didn't ask, didn't even bring it up. I was Mr. Fecking Positive. Told her she looked much better and congratulated her on the continuing recovery."

"That must have confused her, you sounding positive and pretending to be nice."

"Funny, very funny. I need to ring off, I can see Trinity up ahead and the traffic is fierce."

"I'll see you at the room in about twenty minutes."

"I'll wait for you outside the building, I've someone from the college letting us in."

"Thanks, Paddy, see you soon."

Goldsmith Hall faces Pearse Street, just next to the Pearse Street Train Station. It's connected on one side by an enclosed footbridge that goes over Westland Road from the second floor in Goldsmith Hall and connects to the Trinity Sports Center. At the opposite end of Goldsmith Hall stands the Trinity Biomedical Sciences Institute.

Dillon pulled up to the curb behind Suel's car fifteen minutes later. He pulled his An Garda Síochána 'OFFICIAL BUSINESS' sign from the glove compartment, placed it on the dash and climbed out of the car. Suel was standing in front of the building talking to a young woman. He was carrying a black leather briefcase with the shoulder strap slung over his right shoulder. Dillon knew the briefcase contained a camera, evidence bags, latex gloves and a host of items that might come in handy.

"About time, thanks for cutting your tea break short to get on with the business at hand. Marshal Jack Dillon, may I present Miss Tina Ryan, keeper of the keys to all of Trinity College," Suel said.

She was maybe twenty-five, with dark hair, sparkling blue eyes and a wonderful smile.

"Let's just say I'm the low person on the totem pole so I get the honor of escorting the two of you inside Goldsmith Hall."

"Nice to meet you, Tina," Dillon said and extended his hand.

She had a firm grip, a French manicure and about a half dozen silver bracelets around her wrist.

"Come on, let's get you up to the room and I'll leave you to it," she said. Suel pulled the door open and held it for them.

The first two floors of the building appeared to be classrooms and a cafe. "You want to grab a tea or a coffee before you get started," Tina asked.

Dillon and Suel replied, "No," simultaneously. On the second floor, Tina used a key card to gain entry to the actual dormitory area. They walked down an ivory painted hallway, past a number of wooden doors, each with a number. She stopped at the far end of the hall, knocked on the door, then inserted her key card in the lock, after a moment a green light flashed and she opened the door.

"Hello, anyone home? Girls?" When no one answered she said, "I'm sure they're all in class."

The room they stepped into was long and narrow. Oak kitchen cabinets with an oven, a four burner electric range, a sink and a refrigerator lined one wall. The wall between the upper and lower cabinets was covered in

square, glossy white tiles. A metal table with four matching chairs stood opposite the cabinets and a light was
centered in the middle of the ceiling. At the end of the
room a large floor to ceiling window looked out over
Pearce Street. A black, faux leather couch was positioned in front of the window. A coffee table and two
upholstered chairs formed a sitting area. The floor in the
room appeared to be one long sheet of linoleum.

"A lot nicer digs than I had in college," Dillon said.

"Yes, it's quite the step up, but in today's student
market it's what's required" Tina said. "Madeline was in
room number three. I'll leave the both of you to do your
look around. You're authorized to only look at Madeline's room. The other rooms are off limits without ex-
press written permission from the resident."

"Understood," Suel said. "And the room has been
locked?"

"Yes, the doors lock automatically, so remember
that, if you're thinking of using the loo or looking out the
window." Tina smiled and walked down a short hall past
two doors, she stopped at the third door slipped her
keycard in the lock and opened the door. "Gentlemen,
take your time. Please call me when you've finished and
I'll escort you from the building." She held the door for
Suel who stepped into the room. Dillon waited for her to
step back into the hallway before he entered the room.

It was a good thing Dillon waited because once he
stepped into the room and closed the door behind him, it
was obvious there was barely enough space for three

adults to stand within the tight confines of the student room.

TWENTY-SEVEN

They waited a long moment until they heard Tina close the door behind her. "What do you think?" Dillon said.

Suel glanced around the small room and said, "Not a lot of room to throw a party."

The room couldn't have been more than nine feet wide. One side of the room was taken up by a single bed covered with two pillows and a white quilt. A small, built in dresser sat just beyond the head of the bed and an inch below a window with navy blue curtains. A wardrobe with two doors was attached to the wall on the opposite side of the room. Next to the wardrobe was a built-in desk and three file drawers with metal handles. A blue desk chair on wheels was pushed in against the desktop. Three drawers were positioned on the floor beneath the bed. Other than a small desk lamp, a floor lamp standing just next to the window was the only source of electric light.

Suel set his brief case on the floor at the foot of the bed, unzipped a pocket and handed Dillon a pair of latex gloves. They slipped the gloves on as they looked around the room. Suel pulled the camera out and photographed the small room from a half dozen different angles.

An open MAC laptop was plugged in and sat on the desktop. Dillon hit the shift key on the outside chance the screen would go live. Low and behold, it did.

"Whoa, so much for security. Maybe start going through the wardrobe, see if there's anything there. Let me get on this thing and see what the files might bring up."

Suel had gone through the wardrobe, the file drawers in the desk, the dresser drawers and was now going over the bed. He pulled the quilt back, pulled back the sheets, removed the pillow cases and found nothing. He ran his hand between the mattress and the drawers beneath the bed. "Oh? What have we got here?" he said. He was on his knees just behind Dillon seated in the desk chair.

"You got something?" Dillon asked and half turned the desk chair just as Suel stood, lifted the mattress onto its side and leaned it up against the wall.

A bright red battery operated appliance lay on top of the bed frame and next to that, a half dozen red foil condom envelopes with the name Durex emblazoned in blue.

"Bag it?" Suel said.

Dillon thought for a moment. "What? She's nineteen or twenty? Nothing unusual, just a college girl. Yeah, bag it, if for no other reason than the sight could send her mother over the edge. Photograph them first."

"Gee, really? Who would have guessed," Suel said.

The drawers beneath the bed held undergarments, hosiery, socks and some incidentals, but nothing out of the ordinary. Suel returned the mattress and bedding to its original position.

He was in the process of fanning the pages in a half-dozen different books on a shelf above the desk when Dillon tapped a couple of keys on the laptop and said, "Oh, oh."

"What is it?"

"Take a look, an email to our Belfast friend."

"The Cominsky lad?"

"Yeah, complete with a half-dozen selfie attachments."

"Ahh, she can't be that stupid, can she?"

"No more stupid than he is. She sent them in response to his email with a half dozen similar attachments."

"Well, she's not hard to look at, I'll give her that much."

"You got an evidence bag large enough to slip this computer into? I don't want to turn it off in case we need a password to get back online."

"Is it fully charged?"

"Yeah, of course. It's probably been plugged in for the past week."

Suel grabbed a notebook from the upper shelf and handed it to Dillon. "Just to be sure, place that on the keyboard, then close it. With any luck it will most likely slip into the rest mode but won't shut off. Anything else we should go through?"

"I think we've about finished. Another whole lot of nothing," Dillon said.

"Let me give Tina a call to escort us out," Suel said. "We can view the selfies back in the office."

Ten minutes later, Tina knocked on Madeline's door. "Everything go okay?" she said when Suel opened the door.

"Yeah, nothing out of the ordinary, we've left a list of the items we're taking to either view or run tests on, pretty much standard. We're taking her computer and we'll return it when we're finished."

"We received a call from her parents about thirty minutes ago. I haven't returned it yet. Can I tell them it's okay to come over?"

"I don't have a problem with that. Paddy?"

"Not really much for them to see, but I suppose they'll think it might help. Sure, have them come over," Suel said.

Tina escorted them down to the ground floor. Dillon gave her his card and told her to feel free to call with any questions or concerns. They climbed into their respective cars and drove back to the office, Suel carried the evidence bags.

TWENTY-EIGHT

Once back in the office Dillon and Suel ran Madeline Keller's computer down to the computer forensics section. The section was located in a large corner room with maybe a dozen work stations, bunches of cords and wires dangling from the ceiling and computer screens flashing everywhere. A counter ran across the front of the room limiting access to the work stations. The nickname in the department was 'Nerd Central'.

Suel had an attractive redheaded cousin working in the department, she caught sight of Suel as they entered and stepped up to the counter.

"Hi Paddy, what brings you down here? Upset over your access to porn sites being blocked."

"Very funny, Ina. No, we've a computer belonging to a missing person. An American student at Trinity. So far we've come up empty handed in our investigation, but we came across some self-me's on her computer—"

"He means selfies," Dillon said.

"Oh, allow me to introduce the interrupter. US Marshal Jack Dillon, my cousin, Ina. You think you might put a tag on this, see if you couldn't move it towards the head of the line."

Ina brushed a strand of curly auburn hair from the side of her face, ignored her cousin, smiled, flashed a pair of brown eyes and extended her hand to Dillon. "Ina Nolan. It's nice to finally meet you. Heard you've had your hands full keeping himself out of harm's way. You'd need the patience of a right saint."

"Jack Dillon, nice to meet you, Ina," he said as he set the laptop down in front of her. She glanced at the notebook between the keyboard and screen but didn't comment. She took hold of Dillon's hand for a long moment and stared into Dillon's eyes.

"Forgot to mention, Ina fancies herself as a bit of a mystic," Suel said.

When she finally let go of Dillon's hand she looked at Suel and said, "How long has she been missing, Paddy?"

"Five or six days now. Wait a minute, I never told you she was female."

"You're the one who said I was a mystic. Well, that and the sticker on the computer that says, 'Bad Girls Do it Well.' You know, from Bad Girls by M.I.A.," she said in response to their blank looks.

"Yeah, whatever. We just got assigned to the case yesterday and made our way up to Belfast to talk to an acquaintance. Spoke to her roommates yesterday, as well. So far, we're coming up empty handed. Wondered if maybe there might be something on the computer."

"You said on the phone she had a selfie."

"Maybe a half dozen she sent off to a former boy-friend. Looks like they were in response to ones he sent her. He was a student at Trinity at the time," Dillon said.

"Selfies," Ina said shaking her head. "They all think it's the thing to do and no one but the intended will see them. Just wait until she has a fifteen year old daughter who comes across the image of her naked mother. There will be absolute hell to pay."

"Can you put us toward the front of the line. I feel like we're already on borrowed time with her missing for this long," Suel said.

"I might be able to."

"Might be able to?"

"Depends on where you decide to take the Marshal and me for drinks and a lovely evening out."

"Aw, come on, Ina. We don't have time—"

"Not a problem. Maybe you'll be able to think of a way to make time while you wait a month or two for us to analyze the system. Hmm-mmm, a MAC, they can be tricky, you know. I just might have to study up on them a bit before I get started."

"All right, all right, how 'bout Dohney and Nes-bitt's. You two plonkers can drink to your hearts content on my tab. Happy?"

"Suits me. Marshal?" she said and pulled the com-puter across the counter.

"Do we have to bring him?" Dillon said. "Maybe we could just send him the bill."

"Not a bad thought, but we'll no doubt need to be driven home so we had better let him tag along. Here now, out with the both of you's and let me start in on this. You wouldn't happen to know a password, would you?"

"That's why we put the notebook between the keyboard and screen, so it doesn't shut off."

"Umm, I'm impressed. Marshal you must have thought that up."

"I'd love to take credit, but surprisingly it was your cousin."

"Humph, no one more surprised than me. Listen, the two of you, get now, let me see what we can find here."

"Thanks, Ina," Paddy said. Dillon nodded, smiled and they left Nerd Central and headed back up to their office.

"Ina seemed nice. How come you never mentioned her before?" Dillon said. They were standing in the break room, Dillon sipping a cup of coffee that had been on the burner for at least twelve hours and Suel dunking his teabag in a stained cup of hot water.

"Don't go thinking there might be something with her for the likes of you, Dillon."

"Oh, protective, are we?"

"Yeah, unfortunately protective of you. Serve you right if I let you try your luck. She's a pretty little thing who'd have no problem wiping the floor with you."

"What? She likes to fight?"

"No, you daft plonker. She'd just eat you up, spit you out with not so much as blink. I can think of a half dozen decent lads she trampled over just for fun. And that's her recent history. They were all men a lot better than the likes of you or me. So you just smile, act nice and remember to stay the hell away. Oh, yeah, I could see the rusty wheels in that pea sized brain of yours slowly beginning to turn. Thinking, this one looks like she could be fun. Let me warn you, and I'm not kidding, you don't stand a chance."

"She sounds interesting."

"Well, don't come crying to me. You've been warned. The mere fact she's down in Nerd Central should tell you she's a hell of a lot smarter than the likes of you or me. Add to that the red hair, those flashing eyes and that figure, you don't stand half a chance Dillon. I'm not fooling."

"Guess we'll just have to see who comes out on top after Dohney and Nesbitts."

Suel just shook his head, "Suit yourself, I've done my duty. But you don't have any idea what it is you'd be getting into."

TWENTY-NINE

The following morning Dillon got a call from the desk sergeant asking him to come down to the lobby. When he got there the desk sergeant said, "You need to sign for something," and with a nod of his head, indicated a postman seated in a chair against the wall.

"Are you US Marshal Jack Dillon?" The postman read off the front of an envelope as Dillon approached. He was dressed in a matching blue nylon jacket and trousers and carried a green bike helmet in his left hand. "I have a registered letter addressed to you, just need you to sign here next to the X," he said and handed Dillon a pen and a clipboard.

A business envelope with a Belfast return address was attached to the clipboard. A yellow form was attached to the envelope labeled Royal Post with Dillon's name and the station address. Below that was a line with an X next to it. Dillon took the clip board, signed on the line and handed it back to the postman. He tore the top copy off the form, handed the envelope to Dillon, smiled and said, "Have a nice day, sir."

Dillon opened the envelope once he was back at his desk. He unfolded a single page letter with a law firm's name and address at the top and Calvert Cominsky's name listed as one of nine partners. There were two short paragraphs. The first thanked Dillon for meeting with the Cominsky's, listing the date and stating that all questions had been answered to everyone's satisfaction. The second paragraph consisted of two brief sentences basically saying that any further attempts to contact either Colin Cominsky or his father, the charming Reverend Ian, should be directed to their legal representative, Calvert Cominsky. Basically shutting the door on any further talk without Calvert present.

Dillon sat at his chair tapping the empty envelope across the edge of his desk. He pulled out the file they'd received from Calvert up in Belfast two days earlier and made note of the Empire Pub where Colin and friends were supposed to have spent the evening. The names of the three friends were printed at the top of the sworn statements. Dillon googled the three names.

He came up with at least a dozen commercial accounts and business people across Northern Ireland and the Republic that most likely had nothing to do with Colin Cominsky and then there it was, on page two, a photo of four young men, one of them Colin Cominsky. The other three were identified as Noel Taylor, Peter

Jenkins and Jimmy McKenzie. The three young men who had produced and signed the sworn statements.

All four were dressed in team jerseys. The jerseys had white and orange horizontal stripes about two inches wide and orange shoulders. A red line ran across each chest from right to left ending in what looked like a fiery explosion just over the heart. Their hair was messed, one sported a bruise on his chin and all the jerseys had dirt on the shoulders and across the front. The photo had apparently been taken either during or just after a rugby match.

"Hey, Suel, come 'mere and check this out," Dillon called just as Suel put down his phone.

"What is it now, another picture of some young thing with . . . Oh, will you look at that. Belfast Lasers."

"What?"

"They're a rugby team, Belfast Lasers. Sort of a 'B' league, the guys who couldn't make it to the next level. They're always hoping for the nod and every once in a while one of them gets the opportunity to try out for Ulster County or maybe a French team. Still love the game, but either they just don't quite have the skill set or more likely, they had to get a job and support the marriage and maybe a little one. Hey, isn't that your man Cominsky, there on the left?" Suel pointed with a pen.

"Yeah and guess who these three are?"

"Same jersey, I'd guess teammates."

"Apparently. They also happen to be the three who signed the sworn statements saying they were with Colin Cominsky the night Madeline Keller disappeared."

"What are you suggesting? It wouldn't seem unusual that he was out with mates for a pint on any given night. It would almost have to be friends he was with if they spent an entire night out."

"Yeah and they were at the Empire Pub, supposedly."

"You've sworn statements, Dillon. And your man Calvert Cominsky backing them up just by the mere fact he gave them to you."

"Oh yeah, check this out," Dillon said and handed the registered letter to Suel.

"When did you get this?"

"About a half hour ago, came registered and I had to go down and sign for the thing. I don't know, it almost seems heavy handed. I get he's representing his nephew, but I just have the sense we're getting the door slammed in our face and Calvert's on the other side hoping to God we don't ask another question."

Suel seemed to think for a long moment. "Well, if you really want to pursue this I could call Ronnie Maxwell up in Belfast. You can talk with him, see if he knows anything on that pub—"

"The Empire."

"Yeah, I don't know, maybe they've tapes of the night, he might check and see if the lads were actually there. It would add that much more credibility to their statements, take them off your list of potentials.”

“Think he’d do it?”

“Ronnie? Oh yeah, he’d like nothing better than some other knacker besides me owing him a favor down here.”

“Okay, yeah, I’ll give him a call.”

THIRTY

Dillon's cellphone rang, he glanced at the screen, Eric Bergman. "Eric, you survived this morning?"

Bergman sighed. "Long morning. Not a hell of a lot we can do for the parents. I gave them a lift to their hotel."

"The Westin, right?"

"Yeah, they couldn't officially check in until three this afternoon, so they dropped their bags off and we walked over to Trinity."

"Were they going to talk with anyone at Trinity or did they just want to see her room?"

"Planning to do both. We were escorted up to the room, it's in Goldsmith Hall and—"

"Yeah, we were there this morning. Soon as I left the airport, I headed over there."

"Right, they saw the list of items you took. You turn anything up?"

"In a word, no. A sex toy and some condoms, I think Suel listed them as miscellaneous. We also took Madeline's computer, that's pretty much standard procedure.

The computer's down in forensics now. You happen to get escorted by a woman named Tina?"

"Yeah, she brought us up there, none of the roommates were around. I left the Keller's overwhelmed and in the room, and walked out with her, Tina. The Keller's wanted to meet the roommates, and after that they had an appointment with some official at the school."

"I wish I had better news, Eric. Hell, any news would be better than what we don't have."

"So at the end of the day, nothing."

"At least as it stands now. We'd like to talk with the roommates again, but we want to wait until we get the computer analysis. Just in case something turns up there."

"You expecting anything?"

"Expecting anything? No, hoping might be a better description, we've got jack shit to go on right now. I'm starting to wonder if she didn't meet some stranger and either left with them of her own accord or maybe she was drugged. We'll do a follow up checking the veracity of the sworn statements from Cominsky's friends, but that's just routine at this stage. How was the mother holding up?"

"Lois Keller? Poor thing, obviously a basket case. Who the hell can blame her? In all honesty, she probably shouldn't have come and in truth, what the hell is she supposed to do? Just sit and worry back in US? I feel for her, but there's nothing we can do."

"Except find her daughter."

"You think there's a chance?"

"Right now, I don't know what to think," Dillon said.

"Well, I'll let you get back to it, please keep me informed and maybe don't contact the Keller's with any information. If you could run it through me that would help."

"I'll be happy do that, Eric, thanks. You take care."

THIRTY-ONE

illon had barely hung up with Eric Bergman when his cellphone rang again. He didn't recognize the number. "Jack Dillon."

"Marshal Dillon, my name is Ronnie Maxwell. Paddy Suel asked me to give you a call." Ronnie Maxwell, Suel's detective pal with the Belfast police, the PSNI. He spoke with a hard Northern Irish accent and Dillon had to concentrate to understand.

"Yes, DI Maxwell, thank you for calling. Did Suel explain what we wanted to do?"

"Aye, he did a bit, but why don't you tell me."

Dillon went on to explain the Keller case, and the signed statements swearing that all four young men had spent the evening in the Empire Pub.

"Mmm-mmm, Calvert Cominsky," Maxwell said. "He's got a reputation up here, and it's a damn good one. He doesn't miss much. He's well respected. Now his brother, Ian, the lad's father, he's a right piece of work, a bible thumper if ever there was one. Still, your man is popular with a certain group of well-connected folk and he's been quite successful. Now, the Empire Pub is a popular place with the young set. They've security on the premises, and they don't stand for any out of line behavior. On any given evening the place would be crowded."

"Well, we met the father, Ian, not all that happy to see us. Calvert pretty much closed the door on us as far as covering any new ground and to be honest, I'm not sure there is any new ground. I'd just like to verify that the sworn statements are truthful and that everyone was indeed at the Empire Pub for the evening."

"Have you the names of the lads your man was with."

"I've got the names and I can send you a picture of the four of them, along with copies of the statements."

"A picture from the Empire pub?"

"No, they were all teammates on a rugby team, the Belfast Lasers. You familiar with them?"

"In name only. It wouldn't be out of the ordinary that mates on a rugby team would spend a night out with one another at a pub like the Empire. You know, teammates, they can be a pretty tight group. Why don't you send me the picture, and the names? At this stage I don't need to see the sworn statements. I'll ask around. I know the Empire has a number of CCTV cameras, but I'm not sure how long they keep the tapes. Could be twenty-four hours or twenty-four months. Let me give them a call."

"Thanks, DI Maxwell—"

"Please, drop the formality and call me Ronnie."

"Thanks for offering to check this out for us, Ronnie. Give me your email address and I'll have this up to you in just a few minutes."

Dillon emailed the names and addresses of the three young men who signed the sworn statements as well as Colin Cominsky's. He sent the photo of all four of them in their rugby jerseys as an attachment. He spent the next two hours reviewing the sworn statements they'd received from Calvert Cominsky as well as the interviews with Madeline Keller's roommates. There seemed to be a similar word pattern in the three sworn statements which Dillon made a mental note of but, at this stage, it wasn't enough to throw up a flag. At the end of the day, he had a slightly tighter hand on the facts and felt even less assured they had any hope of closing the case.

He shut down his computer, locked his desk drawer and grabbed his coat off the back of his chair. Suel was on his phone and signaled Dillon to wait a minute. Dillon sat on the corner of his desk and waited just a minute or two before Suel disconnected.

"You have plans for the evening?" Suel asked once he hung up.

"I plan to go home, let Lucifer out, eat some left over pizza and maybe have a glass of wine. Why, what's up?"

"I'm just off the line with Joel Dolan."

"Joel the Hole?"

"Oy, one in the same. He's to pay a gambling debt tonight or risk a broken leg."

"And why would that concern either one of us?"

"Guess who he's supposed to pay?"

"You don't mean?" Dillon said.

"I do. One in the same, the always popular Riley Dempsey. The same bollocks we've been looking for over the past six weeks. They're to meet tonight at The Swiss Cottage on Swords Road."

"I'd say it's a meeting we wouldn't want to miss. We can even offer to give Mr. Dempsey lodging."

Suel laughed and said, "Yeah, for the next four years."

THIRTY-TWO

y the time they pulled in, they just barely grabbed one of the last parking spots behind The Swiss Cottage Pub. Over the course of the next four and a half hours they watched the majority of the patrons head home for the night. Now, they were one of only four cars remaining. The lot was large, surrounded by a five foot tall concrete block wall painted white before it had been covered with graffiti. Tall linden trees had been planted about every six to eight feet along the wall.

"Tell me again when they were supposed to be here," Dillon said.

"For God's sake, I've told you twice already. Eight-fecking-o'clock."

"Yeah, that's what I thought you said. And what time is it now?"

"Just a little after midnight."

"Oh, I was hoping I was wrong, but it looks like we got played. Again."

"Bollocks. I'll lock the likes of Joel the Hole up for so long the slimy bastard'll never see the bleeding light of day ever again in his dreadful, worthless life."

"You want to give him a call?"

"That's part of the problem, if I call him, and he's somewhere sharing pints with your man Dempsey, the bollocks is liable to head for the hills and we'll never see the bastard again. I don't want Dempsey thinking we're on his trail. Once we get him it'll take about fifteen minutes to turn him and make him expose a whole host of plonkers. He'll be well worth the wait. I just wish the bastard would get here."

"Any idea where they might be?"

"Would it make any difference? It's not like we could go somewhere and look for them. The piss ants were supposed to be here hours ago, but then neither one of them has ever done anything right in the past. So why would we expect them to change now? We'll wait a bit longer before we call it a night. But, when I get my hands on Joel the Hole he's going to wish . . ." Suel suddenly grew quiet as a dark blue Mercedes pulled into the lot and parked next to the entrance.

The passenger door opened and a heavyset blonde stepped out. She wore a very short, very tight purple skirt and matching stiletto heels. As she headed toward the entrance, she grabbed the hem of her skirt and attempted to straighten it, not that it seemed to make a difference.

The rear passenger door opened and Joel the Hole climbed out, steadied himself against the side of the car and attempted to get his bearings for a moment before he staggered to catch up to the blonde woman. Riley Dempsey suddenly stepped out of the driver's seat, gave a quick look around, placed a cap on his head and headed into The Swiss Cottage, the blonde and Joel the Hole followed.

"Should we go in and get him?" Dillon said.

"Let's give them a minute to get settled, order drinks, and then we'll grab that shiftless bastard, Dempsey."

They waited five minutes, which only seemed like five hours. "Okay, let's go," Suel finally said. They hurried out of their car, across the parking lot and into The Swiss Cottage.

Once they stepped inside, they stopped and blinked for a long moment waiting for their eyes to adjust. The place was almost pitch black with some nondescript music blasting over the sound system. The heavyset blonde was the only person out on the dance floor, dancing by herself. The only illumination came from a large flat screen mounted on a far wall tuned to what looked like a dartboard tournament.

One person sat on the far side of the circular bar in the middle of the room. Although, it was so dark it impossible to tell who it was, the individual did have a cap on his head.

"You go right, I'll go left," Dillon said and took off around the bar. They met at Joel the Hole. Riley Dempsey was nowhere to be seen. They quickly looked around, and Suel waded past tables, half tossing chairs aside in an effort to spot Dempsey.

"Well, there you go," Joel the Hole giggled and took a long drink from his whiskey glass. An untouched Guinness sat on the bar next to his whiskey. "I knew I smelled bacon. Let me buy the first round, gents."

"What'll it be lads? Afraid you'll have to hurry, we're closing in five minutes," the bartender said and smiled.

Dillon glanced toward the door just as a pair of headlights flashed across the glass and sped out of the parking lot. "Oh, for Christ sake, there he goes," Dillon said.

"Looking for a little fun tonight, fellas?" the heavyset blonde was suddenly right behind them. She stood there smiling, attempting to shake seductively. It wasn't working.

"Something to drink, gents?" the bartender asked again and smiled.

"Bollocks," Suel groaned and stormed toward the door.

Dillon and Suel hurried out the door and ran to the car. Dillon was barely in the passenger seat when Suel fired up the engine and screeched across the empty parking lot.

"We don't even know which way he went," Dillon said as Suel skidded left and raced down the street. Two blocks later, he slowed slightly then ran the red light."

"The bollocks is bound to be heading back into city center," Suel said. As he accelerated a set of tail lights appeared in the distance. Thirty seconds later, they slowed when it became apparent the vehicle wasn't Dempsey's blue Mercedes.

"Christ on a cross," Suel swore.

"Maybe we should head back to The Swiss Cottage and grab Joel the Hole."

"There's an idea, and then we'd have herself to deal with. No. The only way he's even getting near this vehicle is if we tie him to the back bumper and drag him behind us."

"Well, I was just thinking—"

"Don't think. You see the state of him? Even if we threatened to lock him up he wouldn't remember or, he'd let us know what he had for dinner when he threw up all over the back seat. The two of them can find their own way home and good riddance."

It wasn't ten minutes before Suel pulled up in front of Dillon's. "Sorry it didn't work out, Paddy. We'll get him sooner or later."

"Only now the bollocks knows we're looking for him so he'll be even harder to find."

"You think the woman might have been with Dempsey?"

"Well, he clearly doesn't have a hell of a lot of common sense so it's a definite possibility."

"Maybe get in touch with Joel the Hole tomorrow and get her name. If she has something going with

Dempsey we might have a better shot watching her instead of cooling our heels in a car for hours on end."

Suel seemed to think for a long moment then shook his head and said, "It pains me say it, but you may have a point. Speaking of which, I'm going to be a tad late coming in tomorrow. Aideen's getting released from James's Hospital in the morning. I'll pick her up, make sure she's settled in at home, then I'll be in the office."

"Any word on who it was?"

"Not yet, but I took your advice and I'm staying low key."

"No one more surprised than me."

"Yeah, well, I also had her locks changed and had motion detector lights installed in the back garden and over the front door."

THIRTY-THREE

Dillon had to attend a briefing at nine the next morning regarding new security measures about to be instituted at Croke Park, the GAA stadium. The meeting lasted far too long and accomplished absolutely nothing. When he got back to his desk, he called Eric Bergman's cellphone.

"Hi Jack," Bergman answered.

"Eric, just checking in. Anything happening with the Keller's?"

"I was hoping you might be calling with something," Bergman said.

"We've got nothing. Madeline's computer is in the forensic lab. We've a detective up in Belfast doing a double check on the three sworn statements. That's more a matter of routine than anything out of the ordinary showing up. You hear from her parents?"

"No, but it's early in the day. I was going to attempt to make a courtesy call later this afternoon. I fully expect to be leaving a message on their hotel room phone."

"Did they talk with the roommates and the powers that be at the school?"

"As far as I know, yes. Beyond that, there really isn't a hell of a lot I can tell you. And other than worry a lot, I don't know what they can do."

"Except get in the way."

"Possibly. As understandably upset as they are, I just don't see them as the type to interject themselves. I mean, where? How?"

"I hope you're right, but they're exhausted and heartbroken. They could do anything."

"Well, if I hear something, I'll let you know."

"Thanks, Eric, same goes for us here. I hope to get a call from our contact up in Belfast later today. Soon as I hear from him I'll let you know."

"Thanks Marshal, talk to you later," Bergman said and disconnected.

Just before noon Dillon's desk phone rang. It was an inside call, but he didn't recognize the phone extension. "Jack Dillon."

"Hello, Marshal. Ina, down in computer forensics. I've got some initial information. If you have some time, you and Paddy could come down and I'll bring you up to date. If it's all right, I'd like to hang onto the computer and do a little further analysis."

"Hang onto it as long as you want, Ina. Actually, your cousin is out at the moment, working on something else. If it's all right, I'd like to come down. You breaking for lunch?"

"I usually just grab a takeout."

"How 'bout you order two? I'll buy and pick them up."

"Oh, you don't have to do that."

"You're right, but it's not every day I get to have lunch with a pretty woman."

"Yeah, right, and in her office. I usually get something from Dublin Wok, you know it?"

"I know where it is, phone in something for both of us, and I'll pick it up."

"How do steam pod dumplings sound? I happen to think they're to die for. Does that sound okay to you?"

"I'm a guy, Ina, I eat whatever is placed in front of me."

She laughed at that and said, "I'll see you in a half hour."

Dillon went around the corner twenty minutes later and picked up their order. The restaurant smelled wonderful and his stomach began to growl loudly as the woman rang him up. He grabbed the bag with the two Styrofoam trays, four sauce containers, chop sticks and hurried back to the station and Nerd Central.

THIRTY-FOUR

s Dillon stepped through the door into the forensics section, Ina said, "Oh, thank God. As you can probably see, I was beginning to waste away." She smiled and struck a sideways pose.

Dillon thought her curves looked beautiful in the blue short sleeve dress. The dress was accented by a small gold cross around her neck. Her hair was pulled back in a tight bun and as she approached he caught the scent of a very lovely perfume.

"You look great."

"Huh, you'll do, come on back," she half laughed. She swung open a gate at the far end of the counter and led Dillon back to a small break room with three tables and maybe a dozen chairs. The walls were painted a pale yellow and the floor was covered with squares of white tile. Two guys were sitting at one of the tables. One was eating a large hamburger. A Burger King bag lay half crumpled on the table. His partner, wearing a plaid shirt with a small notebook and three pens in the pocket, was eating a sandwich he'd obviously made at home. An apple cut into slices sat in a small plastic container in front of him. Neither one acknowledged Dillon or Ina and they didn't seem to be involved in any sort of conversation. He studied them for a long moment, and he realized they didn't seem to be looking at one another, either.

"Any problems?" Ina asked as she pulled two plastic forks from a drawer and handed one to Dillon.

"No, looks like a nice place. I've never been in there before, but only because it would be too convenient. Hey, thanks, but I'll just use the chop sticks."

"Oh, Americans. I suppose you're going to try and tell me you folks invented them," she laughed as she pulled out her chair and sat down. "Mmm-mmm, these are always so good," she said, taking a bite of one of the dumplings.

Dillon stabbed a dumpling with a chopstick and shoved the entire thing into his mouth. Ina stopped chewing, stared wide eyed, but didn't say anything until his stomach began to growl again.

"Oh my God, when was the last time you had something to eat?"

He had to swallow twice before he could answer. "Mmm-mmm, breakfast. These are really good."

"Yes, apparently," she said. "Thanks for getting them. You didn't have to do that."

"Works for me, plus now that I've discovered the place, I'll be back." He stabbed another dumpling and shoved it into his mouth. Ina just stared for a few seconds with her mouth half open.

The two guys at the other table stood and pushed their chairs in. The one who had been eating the home-made sandwich carefully folded his brown paper lunch bag and used it to sweep crumbs from the table onto the floor. They left the room without acknowledging Ina or Dillon. As they walked past she rolled her eyes.

"Gee, really friendly," Dillon said through a mouthful of dumpling.

"Oliver and Desmond, they're okay. Let's just say, social skills aren't always at the top of the list if you're working computer forensics."

"You always seem friendly and vivacious."

"That's 'cause I'm special," she said and fluttered her eyes.

When they'd finished Dillon gathered up the Styrofoam trays and sauce containers and put them in the trash bin. He pushed his chair in and followed Ina out to her work station.

Her desk was one of three in a row with six more in two identical rows behind her.

"Grab the chair at that desk and wheel it over," she directed. "Darcy's taking a vacation day and won't be in."

Dillon wheeled the desk chair over and sat down alongside Ina. Madeline Keller's MAC was on Ina's desk with two manila files resting on top of it. Other than a tea mug, two keyboards and two screens the files and the MAC were the only things on the desk. As Dillon sat down, Ina opened one of the files and handed the other to him.

"These are my notes thus far and that file is yours to keep. I want to do a little more exploration, but it shouldn't take more than a day or two. I've listed her password. It's the first item on the first page."

Dillon glanced at the five random numbers. "How did you ever find that? What is it, the answer to some algebraic formula?"

"No, it's the American postal code of the town she's from. Schleswig, in the state of Iowa."

"Her zip code?"

"Yes, that's what you call it, I couldn't remember. I went back a number of months. She, umm, appears to have garnered some attention."

"You're referring to the selfies she sent to the young man from Belfast. He was a student at Trinity at the time. Apparently, a naked picture is the current way to ask someone on a date," Dillon said as he flipped a couple of sheets and came to an image of Madeline. He flipped to the next page, another naked image of Madeline, this one a rear shot, displaying the butterfly tattoo on her lower back.

"The Trinity lad from Belfast would have received all these images from her," Ina said. "There are three other individuals who sent selfies to her. If you flip the next few pages you'll see."

"Three others?" Dillon said and started flipping pages. He recognized the three faces from an earlier image, Colin Cominsky's rugby teammates from the Belfast Lasers.

"You're saying she exchanged these images of herself with all of these guys?"

Ina shook her head. "Not exactly, it would appear she only replied to the initial contact, that was Cominsky. Of course, we've no way of determining what occurred on a face to face basis. The other three, Taylor, Jenkins, and McKenzie mention something about hearing rumors and asked to be a part. Interestingly, those three emails to Madeline arrived maybe five weeks after Cominsky's and within forty-five minutes of one another. I never did discover an email or an image sent by the Darren Otis individual. I think you said he was the one who left the pub early. Could be he's the only one with some brains and decency."

"So? It's not just chance? These guys obviously thought they were on to something."

"Maybe. But based on the comments, and the images they sent, it seems to me more of a way to sort of give her the finger."

"Was she doing this for money?"

"Not that I could determine, and again, I'm not sure she did anything, other than send a number of images to her then boyfriend, Colin Cominsky. It would appear she did not reply to the images from the other three. Although she did save them."

"And the additional emails are just with these three guys, nothing before, or back in the states, or with others at Trinity, or just in Dublin, or—?"

"Nothing that I could find, and believe me, I tried."

"What the hell?" Dillon said.

"That sort of sums it up," Ina replied.

THIRTY-FIVE

When Dillon returned to his office, Paddy Suel was at his desk on the phone. He waved at Dillon, signaling him over to his desk.

"Just a moment, I'm going to put you on speaker, the Marshal has finally graced us with his presence. It's Ronnie Maxwell," Suel said pressing the speaker button on his phone so they would both be able to hear.

"Hi Marshal."

"Hi Ronnie, you got something?"

"Possibly. I was at the Empire Pub this morning reviewing tapes. Your lads were there, five of them actually. Arrived a bit after five in the evening then left around half seven. I checked, rechecked and checked again, but they did not re-enter the pub. Now, that doesn't mean they didn't head somewhere else and drink the night away. But if they did, it wasn't at the Empire."

"Their sworn statements say they were at the Empire until late in the evening."

"Well, the security tapes present pretty solid evidence suggesting they weren't. They left as a group out a side door. There are camera's covering every entrance and exit, as well as the parking lot. They're on tape driving out of the parking lot and they did not return that evening."

Suel looked at Dillon for a moment then said, "Ronnie, can you secure those tapes for us?"

"Already done, Paddy. I placed them in evidence as soon as I got back to the station. What are you thinking?"

"I'm not sure what to think," Dillon said. "I've come across a couple of other things down here. The fifth individual is probably an individual named Darren Otis. He was not asked to sign a statement because he was supposed to have left early."

"Well, if he left when the other four did, essentially, he did leave early. He certainly didn't return to the Empire, but then neither did the other lads."

"How 'bout we touch base at the end of the day?"

"Just give a yell. Sorry I didn't have better news."

"Glad you caught it, Ronnie. We'll be in touch." Suel said. He disconnected then looked at Dillon and groaned, "Bloody hell."

"You're telling me."

"What have you been up to?"

"I had lunch with your cousin, Ina."

"What?"

Dillon waved the file at Suel that Ina had given him. "Seems our victim was an admired lady. Along with the selfies she exchanged with the Cominsky kid, his three rugby pals sent her images of themselves."

"Naked images?"

"Seems to be the thing to do."

"You're kidding?"

"I wish I was. Apparently, the images arrived within forty-five minutes of one another. It appears she did not receive one from this Darren Otis individual."

Suel shook his head.

"Ina's going through more files on the computer. God only knows what she'll find."

"Was the girl working this angle?"

"Working?" Dillon said, not sure what Suel meant.

"You know? Charging the lads."

"Not that Ina could determine, she only sent images to Cominsky, and those were in response to the ones he sent her. Let's take the worst scenario and say she was charging them. So what? That doesn't mean she doesn't count. Doesn't mean she should be hurt, or threatened, or murdered."

"For God's sake, calm the feck down, I know that. It's just that it adds a complication."

"Not for me."

"Aren't you special. But if she was charging for the images that might mean there could well be a number of people out there we know nothing about."

Dillon flashed a half-second smile then said, "Here's what I'm wondering. How does this jive with Calvert Cominsky and his sterling reputation? Did these guys try to pull a fast one, not realizing the trouble they've created? Or, did he direct them?"

"Sounds like we might be making a return trip to the north," Suel said.

"Let me check a couple of things first. I forgot to ask, how's Aideen doing?"

"She's getting back to normal, more cantankerous by the day. But she's home now and I plan to be there tonight."

THIRTY-SIX

Dillon was at his desk. He had meant to phone the Belfast City Cemetery over the last two days, but between the Keller's arriving in Dublin, Calvert Cominsky's registered letter, searching Madeline Keller's room and going over what Ina had found on the computer, he'd completely forgotten.

A woman answered on the fourth ring. "Belfast City Cemetery."

Dillon gave his name, told her he was with An Garda Síochána working in conjunction with the PSNI in Northern Ireland and said, "I'm calling to verify the date of a recent burial, a young woman by the name of Dawn Davies." He spelled out her first and last names.

"Is she in the Catholic or the Protestant section of the cemetery?"

"I'm sorry, I don't know that," he said, hoping he didn't sound surprised at the question. He thought for half a moment about describing the section they had been in with the Cominsky's but decided his description would only confuse.

"If I could have your number, please. This will take a few minutes and I'll have to call you back," the woman said.

It struck him as strange for a moment, before he realized she probably wanted to be sure he was indeed with the police. Thirty minutes later she called back, apologized for the delay, and proceeded to give him the date of the burial as well as the section and plot number of the grave. He thanked her, hung up and walked over to Suel's desk.

"Well?"

"Finally, something that appears to be legit. The date of the burial corresponds to what Colin Cominsky told us."

"We're still looking at three sworn statements that now appear, in fact, to be false. Given the time they exit the Empire pub, 7:30, they could have driven down here in under two hours and been at the Quays Pub easily an hour before she was left alone."

"You saying she was waiting for them?"

Suel shook his head. "Not exactly. I'm suggesting she could have been waiting for them. She could have been waiting for just one of them. She could have been waiting for the Cominsky lad. She could have been waiting for someone we know nothing about. Or, none of the above and she just wanted to listen to the music."

"Damn it, if only we had the tapes."

"They hold them for forty-eight hours at the Quays and then tape over them again. It's an older system, no digital files."

"I know, I know," Dillon said sounding frustrated, then he thought for a moment. "I think I might head down there, even if the Quays doesn't hang onto the tapes, maybe some places around there do. In order to get to the Quays, you might have to walk past a lot of CCTV cameras."

"I've got to be at Aideen's tonight," Suel said checking his watch. "But you know the shop just to the right of the Quays? It's a food place. What the hell's the name? Oh yeah, Temple Take Out. There's a narrow passageway alongside the building called the Merchants Arch. It leads to Liffey Street and the Ha'penny Bridge. They're bound to have cameras, maybe start there."

THIRTY-SEVEN

Dillon drove into the city center and amazingly found a parking place on Strand Street Great, just across from the Han Sung Asian Market and a short walk to the river Liffey. He made his way over the Liffey on the Ha'penny Bridge, weaving in and out of knots of tourists smiling and laughing as they took pictures with their cellphones. On the far side of the bridge he crossed Liffey Street, went up a couple of steps and through the short, narrow Merchants Arch passageway that led into Temple Bar. At this time of day, and in the nice weather, the area was jammed with people in no particular hurry to get anywhere.

At the end of the passageway, he could see the Quays Pub just fifty feet from where he stood. He turned around, took a step and opened the door to the Temple Take Out. The single room was painted white with glass fronted display cabinets filled with sandwiches, large bowls of salads, pastas, chicken wings and cakes.

He pulled out his An Garda Síochána ID and told the girl behind the counter he would like to speak with the manager.

"That would be me, tonight," she said and smiled. She wore blue jeans, a Temple Take Out t-shirt and a white apron. Her dark hair was parted in the middle and dyed a bright blue maybe three inches above her shoulders. She looked all of sixteen.

Dillon nodded at the security camera attached to the ceiling behind the counter and permanently focused on the customer. "Do you have a security camera covering the outside of the building?"

"The outside? No," she said in a tone that suggested *Why on earth would we?* "That's the only one and it just covers the counter and our cash register."

"Is there a screen I could look at?"

"There is, but I'm not allowed to touch it. It's in my mam's office, and the office is locked. She's not here right now."

"When do you expect her back?"

"Tomorrow morning. We open at eleven and she's usually in here no later than ten."

Dillon handed her one of his business cards. "Would you have her call me tomorrow at her earliest convenience, please?"

She looked from the card to Dillon with a sort of stunned look on her face. "Is this about the dinner I dished up for my boyfriend yesterday? He said he would pay."

Dillon smiled and said, "No, nothing like that. I just wanted to look for someone who may have been walking past. You have a business card for her so I can check in if I miss her call?"

She nodded but didn't move.

"Could I have one of the business cards?"

"Oh, yes sir, just a minute, we've got them right here." She literally seemed to jump over to the cash register, picked up a thick stack of business cards and promptly let them fall out of her hand and scatter across the floor. She picked a couple of cards up and handed them to Dillon, all smiles. "Here you go, you can have two."

"Thank you."

"Her name is Gemma, Gemma Donnelly. I'll leave her a note with your card," she called as Dillon headed for the door.

"Thank you."

Hanely's Cornish Pastries and China Blue were the next two shops along the Merchants Arch passageway. Neither one had exterior cameras. His next stop was the Merchants Arch bar and restaurant. A round, illuminated Guinness sign hung over the entrance, black with the word Guinness in white just below the gold Irish harp and the Guinness signature in red, and there, mounted above the door was a CCTV camera. Dillon hurried inside through the black double doors.

The room had sixteen tables, all filled and a second level with more seating. Incredibly, a small private plane, large enough for one, maybe, hung from the ceiling.

"Go ahead and seat yourself. I think there's an open stool or two at the bar," a woman said. She was short, maybe just an inch or two above five feet with dark hair pulled back in a bun. She clutched a stack of a half dozen menus and she had to raise her voice to be heard over the din of casual conversation.

"Actually," Dillon said taking out his An Garda Síochána ID. "I wanted to speak to a manager."

"Is there a problem?" she said looking up from the ID with a worried look on her face.

"No, at least not here. I just wanted to ask about your CCTV tapes, I noticed the camera outside above the door, wondered if it might have taped an individual walking past."

"My husband's working in the barroom, follow me." She handed the stack of menus to a younger woman, said something Dillon couldn't hear, and hurried towards the barroom in the front of the building.

The barroom was an elegant room with maybe an eighteen foot ceiling painted a shade of burgundy with a large, elaborate, cream colored plaster medallion in the middle of the ceiling from which a massive light fixture hung. At the back of the bar between shelves of liquor bottles was a large mirror and above that in gold letters the words that read, *'Est. 1821 THE GUILD HALL OF MERCHANT TAILORS'*. The windows in front looked out onto the Liffey and the Ha'penny bridge.

She made her way to the bar and called to the bald man in a black apron standing at the far end of the bar.

"Jerry, An Garda Síochána," she said sounding like an arrest might be imminent.

"Be with you in a moment," he said and took his time topping up three Guinness glasses. He pushed the glasses across the bar to a group of people and laughed at something they said before he made his way down to where Dillon stood. "Now, what is it?"

"Your man's with the Garda," she said and indicated Dillon with a frantic nod of her head.

"Hi, Jack Dillon, you're in no trouble here."

"There's a surprise. Jerry O'Hara," he said and they shook hands.

"We're investigating a missing person case, and I noticed your CCTV camera outside in the passageway. I wondered if you kept the tapes. Hoping maybe your camera might have picked the individual up walking past. This would have been about a week ago."

"It's possible. You're American?"

Dillon smiled, knew where this was going and pulled out his ID and badge. "Yeah, I've been assigned to An Garda Síochána, special operations."

The man took the badge and ID, looked at them for a long moment and said, "Dillon? Were you involved in a shooting maybe two, three years back. Out at the airport?"

Dillon nodded, "Terminal Two."

"You saved some lives."

"Not enough, two good men were killed, and a female officer was seriously wounded."

"But you got them, all of them. From what I remember reading in the paper you—"

"Would you have tapes on file from a week ago?"

"The tapes? Yeah, yeah the images are all stored in the cloud nowadays. I suppose you want to take a look."

"If it's at all possible."

He called to the other bartender in the process of filling a couple of wine glasses. "Bobby, I've got to head downstairs, cover for me, it'll just be a couple of minutes." The guy nodded without looking up.

"Not to worry, Annie, I'll take care of this. Follow me," he said and left his wife standing wide eyed at the bar.

THIRTY-EIGHT

Dillon followed Jerry past a gold sign with red capital letters that read **'TOILETS'.** They headed down a steep set of stairs to the lower level. Apparently, handicapped access hadn't quite made it to all of Europe. O'Hara pulled a set of keys from his pocket as he stepped off the stairs and unlocked a door marked private just opposite the restrooms. He flicked a light switch on the wall as they stepped into a windowless room with three desks and a wall of file cabinets. They walked across the room to another door that he unlocked. He reached in the room and turned on the light. Sitting on a white Formica counter running along a far wall were three computer screens. The screens displayed different images of the barroom, the restaurant, the exterior passage way where Dillon had first seen the CCTV camera as well as the main Liffey Street entry and the Ha'penny Bridge. The images were black and white, somewhat bleary and jerky due to a delay in the recording process. That said, they potentially represented the first positive opportunity in the case, slim as it was.

"Here's what we have. Images are stored in the cloud by date, time and location. So, say you just needed the images from the barroom. We can isolate that camera, give you the images based on whatever day and whatever span of time you need and send it to you."

"So, you'd have the images outside in the passage way and on the street from a week ago?"

"Oh, yeah. Sure. But, please don't take offense at this, I don't want you just scanning through them. We had an incident two years back on an assault out on Liffey street. Someone came in from the local Garda station, clicked on the wrong link and ended up erasing a couple weeks' worth of imagery."

"You gotta be kidding me."

"I wish I was. Still happy to work with you and want to help, but what I'll need is a formal request from An Garda Síochána, just to cover us legally. I'll have my bookkeeper email copies to you as soon as that's received. She's really good at this tech shite, honestly it's a bit out of my league. I should mention, that jerking you see on the screen is caused by a five second delay. Just so you understand, the system takes a fresh shot every five seconds so that could conceivably be enough time for someone to walk or run past and not ever be recorded."

Dillon nodded and said, "We address the request to you?"

"I got a better idea." He walked over to a desk and pulled a business card from a small holder. "Here, this is my tech person, Linah Whelan, you can address everything to her. She'll check with me. Like I said, if you have dates and times she can isolate the images and get them to you. I'll give her a heads up when she comes in tomorrow. That take care of it for you?"

"Yeah, I'll have my techie talk to your techie," Dillon said.

Jerry laughed. "This stuff, I tell you, there's a part of me that wishes we could go back to phones you had to dial and manual typewriters."

"You're preaching to the choir."

"Why don't you plan on coming down for dinner some night. We've an extensive menu, great wine, wonderful music. Bring a friend. I'd love to have you as our guest."

"Thanks, that's very kind, but you don't have to do that. And—"

"Okay, but still come on down, please, and bring a guest. I'll be more than happy to charge you both for the meal if that's what you're worried about. Just use that phone number on the card to get in touch with me. I'm here eternally. Just ask the wife."

Dillon extended his hand. "It's been very nice to meet you, Jerry, and I appreciate the help. We'll be in touch first thing tomorrow."

They headed back upstairs. Dillon gave a wave to O'Hara then headed back to the room he'd first entered. Thanked his wife for her help and stepped back into the passage way and headed back past the Temple Take Out and over to the Quays Pub. He stood at the corner, next to the entrance to the Quays and looked up Fownes Street Lower toward the Liffey, a distance of maybe a hundred and twenty feet. He couldn't spot an exterior CCTV camera anywhere.

Directly across from the Quays Pub stood the Temple Bar Gallery and Studio, currently closed, as was the Regent Barber Shop just behind the Quays. There was one business that appeared to be open, the Mai Tai Massage Parlor, maybe fifty feet down the street.

THIRTY-NINE

The door to the Mai Tai Massage Parlor was inset a good eighteen inches. The door was painted a glossy black with a brass mail slot in the middle of the door and a brass doorknob on the left side. Above the door hung a red sign with white letters, 'Welcome To Mai Tai Massage'. Above the door was a window with a small neon sign that read **'OPEN'.** A framed sign attached to the building advertised prices for thirty, sixty, ninety and one hundred and twenty minute massages. Dillon tried the door, but it was locked. He pressed the intercom on the door frame just below a small camera.

"Yes," a pleasant, accented voice answered.

"Are you open?" Dillon asked choosing not to identify himself as a member of the police force.

"Do you have an appointment?"

"No."

"What's your name?"

"Jack Dillon."

Another pause and then a loud buzz before he heard the lock click. He pushed the door open and headed up a steep flight of stairs consisting of fourteen steps and no handrail. With each step the scent of spicy incense seemed to grow a little stronger. At the top of the stairs he entered a small room painted deep purple with a purple shag rug on the floor. A white counter had a sign hanging on the front that read, 'Mai Tai Reception'. Bamboo poles rose from the floor to the ceiling on either side of the reception counter.

A young Asian girl flashed a broad smile at Dillon and said, "Can I help?" Her speech was heavily accented.

"I'd like to speak with your manager."

The smile immediately faded. "There is problem?"

"No. But I would like to talk with your manager, please."

"No problem?"

"No problem," Dillon said shaking his head.

"He not here, you go, now."

Dillon pulled his badge from his pocket, held it in front of the girl and watched as her eyes grew wide. "I'm going to look for him, I promise I won't disturb anyone."

"No, you cannot," she said, although she remained in her chair. Dillon strolled down the purple hall. He passed four doors, two of which were open displaying a massage table positioned in the middle of the empty room. Both rooms were painted in the same purple as the reception room and the hallway. At the end of the hall was a door labeled office.

Dillon opened the door and focused on a man in the process of hanging up his phone. He was young, maybe mid-thirties, lean, with short black hair and a short sleeve black shirt that appeared to be silk. A large man off to the side rose to his feet. He was maybe a hundred pounds heavier than Dillon with a shaved head and a nose that appeared to have been broken more than once, suggesting he had difficulty getting along with people. The room wasn't purple.

Dillon held his hands out in mock surrender and said, "You're not in any trouble. I just have a question and then I'll leave."

"And what is question?" the young man said. With a wave of his hand he signaled the large man to remain in place.

"We're looking for a missing person, she was last seen across the lane at the Quays Pub about a week ago. I'm just trying to get any CCTV tape that would cover the front of your building, in the hope we might spot her leaving and if so, who she was with."

"We not have outside camera."

"Except the one above your intercom."

The young man folded his hands just in front of his chin and tapped his index fingers together, apparently thinking. "That camera cover only our front door. After all, we not want anyone come in here with wrong idea," he said and smiled.

"Can you show me, please?"

He seemed to think about that before suddenly spinning around in his desk chair and tapping a couple of keys on a keyboard. A screen came to life with a live image of the downstairs doorway. Just like he said, the camera was focused on the door and maybe six inches of the narrow sidewalk. In no way would it be able to tape passersby.

The young man spun around in his chair and smiled. "You happy?"

"More like disappointed. I appreciate your time, don't bother to get up. I'll show myself out," Dillon said.

"Sorry we not more help. Next time you here I give you big discount. You enjoy."

"I'll keep that in mind," Dillon said and closed the office door behind him.

Halfway down the hall a woman poked her head out of one of the rooms. "You like favor. Only ten euro. Feel very good. You enjoy."

"Thanks, maybe another time," Dillon said. He waved goodbye to the receptionist, went down the stairs and out onto the sidewalk. It was time to head home.

FORTY

Dillon pulled into the parking space in front of his house and sat behind the wheel for a long moment. After today's infinitesimal progress on Madeline Keller's disappearance, they continued to grasp at straws. Progress was a generous term. Not only had the clock been ticking, but they were virtually out of time, at least statistically, for any sort of positive conclusion. Add to that, last night's disastrous episode at The Swiss Cottage where Riley Dempsey slipped through their hands. If Dempsey had any brains at all he had most likely left the city and disappeared. None of that factored in the additional strain Suel was under with his sister, Aideen, being released from the hospital and her assailant still unknown by all but herself. In a word, things were looking awfully bleak.

He thought for a while longer, didn't come up with any solutions and eventually made his way into the house. He unlocked the front door, took a step inside and flicked on a light. He scanned the front hallway searching for a deposit Lucifer left, but surprisingly couldn't find anything. The door to the sitting room was closed so he walked into the kitchen, expecting to find a mess. Surprisingly, the room was just as he left it that morning, nothing out of place, no paper towels, food scraps or empty meat packages chewed up and scattered across the floor.

He pulled the lid off the cookie jar containing dog biscuits and rattled the top against the jar a few times after he grabbed a biscuit. He heard Lucifer land on the bedroom floor upstairs. No doubt he'd been sleeping on the bed. A moment later, as Dillon looked up the staircase, Lucifer peeked around the newel post.

"Lucifer, what a surprise, you're here and there's no mess to clean up. Come on down and let's get you outside," Dillon said holding up the dog biscuit as an enticement.

Lucifer cautiously hopped down the steps then headed for the front door where Dillon now stood. "Good boy," Dillon said giving some additional encouragement. He followed up by tossing the biscuit out towards his car. Lucifer bounded off the front stoop and snatched the biscuit just after it bounced off the car tire. Dillon watched him for a moment then closed the door and went back in the kitchen.

He opened his refrigerator, pulled out a wrapped plate with a half-eaten chicken breast and mashed potatoes and set it in the microwave. While the plate spun round and the chicken occasionally splattered, Dillon thought of Jerry O'Hara's offer for a free dinner down at the Merchants Arch. He filled Lucifer's food and water dish, pulled the plate out of the microwave and opened the front door and called Lucifer back inside.

His meal, such as it was, lacked a lot, not the least of which was a decent taste. He barely finished half before he'd had enough. He poured himself a beer, went into the sitting room, turned on the television and stretched out on the couch. He woke a little after two in the morning. The television had some sort of fashion show on that he immediately clicked off and headed up to bed. Lucifer was breathing deeply, curled up on one of the pillows. It figured. Right now, even Lucifer seemed to have more sense than Dillon.

FORTY-ONE

The day had begun with a heavy cloud cover and a light rain. Dillon was in the office early, on his second cup of coffee and feeling no more upbeat than the night before. He'd sent an email to Ina Nolan asking her to request CCTV footage from Linah Whelan, Jerry O'Hara's tech person at the Merchants Arch. He gave her the dates and requested viewing hours from nine thirty in the evening to three in the morning and attached the photo of Colin and friends in their rugby jerseys along with a Facebook image of Darren Otis and another image of Madeline Keller even though Ina had the selfies. After leaving a phone message, he'd sent an email to Ronnie Maxwell up in Belfast asking him to get in touch. He'd just sent a phone message to Suel, when his cellphone rang. It was Suel calling him back.

"Yeah, Paddy," was how Dillon answered.

"What's the emergency?"

"Not exactly an emergency. I just wanted to check and see if . . ."

"Not an emergency. It's barely seven in the bleeding morning and you're phoning me? You're interrupting my final ten minutes of sleep. I was in the midst of a wonderful dream. There were these sisters, gorgeous blonde twins, and—"

"Spare me the details," Dillon said.

"Actually, I'm about a mile away, I'll see you in few minutes. Might be nice if you had a mug of tea waiting for me at my desk."

"So? After being bitched at because of the early morning hour I'm supposed to get you a tea? All right, all right, I'll get the kettle going and meet you in the break room."

"See you shortly," Suel said and hung up.

Dillon brought his list of things he wanted to accomplish into the break room, filled the kettle and turned it on. Suel appeared, tossed his coat over his desk chair and headed for the break room just as the kettle clicked off.

"Perfect timing, the kettle just went off."

Suel flashed a half-second smile and turned the kettle on again.

"What? You don't believe me. There, see?" Dillon said in response to the kettle shutting off after a few seconds.

Suel noticed Dillon's list as he carried his mug over to the table and said, "Not that I don't trust you, but I don't when it comes to making tea. What have you got there?"

"Outside chance we might get some images from the Merchants Arch, they've got a CCTV camera, two as a matter of fact. One covering the passage way and the other covering the front of the building and the area across Liffey Street just around Ha'penny Bridge."

"You can thank me later for the tip."

"I've sent a message to Ina to request the tapes from Linah Whelan, she's the tech person for the owner of the Merchants Arch. No other cameras along the passage way and absolutely none on Fownes Street Lower alongside the Quays Pub, which I kind of found surprising."

"Certainly disappointing, but maybe not so surprising, considering the cheapskates."

"I've a call into Ronnie Maxwell."

"Because?"

"I'm thinking of going up today, talking to the lads who made the sworn statements and—"

"You'll need to talk to your man Calvert first, set up something with him, won't you?"

"No, I don't think so. In his letter he only refers to his two clients, his nephew Colin and the reverend. He said nothing regarding the other three. As a matter of fact, I was thinking of asking Ronnie to set things up. Maybe with the local constabulary along it would add a little weight to our questions."

"If he can do it."

"Yeah. Think you could make time to go up with me?"

"When you thinking?"

"Earlier the better, soon as I hear from Ronnie. I'm hoping Ronnie can get us an interview room with the PSNI and since we've got the phone numbers give each

kid a call and request their presence for an informal conversation before we head up there."

"You calling the Cominsky lad, too?"

"Maybe, the letter was addressed to us, but Ronnie
obviously never received one from Calvert Cominsky.
We might just try to have Ronnie contact him. We seem
to have them caught in a lie, whether Calvert Cominsky
knows it or not, and I'd like to add some pressure."

FORTY-TWO

By midmorning the clouds had disappeared, the sky was clear and blue. Dillon and Suel were on the 10:35 train from Dublin's Connolly Station heading back up to Belfast Central. Ronnie Maxwell had promised to meet them at the Belfast Central Train Station. Forty minutes earlier, Dillon had received a copy of Ina Nolan's email to Lena Whelan, the tech person for Jerry O'Hara at the Merchants Arch, complete with an attachment of the official request form listing dates and hours. Ina mentioned she would be using a new facial recognition program to speed up the arduous task of reviewing six hour's worth of grainy, blurry tapes. Suddenly things possibly had gone from *'not a snowballs chance in hell'* to *'half a chance'*.

Dillon turned from the window after watching the outskirts of Dublin pass by and said, "So, how did things go last night?"

"You mean with Aideen?"

"No, I meant with the hot date you had with the blonde twins. Yeah, with Aideen. How's she doing?"

"Physically, okay. Swellings gone. Some discoloration remains. That'll be pretty much vanished in another three or four days. She'll be prancing around town wearing that nose splint for the next few weeks."

"How's her mental state?"

"She'd never admit it, but she's afraid. I was aware of her checking the locks on the front and back door at least three or four times in the middle of the night all the while carrying an old Hurley of mine around with her. She's all the shades and draperies pulled. She's her cellphone with her at all times and she's set up the emergency 999 number on speed dial so she only has to hit the screen once."

"You going back there tonight?"

Suel nodded. "I'll be going back for quite some time until we get this bastard. It's just up to her to tell us who. Unfortunately, right now she just wishes it would all go away. She wants to forget it, blank it out of her memory.

"You talk to DI Walsh?"

"Over to Mountjoy station? Yeah, he's got nothing. Not a reflection on him, but Aideen's not talking, so what's he supposed to do? Poor soul probably has fifty or sixty other open cases just like Aideen's and no one is saying a damn thing."

They were more or less quiet for the final hour of the trip. Suel actually dozed off for a good forty minutes and Dillon figured he had probably been awake and standing guard at Aideen's more than he let on. He woke with a start as they pulled into Belfast Central. Dillon didn't acknowledge Suel's sleeping.

"You let me do the talking. I'll spot Ronnie and introduce you."

"I spoke to him on the phone, for God's sake," Dillon said.

"Did you see him? Do you know what he looks like? Wonderful, a three minute conversation versus my years of dealing with your man, by all means, you lead the way, Dillon."

"Okay," Dillon said and stepped out of the train car with Suel behind him. Not ten feet away was a neatly dressed man standing on the platform with glasses. He was wearing a dark suit and a black trilby hat. " Detective Inspector Maxwell," Dillon called and the man smiled and waved back.

"Oh, for fecks sake," Suel groaned not quite under his breath then shouted, "Ronnie, how you keeping?"

FORTY-THREE

As they drove, Ronnie Maxwell gave them an update. They'd be in a conference room at Belfast's Musgrave Police Station, the only station in Belfast with twenty-four hour accessibility.

"Not that I plan to be there with the likes of you two for twenty-four hours. I called all five lads and scheduled an appointment forty-five minutes apart in a conference room up on the third floor. We come across anything, there's an interview room at the opposite end of the building but based on what you told me I thought it best to begin in pleasant surroundings."

"Really appreciate you making the effort, Ronnie," Suel said.

"Well worth it if we can get some information."

"Anyone suggest they were bringing a barrister with them?" Dillon asked.

"No, but that doesn't necessarily mean they won't. Nothing we can do about that, they're within their rights. I was going to say they all sounded surprised when I called, but shocked might be the better description."

"Be interesting to see if Colin Cominsky brings his uncle."

"I think I told you, your man Calvert Cominsky has a sterling reputation up here. I'd have him with me if I were the lad."

They drove past the Musgrave Station. A five story modern building with red brick and white stone across the exterior. Maxwell put his blinker on and began to turn into the parking area. The parking area had an eight foot concrete wall around it and then mounted on top of the wall was another six or seven feet of steel sheeting painted in broad striped sections of white, red, grey and black. Dillon counted five different CCTV cameras mounted along the wall.

Maxwell stopped at the entrance and a guard stepped out of a small corner structure built of stone and bullet proof glass, wearing a protective vest. He recognized Maxwell, gave him a nod, checked Dillon and Suel's ID's and waved them into the parking area. He watched them for a moment before he stepped back into the corner structure.

They pulled into a parking place and stepped out of the vehicle. "No weapons, lads," Maxwell said. "We'll be going through a couple of detection devices so you might as well place them in the trunk now, or risk having them confiscated."

"I'm clean," Suel said.

"Nothing on me, but thanks for the warning," Dillon said.

The entrance to the building was a square glass outcropping, with a massive roof upturned on the corners in a way that reminded Dillon of the Far East, China or maybe Japan, although he'd never been to either place. They stepped inside as Maxwell held the door to the entry and then Dillon held the next door for Suel and Maxwell. Once inside the building, they passed through a metal detection device similar to a security check at the airport. They were scanned through another device and had their ID's checked again before they stepped onto the elevator.

Dillon thought about people back in the states and wondered what they would think of the security just to enter a police station but didn't say anything.

"We're up on the third floor," Maxwell said. As they stepped onto the elevator, he checked his watch. "The Taylor lad will be our first subject. He's due in about thirty minutes."

"You contacted all of them this morning?" Suel asked.

"Yes, and I'm sure they've been in touch with one another, comparing stories, wondering what the hell is going on. They don't know a thing about the tapes from the Empire pub. I've a copy to run should they have any questions," he chuckled. "As a matter of security, we'll confiscate their phones prior to them stepping in the room and do a check on calls for the past sixty days."

"You need a warrant for that?" Dillon asked.

"We do, five warrants as a matter of fact, and they're all on my desk," Maxwell said as the doors opened and he stepped off onto the third floor.

FORTY-FOUR

The conference room featured a blonde wood oblong table that seated ten. A small window looked onto the park across the street and the glass wall opposite would normally view into the office with a dozen cubicles and staff in civilian clothes although today the drapes had been pulled. The chairs around the conference table had a padded, brown faux leather seat and back. A black plastic tray sat in the middle of the table holding a half dozen plastic bottles of water.

"How do you want to handle this?" Maxwell said, once they were seated around the table. Maxwell had just received the call from the entry security that Noel Taylor had arrived and was in the process of being escorted up to the third floor.

"I think," Dillon said looking over at Suel. "I'd like you to begin, don't introduce us. See if he'll verbally agree to his statement, give him the opportunity to make any changes and once he agrees to the statement as it exists, we'll enter the discussion. Point out the discrepancies, hopefully, that will motivate him. If that doesn't encourage him, we can run the Empire Pub tape and then

I'll speak as an officer from the United States. How long will it take to get information from his phone?"

"No more than a minute or two. They'll have it by the time he steps off the elevator up here," Maxwell said.

"I almost feel sorry for the lads," Suel said just as there was a knock on the door.

"Enter," Maxwell called as the door opened and a woman in uniform held the door open. She wore a short sleeve white blouse with two flapped pockets, a black tie and skirt. One of the pockets had a black name tag attached. Her brown hair was cut short and her jaw was set. She didn't look like the sort of woman you'd give a hard time to. As soon as the young man entered she pulled the door closed behind him. Taylor half turned at the sound of the door closing then looked around at the three grim faced men seated at the conference table.

"Umm, hi," he said and gave a half wave.

Maxwell made a show of studying one of the sheets of paper resting on the closed laptop just in front of him for a few seconds. "Mr. Taylor, thank you for coming, please take a seat," he said and extended his hand toward a seat directly across from Dillon and Suel.

Noel Taylor looked like an average college kid. He wore a blue pin stripped shirt with a button down collar and jeans that appeared to be clean. The shirt was untucked as was the style. His dark hair was neatly trimmed along the sides and slicked in a short spike on top. He appeared to be in very good physical condition, no doubt from playing rugby. Once seated, he swallowed nervously a couple of times.

Maxwell smiled, turned on a recorder, stated the date and time and listed everyone in the room. He made a point of mentioning that Suel was with Dublin's An Garda Síochána, and that Dillon was a United States Marshal attached to An Garda Síochána. Taylor glanced nervously across the table as Dillon and Suel's names and positions were mentioned.

"Thank you for making time on such short notice to come down to the station, Mr. Taylor. We just wanted to clear up a few questions we had with your statement regarding the disappearance of Madeline Keller down in Dublin."

Taylor glanced back and forth, nodded and focused on the table.

Maxwell smiled and handed a copy of the signed, sworn statement to Taylor. "If you wouldn't mind reviewing this just to make sure, based on your memory, that you remain in agreement with everything you've sworn to," Maxwell said. He paused for three beats and added, "Under penalty of law."

Taylor gave a worried glance as he took the copy of his statement.

He looked down at the statement in front of him as if he was about to read. Dillon couldn't be sure, but he thought Taylor's eyes seemed to be staring vacantly, focused on a single spot, not moving from left to right which would be the case if he had actually been reading. He swallowed nervously a few more times.

When he looked up he appeared about ready to cry, nodded and in a soft voice said, "It's . . . it's okay, I think."

"You're sure? Because right now you could change anything that isn't correct and we'll simply accept the change. We realize things can get confusing and sometimes with a little time, after five or six days, things become a bit more clear," Maxwell said. "See, the idea of being associated in a kidnapping, a rape, or possibly even a murder is a very serious charge and we will pursue our investigation with all due speed. It's what we're paid to do, and believe me, we know how to do it. So, please double check the statement and make sure you don't wish to change anything or maybe add an additional fact or two that now comes to mind?"

"No, no, we, I mean, I, umm, everything is correct, it looks just like what I remember."

"You're sure? Because as you probably know, we're going to be talking to everyone and if someone adds something that contradicts your statement, well, then you've got a problem. You see?"

Taylor gave a slight nod.

"Would you mind speaking so the recorder can pick it up for the record. You understand what I've just told you?"

"Yes, sir, I understand," he said in barely more than a whisper.

"So you're saying you all remained at the Empire Pub the entire evening?"

"Yes, sir," Taylor said, his voice a bit stronger.

Maxwell picked up his copy of Taylor's statement. "You said, let's see, ahh, yes. You state that, 'We arrived around half past five in the evening and didn't leave until right before they closed. We chatted for maybe five minutes in the parking lot and then I went home.' That's what you wrote here, what you swore to. Right?"

Taylor slowly nodded as if he knew the next bit was not going to go his way.

"Could you speak, please."

"Yes sir, I went right home."

"I'm going to ask you one more time. Is there anything you wish to change, now, after having some time to think about it. Maybe you suddenly remember something, it happens, we all forget things until we're reminded. Anything you want to change?" Maxwell said.

"N-N-No, sir," Taylor said, not sounding all that sure.

"Interesting," Maxwell looked over at Suel.

With a nod of his head Suel indicated Maxwell should continue.

"Here's what I'm not quite understanding, Mr. Taylor. See, as it happens I was at the Empire Pub, just yesterday. Did you know they have CCTV cameras? A number of them, as a matter of fact. So, of course, they were only too happy to provide us with tapes of the night you were there."

The color seemed to suddenly drain from Taylor's face.

"I'd like you to take a look at this," Maxwell said as he flipped open the laptop and tapped the return button. A grainy black and white image appeared of five of them gathered around a high table. Three were seated on bar stools, two were standing, the table was littered with empty glasses. Colin Cominsky appeared to be heavily intoxicated. The next few images showed all but one of them draining pints of beer. The next dozen or so images showed them beginning to slide off their stools, followed by four images as they passed through the crowded barroom, another at the door, a half dozen walking out to the parking lot and images in the parking lot, and finally, images of headlights as a pair of cars, a two door blue compact with a white top and an older black SUV exited the parking lot. The entire license plate on the SUV could be read, but only the last three numbers, 471, on the compact's license plate were visible.

Taylor's bottom lip began to tremble.

"Now, just for a sense of clarification, help me out. Do you have any idea who, exactly this SUV is registered to?"

Well, umm, that's me mum's car. I was driving it that night."

"Interesting, your mother's car. I bet she'd be proud right about now. What do you think?"

"No, sir, not exactly."

"Not exactly. Noel, you'll notice that the date and time are posted in the lower righthand corner of each image," Maxwell said. "Looks to us like you lads left sometime after seven. Now, if I'm not mistaken, the Empire closes at one-thirty in the morning. Care to enlighten us where you were for the next six hours? Because right now, we're thinking you all drove down to Dublin and grabbed the Keller girl in your mum's car. "

FORTY-FIVE

oel Taylor gave an audible swallow. His eyes began to water, as if he was about to cry.

"Okay, okay, look, you've got it all wrong. Colin was in a bad spot. See. They'd just buried a good friend of his a week or so before—"

"Who was that?" Maxwell said.

"Ah, Dawn, Dawn Davies is, or rather was, her name. She'd been sick for a while, couple of years with cancer and it finally took her life. Colin said he was going to find a cure for the cancer. It's why he left Trinity and transferred up here to Queen's. Well, that and I think his father probably made him leave Trinity after the girlfriend down there dumped him."

"Go on."

"So, we're buying him pints and well, he wasn't feeling any pain and Jimmy sort of had the phone number of a girl that for a few quid she'd maybe give Colin a gobble. We all kind of maybe chipped in and were gonna get him, umm, taken care of, you might say."

"By Jimmy you're referring to James McKenzie?"

"Yes, sir."

"And you paid this woman to have sex with Colin Cominsky?"

"Not really. I mean, that was sort of the idea, but he was so drunk that he maybe, sort of passed out. She just took our money and then threatened to call security if we didn't leave the building. So we ended up driving over to Dorys to get some fish and chips into Colin so he'd sober up. His father, the reverend, doesn't like drink, calls it sinful. We dropped Colin off at home a little after midnight, once he was able to walk himself to the door."

"Who, exactly, do you mean when you say we?"

"Umm, all of us, well except for Darren Otis. He went home when we left the Empire."

"I'll need names," Maxwell said and made a show of getting ready to write.

"Well, it was Colin Cominsky. Jimmy McKenzie. Peter Jenkins. Oh, and myself, of course."

"Why did you falsify your statement?"

"We thought it was the least we could do for Colin. His girlfriend broke up with him, Dawn Davies died, the reverend made him leave Trinity. We didn't know any-thing about Madeline being missing, at least not when we wrote those statements. We thought it was because we paid that woman to go down on him, and I mean, it never even happened. Like I just told you, she took our money and then threatened to call security if we didn't leave. We just didn't want him to get into any trouble with his old man. Colin's really a good lad, and well, the reverend is a bit of the old time religion sort of wanker."

"So, tell us about your relationship with Madeline Keller?"

"Madeline?"

"Yes, Madeline Keller."

"I never met the girl. I only know her from what Colin told me."

Maxwell stared at Taylor for a long moment and gave an audible sigh. He turned the laptop around, ran his fingers across the keyboard bringing up Taylor's selfie, an image of him standing naked in front of a bathroom mirror. He spun the laptop around so Taylor could get an unobstructed view of the image.

"Oh shit," Taylor said as tears began to flow down his cheeks. "I . . . I . . . I'm sorry I ever sent it. I shouldn't have done it. We all thought it would be funny. I know that's stupid, but after she broke up with Colin, he sent me the images of her, and I, maybe sort of sent them to the other lads. I guess we all sent selfies to her. You know, we thought it would be funny, kind of telling her what she was missing out on or something. But I never met her in person. I don't think any of us did, ever."

"Whose brilliant idea was it to send your selfies to Madeline?" Maxwell said.

"Umm, that may have been my idea. Now, I kinda wish we didn't do it. We just sort of did it on the spur of the moment."

Dillon leaned forward across the table, suddenly red faced and spoke in a low growl with his jaw clenched. "Listen to me, you over privileged little prick. You have just one chance to come clean and tell us what the hell happened. So help me God, if you lie, you will not make it out of this room alive."

Maxwell's eyes grew wide and he sat there in shock. Suel placed a hand on Dillon's belt, holding him in his chair so he wouldn't leap across the table.

"No, no. I'm telling you the truth," Taylor said, crying openly. "I never, ever met her. We just thought it would be funny, you know, since she broke up with Colin. We just wanted to get even, for Colin's sake. Honest, you gotta believe me, I would never hurt her. I wouldn't even be able to find her, I've never, ever, even been to Dublin. You can ask anybody. Even ask my folks."

Dillon pointed a finger at him and said, "You better pray to God that you're telling me the truth and your little dumb fuck friends back you up. Because if they don't . . ."

"No really, I'm not lying. I'm sorry for what we did. I really, really am. We didn't mean to cause any problems we just thought it would be funny. We didn't know she was going to disappear," Taylor said and broke down sobbing.

FORTY-SIX

Maxwell escorted Noel Taylor out of the room and placed him in an interview room at the opposite end of the building.

Once they were alone, Suel said, "That was quite the act, Dillon. For a moment there I wasn't sure if you were going to leap across the table and strangle the little wanker."

Dillon took a deep breath and said, "It was no act. A bunch of spoiled, privileged, little bastards sending naked pictures to some girl who's busting her ass in school trying to make something of herself. Her mother's gone crazy, there's not a damn thing her poor father can do to fix any of this, and these, these, little pricks are getting together to get their story straight. Paying some street hooker to service their drunken pal, apparently just an average night out on the town for all of them. And isn't this just great, the kid's old man is some sort of religious zealot. How's that working out? God, I just want to scream."

"I think you did," Suel said. "I do have to remind you that she sent those pictures of herself."

"Yeah, I know, but she sent them to her boyfriend. They were supposedly in a damn relationship. Was it stupid? Hell, yes, it was stupid. It was beyond stupid. But that doesn't give him the right to send the images around to his pals."

Suel gave Dillon a look. "From what we just heard, it was this Taylor lad who sent them around and—"

"I know, I know, but damn it. Unfortunately, we both know where in the hell this investigation is probably headed. The odds of us finding this girl alive, at this late date, are about one in a million, and there's nothing we can do about that. Damn it."

The door opened a few minutes later and Maxwell stepped back in and looked at Dillon.

"Ronnie, I'm sorry. I apologize, it won't happen again. Just listening to that kid, Jesus Christ. We got a girl missing, odds are at this stage she's not alive, and this bunch of spoiled brats are all chipping in to pay for a prostitute. I want to wade into the middle of them with a baseball bat and just start swinging."

Maxwell shook his head and said. "I was thinking the same damn thing, except we'd use a hurley. I wouldn't have minded you beating the little plonker. I was just worried about scuff marks on the table when you jumped across. What do you think?"

"Think? About getting ripped off by the hooker and then buying fish and chips? It sounds so damn stupid, I'm thinking it almost has to be true. Any way we can see if that Dorys Fish and Chips has a record? Either images or I'm thinking if they all put money in to pay the hooker maybe they used a credit card for the fish and chips."

"Already made the call and have someone checking on it. Hopefully, we'll have some sort of confirmation in a bit. Thing is, if that story holds up, I don't see how any of them could have made it down to Dublin before the pub closed. It would be next to impossible."

"Who's next on the list?" Suel asked.

"The Jenkins lad. He's being escorted up as we speak. Same routine as before?"

"I don't see any reason to change," Dillon said.

"Works for me. I'll make sure Dillon doesn't scuff the table top, talk about needing a hurley," Suel said.

A few minutes later there was a knock on the door and the same female officer, looking just a little more severe, walked into the room.

"Hold on a moment before you let him in here," Maxwell said. Once she closed the door he said, "I took our first individual down to interview room three. I was planning to leave him there for a few hours, but on second thought I'd like you to escort him from the building. Unless something earth shattering develops, we'll be sending all of them back out of the building. Does that sound all right to you two?"

"I don't have a problem with that," Suel said.

"As long as we have access as things develop, I'm fine with that," Dillon said.

"Okay, bring in the next one and then escort the Taylor lad out of the building."

A strapping, ginger haired, young man followed her in and stepped up to the table. He wore blue jeans with a designer label above the left front pocket and a Belfast Lasers t-shirt. He was large, maybe six foot three, with brown eyes, a clear complexion and a red scar about an inch long running down the side of his chin. The lower half of a tattoo on his right bicep extended below the shirt sleeve. His jaw was set and his gaze was cold.

"Is it all right if I sit down," he said as the door closed behind him. He didn't seem to appear concerned.

Dillon, and in fact all of them were familiar with the act. A lot of bravado suggesting he wasn't about to be intimidated. The type who usually had themselves tied in knots about three minutes into the interview.

"Please, have a seat, Mr. Jenkins. We want to thank you for coming down here this afternoon and—"

"Didn't really sound like you were giving me much of an option on the phone. Well, here I am. So, let's get this over with and I can get back to my day."

Maxwell smiled. "Just a couple of questions regarding your statement. Hopefully, we can get them cleared up. Let me just record this, in the event someone has a question later on, we won't have to bother you." He pressed the record button, stated the date and time along with listing everyone in the room. As he mentioned Suel and Dillon, Jenkins flashed a quick look across the table at them. Once finished, Maxwell smiled and slowly slid a copy of his signed statement over to Jenkins.

"Now, you've made your statement and signed the document, swearing that everything is true to the best of your knowledge and we just thought it might make sense if you—"

"I'm standing by the statement. We all are. It's why I added my signature. What you see there is exactly what happened that night. We were in the Empire Pub until it closed."

"And it closed at around one-thirty I believe. Correct?"

"If you say so. As you can see, I don't wear a watch," Jenkins said, lifting his muscular left arm to prove the point.

"Oh, interesting," Maxwell said as the first signs of doubt began to creep across Jenkins face. "I would still advise you to carefully read your statement. In my experience, after close to a week, some items that you initially forgot may creep into your memory and you are at liberty to add or change anything you wish at this time."

Jenkins slid the statement back towards Maxwell. "No thanks. Apparently you weren't listening. I just got done telling you, everything there is correct. Exactly as I remember."

"You sure, Mr. Jenkins? We always urge individuals in an interview, prior to arrest, to double check."

Jenkins flinched visibly at the word arrest, then seemed to regain his composure. "No, I know what we did that night, we drank pints in the pub with our pal, Colin. He's had a tough couple of weeks and it's what mates do. It's what you do if you're a good mate," he said, maybe suggesting Maxwell wouldn't know what good mates do.

Maxwell pursed his lips and nodded for a long moment. "Thanks for enlightening me. Let me tell you what good investigators do, Mr. Jenkins. We search for the truth, we check out statements, we examine the facts. And when someone states for the record that they were in a pub until close we actually go to the pub. You know why, Mr. Jenkins?"

"Umm, to ahh, talk to the staff?"

"Sometimes, of course," Maxwell opened the laptop, clicked some keys and spun it around so Jenkins could watch the images flick past. "But what's the old saying? A picture is worth a thousand words. We've got a lot of pictures from the Empire Pub. You see, they have CCTV cameras all over the place, inside and out. So we've got pictures of you and all your *good* mates. Oh, by the way, while you're watching you might just make note that the date and time are posted right there in the corner. Now, we have pictures of you in the pub, drinking pints until around half past seven when you all decide to get off your lying fat asses and leave. Care to tell us where you were going? Oh, and let me warn you, we've already spoken to some of your *good* mates. So anything you say, any lies you tell, will be held against you, and I will be making damn sure that you are charged. Do I make myself clear?"

All the bravado from a moment earlier had suddenly disappeared. Jenkins gave a slight nod then pulled the copy of his statement back in front of him. "Maybe I should just check this one more time."

"Probably a good idea," Maxwell said and flashed a quick smile at Dillon and Suel.

Over the next thirty minutes, in between answering questions, Jenkins crossed out a major portion of his signed statement and wrote two additional pages that more or less corroborated the version that Noel Taylor had provided. Yes, they left around half past seven. After making a phone call, they drove to council housing, a place named Towerview, and pooled their money to pay a hooker named Molly who kept the funds and threatened to call security if they didn't leave. They finished up with fish and chips at Dorys, and paid for them by using Colin Cominsky's credit card. With Cominsky asleep in the back seat, Noel Taylor dropped Jenkins off at his apartment a little after midnight and Jenkins went to bed. Jenkins did not own a vehicle and did not travel down to Dublin that evening nor any time since.

Towards the end of an hour Maxwell slid a note over to Dillon and Suel with three words written on it. 'Send him home?'

Dillon and Suel read the note, nodded and when the officer appeared to escort Jenkins from the room Maxwell instructed her to bring him down to the lobby and send him out the door.

"Mr. Jenkins, you're not to leave the city limits of Belfast for any reason without first checking with this office. You have my card and my phone number. Feel free to contact me at any time. If, for any reason, you leave this city, we will find out and you will be placed under arrest. A word of advice to you. It would be unwise to contact or interact with your friends. We will be watching all of you. Do I make myself clear?"

Jenkins gave a frightened nod.

"I'm sorry, I would appreciate it if you would speak up. In the event you choose not to follow my instructions we'll have it on tape. Now, I'm going to ask again and I expect to hear an answer. Do I make myself clear?"

"Yes, yes sir."

"Very well. Officer, if you would please get Mr. Jenkins out of our sight and release him in the lobby."

When she opened the door Jenkins literally ran out of the room.

"Are we ready for Mr. Darren Otis?" Maxwell smiled.

FORTY-SEVEN

As with the two young men before him, Darren Otis was escorted up to the fourth floor and shown into the room by the stern looking officer. He was noticeably smaller than Taylor or Jenkins. Dillon guessed his height to be about five feet five inches. He had blondish hair with maybe just a hint of a reddish cast. His hair was a bit long on the top and combed straight back. The sides and back of his head were shaved. He was dressed in grey trousers and wore a starched blue shirt with a button down collar beneath a navy blue sport coat. He nodded politely and looked from Maxwell to Dillon to Suel and back to Maxwell and said, "Good afternoon."

"Mr. Otis. Please, have a seat," Maxwell said.

"Thank you," he said and sat down. He folded his hands in front of him and waited politely.

"We're going to record this, just in case we have a question later on. We can check what is said and we won't have to inconvenience you to come back in."

Otis nodded.

Maxwell repeated the standard lines of date, time and who was in the room. Then said, "Now, Mr. Otis, of the four friends who joined Colin Cominsky on the evening in question, you were the only one who was not requested to fill out a sworn statement. Do you happen to have any idea why that was?"

"I don't know for sure, sir. But, I think it was because I left the group at the Empire Pub. I had to get home and study. I'm a finance major and I had an exam the following morning. So, I was in the dark about anything that went on later that night."

"I see. And where do you attend school."

"Queen's, like the others, although Colin just transferred in. I'm third year."

"What was the exam in?"

"Finance, it's my major."

"And how did you do on your exam?"

"I think I did all right, I haven't actually gotten the exam results yet, you know, fingers crossed and all that."

"Who teaches the course?"

"Professor Winton Varley, I rather like his course."

"Do you now?"

"Yes, sir. But then I've always wanted to work in finance or maybe become a banker. Always been good with numbers. The lads give me a bit of a hard time about it, but that's okay."

"And you play rugby?"

"Afraid not, sir. I did for a few years, but I wasn't exactly blessed with the size you need to play at university level."

"Did you try out for the Belfast Lasers?"

"No, sir. Unfortunately, that's pretty much by invitation only. Not that I fault them for it, it just pushes me out because I'm that much smaller. I try and go to most of their matches, but honestly, if I was out on the pitch with the size of the players in that league, I'd probably end up in traction in the Royal Victoria just a few minutes into the first half. Everyone at that level is charging around on the odd chance they might get a shot at playing at county level, or God forbid, playing for Ireland or one of the French teams. Much as I loved it, I'm out of the league, sort of speak." He smiled for a moment at his humor.

Maxwell smiled back for a brief moment. "But you were with the lads the other night at the Empire Pub?"

"Yes sir. I was there with them for a bit, but then everyone decided to leave. Like I said, they had something they were going to attend to and I had to get home and study. They were still seated and in the process of finishing up when I left."

"What time would that have been?"

"Oh, not too late. I think maybe half past seven or so. If I recall, I was home at my desk reviewing tax formulas by eight that evening."

"Where'd everyone else head off to?"

"After pints at the Empire? I believe they drove over to an apartment to see someone for a few minutes, then they ended up at Dorys for some fish and chips."

"Who'd they see in the apartment?"

"I'm sorry, but I don't know her name."

"A girl? Someone from school?"

"No, sir. I don't believe it was someone from school, sir."

"What makes you say that?"

"I think I would have known who it was, we all run in pretty much the same group. I do think Colin was maybe sleeping. He might have had a little too much to drink. We were all buying him pints, you know. I mean he wasn't driving and he'd had a tough couple of weeks."

"He was sleeping?"

"Mmm, maybe passed out, I'm afraid."

"You ever hear of Madeline Keller?"

"Yes sir, of course. Isn't that why you're all here? I heard she was missing. Is that true?"

"Did you ever meet her?"

"No, sir. Never did. Umm, I do know that she broke up with Colin and he did send some pictures of her to all of us. She, ahh, didn't have any clothes on in the pictures," he said, now staring down at the table top, apparently embarrassed.

"Do you still have those pictures?"

"No, sir. I deleted them. I think there's a way to still get them from my phone, but I don't know how to do that and I don't want to see them anyway. She sent those as a private message to Colin and they were for his eyes only."

Maxwell raised his eyebrow towards Dillon and Suel, both of whom shook their head no.

"Darren, I want to thank you for your time."

"Thank you, sir."

"Let me text the escort. You're free to leave and best of luck on that finance exam."

"The exam? Oh yeah, sorry, was just thinking, I hope you find her, Madeline, and she's okay. I would have liked to meet her someday."

Maxwell smiled as the door opened and Otis was escorted down to the lobby.

"Pleasant change of pace after the first two. Nice to once in a while run into a young man who actually gets it," Suel said.

Dillon just sort of shrugged, feeling like the guy was almost too accommodating. "Would you excuse me for a moment. I need to use the loo."

"We've James McKenzie on his way up in just a moment," Maxwell said.

"I'll be back before he darkens the doorway."

Dillon left the room, hurried around the corner and down the hall. He placed a phone call to Ina Nolan, left a message, then hurried back to the conference room. Just before he turned the corner he saw the elevator door open and the stern looking escort stepped out. He hurried back into the conference room and was nicely settled by

the time the door opened and James McKenzie stepped
into the room.

FORTY-EIGHT

James McKenzie was a nice enough looking young man with neatly trimmed dark hair and brown eyes. He wore a black sweater over a black t-shirt and jeans. His shoes were polished. Like Taylor, Jenkins, and for that matter Colin Cominsky, he was large and solid. Dillon immediately thought of the comment Darren Otis made about ending up in traction in the first minutes of a rugby match with these guys.

"Mr. McKenzie. Please, have a seat," Maxwell said.

"Thank you," McKenzie said in a raspy voice and cleared his throat.

Maxwell recited his standard lines, date, time, everyone's name and then smiled at McKenzie and said, "Bit of a cough?"

"No, sir. Just a little nervous about all of this."

"Nothing to be nervous about, son," Maxwell said sliding the copy of the signed statement over. "We'd just like you to take a moment, review what you've stated and feel free to make any changes you see fit. It's not at all unusual that after a few days something might have popped into your head that you forgot to mention." Maxwell lowered his voice. "Or, perhaps you wish to adjust because you know your original statement was, in retrospect, simply wrong."

McKenzie grimaced, pulled the statement in front of him and began to read as it lay on the table. He licked his lips a number of times and gradually sort of circled his arms and hands around the statement in what appeared to be a subconscious attempt to hide it. He seemed to read through the statement at least three separate times before he looked up at Maxwell.

"Mmm, there might be a couple of things I would like to adjust here if that's okay."

"Oh, really?" Maxwell handed a pen to McKenzie.

"Yes, sir. See, we sort of didn't quite stay til close. We actually went and got some fish and chips."

"Best to make that adjustment then, go ahead, feel free to cross out the inappropriate lines and just write your adjustment on the back."

McKenzie wrote a couple of quick sentences then looked up and flashed a quick smile.

"Good. All set? Is there anything else you'd care to add?" Maxwell asked.

"I think that's about it."

"Really? Well, you seem to have finished much faster than the other lads we've spoken to. They made change after change. Of course, that was after I mentioned that, should you be swearing to any falsehoods, well, jail is the logical result. After you're found guilty, of course. And, once that's the result, and you have jail time on your record, well, good luck getting any sort of decent job. But I'm sure you know all that. I'm just amazed that the other lads made all sorts of changes. Maybe you should just take a moment and really think about the consequences before you decide to hand that statement back to me," Maxwell said as he passed a number of blank sheets of paper over to McKenzie.

McKenzie looked at Maxwell for a long moment before he suddenly picked up the pen and began to feverishly write. He wrote for a good fifteen minutes while Maxwell, Suel and Dillon silently watched. When he was finished he reread what he wrote, twice, before he handed the pages back to Maxwell.

Maxwell scanned the copy then looked up at McKenzie. "It would appear from your corrections here that about the only thing you agree with in your initial statement was that you were at the Empire Pub."

"I sort of added a couple of things."

"Like leaving five hours earlier than you originally stated. Interesting. You mention you went to see a friend of Darren Otis?"

"Yes, sir, but we just talked with her, umm, Molly."

"Talked with her? As one would do, I suppose. Tell me, was Darren with you?"

"No, sir, I think he went home."

"Well, if Darren wasn't with you, how did you find this Molly? Had you met her before?"

"No, sir, umm, Darren gave me her phone number and I called her."

"Did he give you her phone number that night?"

"Yes, sir," McKenzie said, looking like he was ready to cry, knowing where this was going.

"This wouldn't happen to be a particular young lady from Towerview you went to *talk* to, would it?"

The color drained from McKenzie's face at the mention of Towerview. "I think that might be where she lived."

"Think or know?"

"Yes, sir, it was Towerview."

"And you just wanted to talk?"

"Well, no, umm, not exactly, sir."

"Seems to me that's an important fact you omitted. I think it would be best if you added that along with a full explanation of purpose, money involved and results. I should mention, James, that failure to honestly comply will get you locked up. Put you at the mercy of all the degenerates behind bars and, at that point, there just isn't an awful lot we'll be able to do for you."

After writing furiously for another ten minutes, McKenzie passed his statement, now consisting of five freshly written pages, over to Maxwell.

Maxwell took a few minutes to read the pages then looked up at McKenzie. "So, the woman at Towerview, the one you were going to pay to service Colin Cominsky was named Molly?"

"Yes, sir."

"No last name?"

"Darren didn't tell us one. He just gave me her number and, when I talked to her, she said she would be waiting for us in the parking lot. We pulled in, Peter handed her the money. She took one look at Colin passed out in the car and told us to leave or she was going to call security."

"And Colin had that much to drink that he was unconscious?"

"Yes, I mean no, not exactly. See Darren wanted to add something to Colin's pint."

"Add something?"

"A roofie, maybe, I guess."

"A drug?"

McKenzie nodded.

"Please answer yes or no for the recording."

"Yes, sir, umm, a drug."

"What did it look like?" Dillon said.

"It was just a little pill, to be honest, I didn't think anything of it, thought it was maybe a joke. Thought it just might make his pint taste funny, but that was all."

"Was the pill white?"

"No it was sort of a grey-green?"

"Sounds like Rohyponl, but that changes the color of the drink so you can see that it's been drugged. Didn't anyone see that?"

"I don't think that would work because Colin was drinking Guinness and it's black."

"Did Otis have more than one of these pills?"

"I don't know. Honest, I really don't. I think I was the only one who saw him drop it in Colin's pint and I didn't think much about it. Besides, since he passed out, the deal with Molly didn't actually happen and even though she, umm, took our money, it was kind of okay because Colin didn't have to wake up and face the embarrassment. You know? Honest." McKenzie had tears running down his face at this point and he looked from Maxwell to Dillon and then Suel hoping for some sort of support or possibly an affirmation.

They talked for another five minutes and then Maxwell sent a text message to the police escort. Once McKenzie left the room, Maxwell said, "Do you want to have Darren Otis picked up?"

"Not quite yet," Dillon said. "Let's see what Colin Cominsky can remember?"

"Well, be prepared," Maxwell checked his phone. "I received a text message about fifteen minutes ago. He's waiting in the lobby with his barrister."

"That'll be his uncle, Calvert Cominsky," Suel said.

Maxwell seemed to think for a moment. "If nothing else, we can just have a short meeting with them, let them know the statements turned out to be completely worthless. The barrister will no doubt request a copy of the recordings and the revised statements. Since no charges have been filed, I don't see any particular reason to comply with that request. What's the lad going to tell us? Based on what McKenzie just swore to, he was drugged, unconscious. Christ sake, virtually anything he tells us is going to be inadmissible.”

“Let’s bring them in and keep everything close to the vest. There’s a chance Colin doesn’t realize he was drugged. Maybe he just thinks he had too much to drink. I want to get a read on them passing Madeline’s selfies around. See if we can pick up anything regarding the others,” Dillon said.

“Let’s have at them,” Suel said and rubbed his hands together like he was about to sit down to dinner.

“Suddenly your man, Darren Otis, isn’t looking so golden,” Maxwell said.

FORTY-NINE

This time when the escort opened the door, she looked more like she was just about out of patience, rather than simply stern. She never entered the room, but instead took a step back as a red faced Calvert Cominsky suddenly charged in. He attempted to grow a shocked look as he focused in on Dillon and Suel. The routine struck Dillon as a poorly practiced maneuver and he didn't react.

"Bloody hell. I thought I made it perfectly clear I wanted to be informed when either of you wished to speak to Colin. It is his right to legal counsel under the laws of the United Kingdom and as such—"

"Pardon me, Mr. Cominsky, is it? I don't believe I've had the pleasure," Maxwell said. "I'm DI Maxwell, PSNI. Neither Detective Inspector Suel nor US Marshal Dillon intend to do anything but listen. Since you are here, it would appear that you have not been denied access. You are indeed within your rights and those of your client to ask questions, offer advice or leave if you so choose."

Calvert Cominsky appeared about to speak when Maxwell raised a hand and said, "Please. You might, however, find it worth your while to have a seat and, at the very least entertain the questions I pose. You are always free to advise your client not to comment."

Cominsky gave an exasperated sigh as he pulled a chair out from the table and sat down. "Sit," he commanded his nephew Colin who immediately did just that, pulling out a chair that placed his uncle between himself and Maxwell. He sat down, stared at the table and sort of hunched over as if he expected the roof to fall in. Dillon noted that the neatly trimmed beard from the other day had been completely shaved.

Again, Maxwell went through his opening routine of date, time, place and who was present in the room. When he had finished Calvert said, "I should like to state for the record that this interrogation of my client is beyond the pale. Furthermore, the fact that Detective Inspector Suel of An Garda Síochána, and US Marshal Dillon choose to participate in this affair after being informed, in writing, I hasten to add, that I am to be present at any interaction with my client, is simply beyond belief."

"Which, Mr. Cominsky, is exactly why I am conducting this informal interview," Maxwell said. "DI Suel and Marshal Dillon are merely here to listen and perhaps confer with—"

"From the little we've been able to glean from the lads subjected to this atrocious undertaking prior to our appearance, both individuals have been fully involved and went so far as to physically threaten at least one of the participants. All this, I hasten to add, in a nation where they have absolutely no legal authority. For the record, I wish to state that we provided written and sworn statements regarding the evening in question and, following our momentary appearance here, I intend to file a formal complaint."

"Oh, by all means, Mr. Cominsky, please do that. It's certainly within your right and purview. As it is within my right and purview to question the veracity of those statements regarding the disappearance of a young woman. Without going into any specific detail we've found the sworn statements to which you so eagerly refer are complete and utter fabrications. Each and every statement has been withdrawn and rewritten." Maxwell held up a sheaf of almost two dozen sheets of paper.

Both Calvert and Colin Cominsky's eyes grew wide. "I shall demand that those are not entered as evidence and that—"

"Just hold on a minute. You're getting ahead of yourself. No one has even been charged yet. To my knowledge, you do not, with the exception of your nephew, represent any of these individuals. We are simply in the early stages of an ongoing investigation and are in the process of gathering facts. I hasten to remind you that, in fact, you provided these statements to DI Suel and Marshal Dillon. Being responsible law enforcement officers, they simply asked the appropriate authority, in this case the PSNI, to investigate and determine the veracity of the statements provided to them. We've begun to investigate and found the statements completely false. Rather than prosecute, which is within our purview, we've turned a blind eye and are in the process of accepting corrected revisions. If you have a problem with that, I will gladly haul each individual back in here and charge them with falsification of fact in a missing person case. Would you like me to do that?"

"I view that as a threat, Detective Inspector."

"View it as a promise."

"I want to see those statements."

"If and when someone is charged, and you are providing legal representation for that individual, then you may certainly request to see the statements and they will be made available to you. Until that time, you have no justification."

Calvert Cominsky stood and signaled Colin to do the same. "It's been informative, gentlemen," he said and headed toward the door with Colin in tow.

"Thank you for your time," Maxwell called just before the door closed.

Suel chuckled and said, "Well done, Ronnie."

"What do you think?" Dillon said.

"What do I think? The usual, if they wouldn't barge in here all full of themselves they'd be walking out with a lot more information. I'd say there's a pretty good chance that if the Cominsky lad was indeed drugged, he has no idea. An act which, as dreadful as it appears, would basically release him for any sort of culpability or responsibility. But, as always seems to be the case, they come in full of themselves, attempt to lord it over everyone, and leave in a huff."

"Next step?" Suel said.

"Let's see what we can learn from the phone records. That's going to take at least a day, possibly two."

"In the meantime, we've got some CCTV tapes An Garda Síochána is running a facial recognition program on. It's slim, but maybe something will turn up," Dillon said.

"Truth be told, yeah, the bastards gave false statements, but in a way the revisions provide an even tighter defense. We'll check with Dorys, but if that receipt shows up with someone's credit card, it just about eliminates the four of them as suspects," Maxwell said.

"Which leaves us with the golden boy, studying at home" Dillon said.

"Bollocks," Suel groaned.

FIFTY

uel shook his head and said, "God, we need something to happen here, a break of some sort."

He and Dillon were on the train heading back to Dublin. Dillon was staring out the window, deep in thought, not really seeing the countryside as it flew by. He turned and faced Suel sitting across from him. "You spending the night at Aideen's again?"

"I'll be doing that from now until doomsday. I can see her beginning to settle into the idea that somehow the whole thing was her fault and if only she hadn't done or said something to set this fecking knacker off, the damn assault would never have happened."

"Think he might just stay away?" Dillon asked.

Suel shook his head. "It's almost time for him to send her some sort of gift, a necklace or maybe a day at a spa, and then ask her why she made him hit her. I expect him to make an appearance in the near future."

Dillon nodded. "Unfortunately that's not an uncommon reaction to an assault between a couple."

"Oh, for Christ's sake. If only she'd give me a name. I don't even know if they were or are a couple. I'd love to get hold of the bollocks, take him out in a boat and see if he would be able to swim maybe ten miles back to shore."

"No idea of who?" Dillon said.

Suel shook his head. "Not a one. I've no idea if he even knows I'm spending nights there. Given the ferocity of the assault, the fact that she's frightened to death, and life being what it is, I'm fairly confident he'll show up again. Sooner rather than later. She's not left the house since she was released from James's hospital."

"Is she talking to you yet?"

"A bit, slowly but surely she's returning to her old, disagreeable self."

"There's progress, of a sort. Anything from DI Walsh?"

"Not so much as a peep, but what in the hell is he supposed to do? Aideen won't say a bleedin' word, won't name the bollocks."

Once back in Dublin and out of Connolly Station, they said their goodbyes. Suel was parked just across the way on Talbot Street. Dillon's car was four blocks in the opposite direction.

It was after seven and Dillon stopped in the Drumcondra Tesco on the way home. He picked up a frozen pizza and a tub of sea salt caramel ice cream for dinner and drove home. He parked in his front garden, pulled the wrought iron gates closed behind his car, and headed into the house.

As Dillon stepped into the entryway, Lucifer poked his head out of the kitchen door. He had a yellow Styrofoam tray in his mouth that had held a chicken breast from two days earlier. He stared at Dillon for a long moment before he leaped onto the landing, bounded up the staircase, and disappeared, never letting go of the Styrofoam tray.

Dillon walked into the kitchen, carefully stepped over the trash items scattered across the floor and turned on the oven. He placed the ice cream in the freezer, the pizza on the counter and set about cleaning the mess scattered around the room. He placed the pizza in the oven then pulled a biscuit from the jar and called upstairs to Lucifer.

No response.

He called a couple more times with no result then said, "Lucifer, biscuit. You want a biscuit?" He heard the dog jump off the bed, envisioned him stretching for a moment and then right on schedule, a dark head peered around the newel post.

"Come on, outside," Dillon called and waved the dog biscuit. Lucifer bounded down the stairs and headed for the front door. Dillon opened the door and tossed the dog biscuit out onto the concrete pad. Lucifer jumped off the front stoop and as usual, caught the biscuit on the first bounce.

When the kitchen timer went off he pulled the pizza out of the oven and set it on a cutting board. He opened the front door, called Lucifer into the house and went back into the kitchen. He cut the pizza into triangular pieces, went to pick a piece up and immediately dropped it. He waved his hand in the air for a moment before licking the hot cheese from his finger tips and checking for blisters.

He thought about Suel and his sister, Aideen. Remembered Suel's comment, it being just about the time when whoever assaulted her would make an appearance. He worried about the two of them, Suel and Aideen, for the rest of the evening.

FIFTY-ONE

Early the following morning Dillon was at his desk. He left a message for Ina Nolan, his second message, counting the one he'd left yesterday while up in Belfast. He sat and re-reviewed for the umpteenth time the file on Madeline Keller. Unfortunately, nothing new presented itself. At exactly nine o'clock his phone rang.

"Jack Dillon."

"Morning, Jack. Eric Bergman, just checking in. Anything develop up in Belfast yesterday."

"Yes and no. The three pals of the former boyfriend, Colin Cominsky, retracted their original statements."

"They did?"

"Yeah but hold on. They had failed to mention a visit they made to a woman to pay for services—"

"What?"

"A prostitute. Apparently, they all chipped in to pay her to service the Cominsky kid. Unfortunately, one of these idiots had slipped Rohyponl, a roofie, into Cominsky's pint and he was incapacitated."

"What the hell?"

"Yeah, the woman takes one look at Cominsky, basically comatose in the car with his three idiot pals, grabs their money, rips them off, and threatens to call security if they don't leave. They end up at some fish and chips place until around midnight, paid for the food using Cominsky's credit card, who, no doubt, was still probably comatose out in the car and then they go home. Our PSNI contact up there is verifying all of this, but on top of being beyond stupid, it's looking like an air tight alibi. I doubt there was any way they could have made it down to Dublin and somehow connected with the Keller girl. Hopefully we'll have confirmation by the end of today or early tomorrow."

"So you're back to square one?"

"Your question suggests we actually made it off square one. The PSNI did apparently obtain cellphone records from all five of the group and that's part of what they'll be checking, but I fear the phone records are going to confirm these updated statements. Which will simply confirm they're all guilty of being stupid, but not much beyond that."

"Back up, you said all five of the group?"

"Yeah, four were with Cominsky for the night. One supposedly went home to study for an exam the next morning. The guys with Cominsky all confirmed that he left around half past seven."

"Jesus," Bergman said.

"You're telling me. Are her parents still over here?" Dillon said.

"Yeah, not that they're doing much other than running into dead ends. I genuinely feel for them. They've spoken with the roommates three or four times as a group, I think twice on a one to one basis. They've probably met with three or four different staff at the school. They've walked around the area of Temple Bar a number of times, interrogated staff at the Quays Pub and they've contacted someone at the Irish Independent."

"The newspaper?"

"Yeah. Fortunately, I gave them a reporter's name I know, Ciara Bannon. She called me after she met with them."

"And?"

"And she's going to poke around a bit, she's of the opinion that this could well be a case of the Keller girl on an adventure over to the continent, Paris, Rome, wine country, who knows? She promised to get back to me if and when she actually writes anything. You want me to pass on your name?"

"Mmm-mmm. Maybe wait for a bit. I don't want to take the chance of an article appearing in the paper and possibly serving as a warning to someone out there."

"What do you think?" Bergman said.

"To be honest, Eric. I'd love it if this were a case of a girl going off on an adventure trip of some sort. Honest to God. But, it doesn't fit the Madeline Keller profile. She was a hard charging student at Trinity. One of the bright ones in her high school class. For her to take off like that would be contrary to the way she operates. And, then not connect with her parents? No, I don't see that happening. Hell, which option is better? We determine she was murdered? Or, she's listed as a missing person and for the remainder of their days her parents can wonder what the hell happened and maybe cling to the razor thin chance she's out there, still alive somewhere."

"You're thinking she was murdered?"

"Not officially, but yeah. It's day nine and we don't have shit. That's not good. How long are the parents over here?"

"Open ended and, under the circumstances, the airline would adjust any plans they have. I would think, at some point, they'll pack up and head back to Iowa, but that's a huge decision."

"The mother doing any better?"

"No, in a word. Poor thing is exhausted and who can blame her. Sooner or later, her husband is going to have to get her home and under some proper medical care. It's becoming more and more apparent she's going to need some serious help."

"Anything develops, Eric, I'll let you know, but like I said, if nothing turns up on the phone records of these guys in Belfast, it's going to turn out to be just one more dead end."

Bergman gave a sigh and said, "Damn it. Okay, Jack, keep me posted."

"I will, wish I had more for you."

"Yeah, me too," Bergman said and hung up.

Dillon's phone rang ten minutes later, Ina Nolan. "How'd things go up in Belfast?"

"How they'd go?" Dillon said. "Let's just say it shut the door on a number of potential options."

"Mmm-mmm, not good."

"Yeah, that about sums it up. We caught them conspiring on their sworn statements. But, when the truth came out, it pretty much erased them as suspects. Actually gave them a much tighter alibi in the end. The PSNI is in the process of confirming this latest version, but I'm guessing the facts will corroborate what we learned yesterday and our strongest investigation to this point is going to turn out to be a dead end. Where do we stand with the facial recognition on the CCTV tapes?"

"We haven't begun yet, but only because I haven't received the tapes from the Merchants Arch."

"What?"

"They sent them over, but we couldn't open the file format. One of our techies, in fact Desmond, is on his way over there now to get the file formatted properly."

"Who is Desmond?"

She laughed. "Remember the brainy techies the other day when we had lunch in the break room?"

"The two guys with the charming personalities."

"Yeah, right. Oliver and Desmond, never Des by the way. Desmond was the one in the plaid shirt."

"With the pens and the small notebook in his pocket?"

"That's him. You can laugh all you want, but if he can't format that file so we can examine it, no one can. He's damn near a savant."

"When will you have it?"

"Hopefully, sooner rather than later. Whenever I get it I'll jump on it immediately."

"Keep me posted one way or the other. If you don't find anything through your program, would it make sense if I went through it?"

"You're talking about hours and hours?"

"Does the term grasping at straws mean anything?" Dillon said.

"Let me see if we come up with anything and go from there," Ina said and hung up.

FIFTY-TWO

Suel entered the office just before the noon hour. "Working banker's hours?" Dillon said and handed him a fresh mug of tea.

"Oh, lord, hell of a long night. Thanks for this," he said and slurped tea from the mug. "Some plonker prowling around just after midnight. I can't be sure, but I think I heard some bastard at the front door trying to use a key."

"What did you do?"

"Sat in the dark and waited, but nothing ever happened. I'm thinking he had a key, I'm betting it's how he got in before, but I had the locks changed. I grabbed an hour or two of sleep once the sun came up. I checked this morning and somehow he was able to unscrew the bulb just enough in the motion detector in front so that it didn't come on."

"That explains why you look even shittier than usual. You mention any of this to Aideen?"

"No, I'm still trying to get her calmed down enough so she'll give me a name. This would have only set her off. Anything on the missing Keller girl?"

"No, in a word. I don't want to call Maxwell and put any undue pressure on him. I'm sure he's doing all he can, but I've got the feeling it's becoming more and more of a dead end. I talked to Ina awhile back."

"Did they find anything?"

"The tapes were sent over in some format they couldn't use. They've got one of their tech people over at the Merchant's Arch now. She seemed to think he'd be able to make some adjustments and they could get on with it. Honestly, at this point, it's an awfully slim chance, but it's all we have."

"What options do we have if they don't find any-thing?"

"Go back to the other places in Temple Bar with CCTV cameras and see if they might have anything. There's easily a half dozen different ways out of the area. It just so happened that the Merchants Arch seemed to me to be the most logical. Surprise, surprise they even had cameras and tapes."

"Provided we can examine them," Suel said and slurped more tea. He grimaced after swallowing.

"You got any ideas?" Dillon said.

"Yeah. First off, let me call my close personal friend, Joel the Hole. Riley Dempsey is still out there, somewhere, and we still need to get him."

"You don't think he's gone into hiding after our fiasco the other night at The Swiss Cottage?"

"Oh, as a matter of fact, I'm sure of it. Joel the Hole doesn't know it yet, but he's going to tell us where

Dempsey is and he's going to give us the name of the woman who was with them. Hopefully, she was stupid enough to end up with Joel the Hole the other night. Which means, Riley Dempsey is either with her now or there's a good chance she knows where he is. Either way, I intend to find out."

FIFTY-THREE

Dillon had just slid into Suel's car in the parking lot behind the station.

"Let me try this idiot one more time," Suel said.

"You've already called him three times. You said you left him a message about twenty minutes ago and yelled at him to call back. He's either passed out, or he knows it's you calling. Either way, he's not going to answer."

"Oh, he'll answer, at least he better. You're right, I did leave him a little love message on my last call. Let him know just a few of the things that are going to happen if we don't talk and soon."

Suel hit a speed dial button as Dillon said, "I think we should just head down to Temple Bar and start seeking out other CCTV cameras. Although, at this late date, I doubt too many of them hang onto their images."

"What's with all the negative vibes? I thought you Americans were always supposed to be positive and—" Suel suddenly shouted into his phone, "Do not hang up yer fecking phone, Joel. I swear to God you hang up on me and you'll find yourself in an isolation cell in *The Joy* for the next month. You hear me?"

Dillon watched Suel's face turn beet red.

"I don't give a damn and I'll not be listening to any more shite from the likes of you. Now, either you tell me where Riley Dempsey is, or I'm going to bring you in and have you drawn and quartered. You hear me?"

Suel shook his head. "I don't give a tinker's damn about that. Where in the hell is he? Well, you should have thought about that before you started down this path." Suel pounded his fist against the steering wheel. "That is *so* not my damn problem. And is she the blonde woman you were with the other night at The Swiss Cottage? What's her name?" Suel demanded and made a movement with his hand at Dillon to indicate writing. Dillon pulled a pen and a small note book from his coat pocket and had a momentary image of Desmond from forensics in the plaid shirt.

"Yes, go ahead, first name Shanessa," Suel said and then spelled it out for Dillon. "Last name Leary."

Dillon held the notebook up to Suel to show him what he'd written and Suel nodded once he read it.

"And where does she live? In Tallaght. Is that the new council housing? What's the house number? Well then, how in the hell am I supposed to find it? Well, you had better think, you worthless plonker, or you'll find yourself hanging by your bleeding thumbs before the day is out. Third one on the left with the blue door. Much better. Now then, Joel, my dear friend, do I need to warn

you about phoning the likes of Miss Leary or that bollocks Riley Dempsey? All right then, against my better
judgement, I'm taking you at your word, Joel. So, you'd
better not be playing me or there will be hell to pay. Understand?"

Suel clicked off his phone and looked over at Dillon.
"What a bleeding maggot."

"But he told you where she lives," Dillon glanced at
his notebook. "This is her, Shanessa Leary?"

"Supposedly. But you can barely take half of what
Joel the Hole tells you. If his lips are moving there's a
good chance your man is telling you a lie. Sheehy Skeffington Meadows, it's new council housing. Supposed to
be nice, at least for the moment. Just moved people in
this past July, sixty-nine units in all. Let's see what we
find."

It was a twenty minute drive to Tallaght and another
ten before they found Sheehy Skeffington Meadows.
Suel drove slowly down the street, past a large cul-de-
sac with a sort of long, triangular patch of dirt in the center. Six young trees had been evenly planted around the
patch of dirt. The units looked shiny and new. Although,
three of the low walls in front of the units were already
marred by some sort of illegible black graffiti. As they
drove past the cul-de-sac, Suel said, "Look on the left
hand side and see if the third door in is painted blue."

Dillon glanced back at the twelve attached units.
The first two doors were a bright red with the third one

blue. "It's blue. Third unit in. It has an all stucco front, the first two have brick fronts on the first floor."

Suel nodded. "That matches what Joel the Hole told me." He pulled around the corner and stopped three doors up.

"What are you doing?" Dillon said.

"Council housing, it's done on a plan. The front lay-out on this unit is the same as the Leary woman's over on the next street." Suel stared out the window at the unit. "Just behind the front door, there'll be a staircase heading up to the second floor. We've got two small bed-rooms looking out over the street on the second floor. There'll be a hallway with the bathroom opposite the first bedroom and two small bedrooms on either side at the end of the hallway. Three bedrooms in all. The front door has a window to the left, that will be the sitting room. A door will lead back to the kitchen and the dining area. There'll be a back door. The back garden will be walled so if our man makes it out the back he's going to have to get over a number of walls to get to the street. His only access to the street is at the corner. If he makes it out the back and over a wall, our best option will be to head out the front and wait for the bollocks at the cor-ner."

Dillon nodded, hoping he would remember every-thing and said, "I'm ready if you are."

FIFTY-FOUR

uel drove back and took a right hand turn, driving around the cul-de-sac and the triangular patch of dirt. He pulled to a stop in front of the unit just to the right of the blue door. They casually climbed out of the car, glanced around, then hurried up to the blue door. Suel rang the doorbell.

Dillon looked around the development as they waited, there were only two cars parked in front of almost fifty different units. Directly across the dirt triangle he noticed the curtains move in a front window. Someone checking them out.

The door suddenly opened and before them stood the same heavyset blonde woman they'd seen at The Swiss Cottage. She wore a loose fitting blue silk dressing gown that just barely hung to her thighs. She held a glass of what appeared to be whiskey in her left hand. She studied the two of them for a long moment before she gave a broad smile once she recognized them and said, "So, decided to change your mind, did ya's? Come here looking for a little party?"

"Shanessa Leary?" Suel said.

"You can call me anything you want, big man. Name your pleasure."

"We're looking for Riley Dempsey. He's wanted on multiple assault and drug charges as well as—"

"I haven't seen him since the other night when you two scared him off. You're welcome to come inside and have a look. Who knows, you might just find someone else you're interested in," she said with a smile and stepped back to hold the door for them.

Suel moved inside, gave a quick glance, and started up the stairs. He indicated the small sitting room off to the left with a wave of his hand and Dillon hurried into the room. The small flatscreen was positioned on a wooden chair opposite a worn couch and tuned to some sort of game show. An open bottle of Dead Rabbit whiskey sat on the floor next to the couch. Another whiskey glass was on the floor next to the bottle.

Dillon gave a quick look behind the couch then hurried into the kitchen. The wall to the left had cabinets, four on the top and four on the bottom. Centered in the middle was a four burner range with a hood fan overhead and an oven below. To the right, in the corner was a small white refrigerator and to the right of that, against the back wall was a kitchen sink. A small wooden table with two unmatched chairs were positioned below a window. The door leading out to the back garden was closed. Dillon could hear Suel's footsteps hurrying down the hall overhead.

He tried the doorknob on the door leading out to the back garden, found it locked, and looked at Shanessa Leary leaning against the doorway leading into the sitting room.

She smiled as she sipped from her glass. "Told you he wasn't here. See anything else you might like to examine?"

"Yeah. As a matter of fact, the glass in your sitting room in front of the couch. Who is that for?"

"Always hoping someone might stop by, I never like to drink alone. Maybe you'd like a little sample," she said and began to spread her arms.

"Dillon?" Suel called from the front of the unit.

"Nothing worth seeing back here," Dillon replied and headed into the sitting room. As he passed Shanessa Leary she gave him a quick grope on his rear.

Suel stood by the front door holding a pair of worn jeans and a faded black t-shirt advertising the Cabra Club. "Look what I found," Suel said holding the t-shirt out between his thumbs and forefingers.

"Umm, I think those are mine?" Shanessa said.

Suel held up the jeans as if to study them then looked at plump Shanessa in her silk robe. "I highly doubt it," he said.

She smiled. "Sure I can't talk you two into a whiskey? I was just telling your friend here I hate to drink alone. Never thought I might be lucky enough to have two visitors."

Suel tossed the jeans and t-shirt onto the staircase and said. "Tell your man, Riley, we'll get him sooner or later and when we do . . ."

"I told you before, I haven't seen him since the two of you chased him off."

Suel indicated the front door with a nod and headed out to the car with Dillon close behind.

"Stop back anytime," Shanessa called from her front door. She stood there sipping with a smile on her face and her silk robe undone.

"Good Lord, the cheek of your woman. We'd almost be doing that plonker, Riley Dempsey, a favor by picking him up. You'd sure as hell want to have your shot record up to date before you got very close to that one."

"I'm not sure they have shots for all that."

"Incredible, damn it. My God, we can't seem to get a win anywhere."

Dillon's phone suddenly signaled a text message coming through. He pulled his phone out and swiped a finger across the screen.

"Ronnie Maxwell?" Suel asked.

"No, Ina. The files from the Merchants Arch just came across and she can finally access them. She's going to run them through the facial recognition program."

"Finally, something goes our way, maybe. Let's head back to the station."

As Suel drove, Dillon sent a text message to Ina Nolan.

'Heading back to station. Madeline Keller wore blue jeans, white or grey silk tank top with spaghetti straps and white Nike shoes with the swoosh logo on either side.'

A moment later her reply came across.

'So noted. Based on length of tapes will hopefully have something later this evening.'

FIFTY-FIVE

Dillon was sitting at his desk. He was the only one in the office at this late hour. Suel had left for Aideen's a little before six. DCI McCabe departed about forty-five minutes after Suel. That left a couple of people grinding out paperwork, but the last of them had left almost an hour ago.

He was going over the Madeline Keller file for the umpteenth time, trying to look at it from all sorts of different angles, and reviewing yet again the three adjusted statements. He kept thinking about the reaction from Calvert Cominsky at Belfast's Musgrave Street Police Station and still he came up with nothing.

On a whim he sent a text message to Ina Nolan.

'Stomach growling. Not sure if you're still here. Going over to grab a takeout at Dublin Wok. Can I get one for you?'

If she didn't answer in the next ten minutes he would just head home. Although, he wasn't looking forward to the left over pizza waiting for him in the refrigerator.

Her reply came through about 30 seconds later.

'Perfect. Just finishing up. Questionable results. Ready by time u get here with sustenance.'

He phoned Dublin Wok, ordered two steam pod dumpling takeouts, and hurried over ten minutes later to pick them up. He literally ran back to the station then knocked on the security door to the forensics section. Ina opened the door a moment later.

"Thank God. I was beginning to think I was going to waste away," she said and grabbed both Styrofoam trays from Dillon. The office was dark with the exception of the lights over her work station. He followed her as she hurried into the break room.

"Afraid all we have to drink is some weak tea or coffee that has probably been on the burner since yesterday morning. I'd stay away from both if I were you."

"Not a problem, I've got it covered," Dillon said and pulled out two plastic bottles of Coca-Cola from his jacket pockets.

"Oh, you are so wonderful," she said and sat down at the table. She lifted the lid on her Styrofoam tray, jabbed the plastic fork into one of her dumplings and inserted the entire dumpling into her mouth."

"Copycat," Dillon said.

"Oh, I don't even care," she said in response to Dillon's smile. "I'm starving."

Dillon waited until she had worked her way through three quarters of the meal. He pushed what was left of his tray away and said, "So, your last text didn't seem to sound all that promising. Questionable results?"

"Mmm-mmm," she chewed, swallowed and speared another dumpling. "It's just that I always hope for a ninety-nine point nine percent match. The images are all scored in case you didn't know. We got exactly one potential image match, and it rated fifty-nine point seven percent."

"Was it the girl, Madeline?"

"No, although there is a woman in the three images and she is wearing a tank top with spaghetti straps. But no facial image available for comparison, unfortunately the shots are from the rear, so it's just a bit of conjecture on my part. The fifty-nine point seven percent match was actually to the Darren Otis image you provided. The images, there are three, were taken as they're crossing the street and stepping onto the Ha'penny bridge."

"Right outside of the Merchants Arch," Dillon said.

"Yes. Two images of them crossing the street and then one almost, but not quite out of range as they start across the bridge. In that image he's turned and might be saying something to her. They're fairly close together, but it doesn't look all that romantic. He's got his right arm around her shoulder and then seems to be holding her left arm with his left hand, like he's steering her or something. Umm, you'll have to see it to understand my description. Anyway, almost out of range, a bit blurry, and a side view so that's why only the fifty-nine point seven. Wish it was better."

"Well, it sounds better than all the nothing we've had so far. Let's go take a look."

"Let me just finish this," she said, stabbing her last dumpling. She chewed, swallowed, and glanced over at Dillon's Styrofoam tray. "Umm, are you going to eat the rest of yours?"

"No, you want it?"

"Would you mind? I skipped lunch and literally was about to die from the hunger."

"Help yourself," Dillon said and pushed what was left of his tray across the table to Ina.

"Mmm-mmm, thanks, won't be but a minute," she said, crammed one of Dillon's dumplings into her mouth and smiled.

FIFTY-SIX

Ina said as she settled into the high back black leather desk chair in front of her work station Ina said, "Pull that chair over." Dillon pulled over a grey chair on wheels that looked like it came from about 1960. One of the wheels squeaked as he rolled the chair across the tile floor.

Ina's fingers raced across her keyboard and a moment later the large screen in front of them came to life. A blurry black and white image of a head filled most of the screen with three rows of option buttons running across the bottom. The buttons seemed to offer everything from size adjustments to color changes. Ina clicked some more keys and the image reduced in size and became much more defined although it still appeared blurry.

"This is the best one of the three," Ina said.

"And it's a sixty percent match?"

"No, fifty-nine point seven percent."

Dillon looked at her for a moment to see if she was joking, she wasn't. Then again, she was in the business of being exact.

"You can see by the side view that he's almost got his head buried in her hair. It's tough to get any sort of affirmation. But, notice how he's got hold of her, the arm around the shoulder and you can just catch a bit of his left hand. See? Holding on here, just below her elbow," she moved a mouse back and forth causing an arrow on the screen to circle the small exposed portion of his left hand. "And it looks like he's got her purse over his left shoulder, like maybe she's too intoxicated to carry it. I wish we had something more definitive for you, but—"

"This works. I recognize him." The hair was exactly as Dillon remembered. Blondish and slicked back on the top, a couple of strands hung over the shaved side of his head dangling close to his ear. "The Golden Boy. His name is Darren Otis."

"You sure?"

"Very. Met him just yesterday. Funny. At the time he seemed to be the least likely, but there's no mistaking it. That's him. The silk top with the spaghetti straps and the jeans fits the clothes description her roommates gave us. That purse looks like it could be denim which matches what the roommates said. Look, you can even see the Nike Swoosh logo on her right shoe." Dillon made note of a wrist watch around her right wrist. The watch appeared to have a black leather strap.

"Were they dating?"

"Not as far as we know. There's the suspicion he may have drugged her drink. We suspect he did the same to her former boyfriend earlier that night up in Belfast. Might account for him carrying the purse."

"Drugged her drink?"

"Rohyponl, we think."

"But that clouds a drink, for exactly that reason, so someone can't drug you."

"That works great if you're drinking white wine or vodka. The guy up in Belfast was drinking a pint of Guinness. Same thing she was drinking at the Quays, only half pints, but based on the way she looks here, if she was drinking Guinness she never would have known her drink was drugged. You're right, there's nothing romantic about the way he's hanging onto her. I suspect she's so drugged up she can't walk a straight line."

"Still, at fifty-nine point seven percent, any defense will tear this image apart in court," Ina said.

"Probably, but it's a start. What about the other two images?"

"Let me bring them up here. There's more of the same except their backs are to the camera so there is absolutely no chance of any sort of facial recognition."

An image suddenly appeared on the left hand side of the screen and a moment later another image just to the right. Ina wasn't kidding, just two figures heading across the street toward the Ha'penny Bridge. The images were almost identical. Still, to Dillon's mind, it was definitely Darren Otis more or less steering a drugged Madeline Keller.

"You down there very often?" Dillon said.

"Temple Bar? Just on the rare occasion. It's all tourists and college kids. Now, mind you, if I was nineteen or twenty I'd probably be down there every night."

Dillon studied the two images for a long moment. "Can you blow those up a little. I want to get a closer look at his jacket."

Ina ran her finger over the keys for a few seconds and the images increased by about twenty-five percent.

Dillon stood and leaned in toward the screen studying the back of Darren Otis's jacket. It appeared to be leather, maybe brown leather. The back consisted of two vertical panels with a seam running down the center. The back of the collar was ribbed. He thought he may have seen the jacket on some of Maxwell's images from the Empire pub, but he couldn't be sure. A scrape or possibly a slight tear, maybe three inches long, appeared on the back of the upper right shoulder of the jacket.

"What do you think?" Ina said.

"I think I'd like you to forward all three images to me and I'll send them to our man up in Belfast. Looks like we might be heading back up there tomorrow."

"May I make a suggestion?"

"By all means."

"Let me forward them up to him. No offense but coming from this department it will add just a bit more weight. I'll send them to you and you go ahead and send them, too. With both of us sending them they'll almost be required to put this on the front burner."

"I'd like to talk to the lad tomorrow and if we can get hold of that jacket, I have a feeling we'll finally be moving in the right direction, for a change."

"Send me the PSNI man's address and I'll have them up there in about sixty seconds."

"Thanks, Ina. Let me run upstairs and I'll send it your way. Much appreciated. I owe you."

"Yes, you do. Now off with you so I can send that up to the PSNI and get out of here. It's been a long day."

When Dillon turned on his computer the email with the three images from Ina was waiting for him. He forwarded it to Ronnie Maxwell with a request that Maxwell phone him first thing in the morning regardless of the time. He sent her Ronnie Maxwell's email address then hurried back down to forensics and knocked on the door. Ina answered with a purse slung over her shoulder and a look of disappointment when she opened the door and saw Dillon.

"Now what is it?"

"Nothing. Relax. I just wanted to thank you and walk you to your car."

She gave him a look like she didn't quite believe him.

"Honest," he said.

"Okay. Yeah, much appreciated."

She was parked in the far corner of the lot and when they got to her car Dillon held the door for her as she slid in behind the wheel. "Thanks again, Ina, I really appreciate you going the extra mile. You've given us the first real break in this case. Very much appreciated."

She smiled. "Thanks. Just doing my job and thank you for walking me to my car. That was very nice. But, you still owe me," she said, then closed and locked the car door, started the engine, and drove off giving him a quick wave.

FIFTY-SEVEN

Dillon thought about calling Paddy Suel then looked at the clock on his dashboard, it was well after eleven. Still, he was so excited about the image of Darren Otis he knew he wouldn't be able to sleep. He decided to drive past Aideen's and see if they might still be up. It was close to midnight when he pulled off Phibsboro Road and headed towards Shandon Gardens, Aideen's street. There was about a zero percent chance Suel was up. But, as long as he'd come this far he might as well check. Sure enough, he drove past Aideen's and all the lights were off.

It was worth the try he thought and continued down the street and around the corner. As he turned the corner his headlights caught a figure on the sidewalk walking towards him. Dillon almost didn't see him because he was dressed all in black. He did notice the bottle the figure was carrying, wine or maybe whiskey. And then, as he drove twenty feet further, he thought, *was that a sock hanging out of the top of the bottle?*

He pulled over, got out of the car, and ran to the top of the road. The figure continued down the sidewalk, possibly heading to Aideen's, or maybe just walking home. Dillon wasn't sure so he began to follow, picking up his pace as he went.

Suddenly, the figure stopped, gave a quick glance up and down the street, apparently didn't see Dillon, and opened the front gate to Aideen's.

Dillon took off at a run. He hadn't taken five steps when a small flame appeared. A lighter? A moment later a larger flame ignited whatever had been stuffed into the top of the bottle. The figure took a half step forward and appeared to wind up, ready to throw a Molotov cocktail through the front window just as the motion detector light above the front door flashed on.

As the figure raised his arm to shield his eyes, Dillon shouted something. Although later, when interviewed, he couldn't recall what he had shouted. He did remember pulling his pistol from his belt, firing a shot and suddenly the figure was screaming and flailing his arms, engulfed in a ball of flame.

By the time Dillon made it to Aideen's the man was on fire writhing on the ground. A puddle of flaming liquid and broken glass continued to burn across the lawn, the sidewalk, and the front stoop. Dillon took hold of the man by the wrists, dragged him out of the flames and into the street. As he rolled him in an effort to extinguish the flames the man groaned and whimpered.

By this time, a number of lights had flashed on up and down the block, not the least of which were all the lights in Aideen's unit. A moment later the front door tore open and Paddy Suel stood bare chested with a pistol pointed at Dillon.

"Don't shoot, Paddy, it's me," Dillon shouted.

"Dillon, what in the hell are you doing? Did you fire your weapon?"

"Call emergency services, Paddy. This bastard here is going to need attention."

The man let out a high pitched raspy groan. His jeans and what was left of his shirt smoldered. It appeared a good deal of his hair had been burned off. The right side of his face and his right arm were scorched and blistered. Dillon patted the man's pockets and checked his belt for a weapon. He rolled him over on the sidewalk none too gently using his foot and checked his back side.

The man gasped and groaned.

"What in the bloody hell is going on," Suel said, suddenly right behind them.

Dillon visibly jumped, took a deep breath and shoved his pistol back in his belt. "I was gonna stop by, but it looked like you were already in bed. So, I went around the corner ready to head home and saw this bastard carrying a bottle. The more I thought about it, the more it didn't seem to make sense. I followed him and all of a sudden he's in your front garden ready to throw a Molotov cocktail through the window. I don't know if I shot him or the bottle. All of a sudden he burst into flames."

"Help me, help me," the figure at their feet groaned.

Dillon looked down at him and for the first time noticed a slit running from the bridge of his nose across his left cheek. He remembered the Mountjoy Forensics Team bagging the stem on a wine glass with blood on it. Dermot Dugan, the next door neighbor had said the man who assaulted Aideen had run out the door with his hand covering the left side of his face. The odds of finding whoever assaulted her suddenly seemed to have improved.

"What the hell is your name?" Suel growled.

"Help me, I need help—"

"You got one more chance to tell me your bleedin' name or I'm going in to get my matches and I'll come back and roast the hell out of the you."

"Help, me, please."

"That's it, you're gonna be a bar-b-que," Suel said and turned to head for the house.

"He's not kidding, pal, and believe me, no one is gonna stop him. What's your damn name?"

"Tommy, Tommy Brody. Please, you gotta help me. I'm dying here," he said and let off another long groan.

"You're beyond help, Brody. You're just damn lucky my partner shot you because if I'd gotten hold of you it would be a slow death. Like beating up women, do you?" Suel said. He stepped on top of Brody's right hand with his boot and ground it into the sidewalk. In the distance they could hear a siren suddenly growing louder drowning out Brody's screams.

Eventually, Dillon reached for Suel's arm and pulled him off the hand. A moment later a flashing light rounded the corner and sped toward them. As the officer stepped out of the vehicle, Dillon and Suel identified themselves. A few minutes later, an ambulance rounded the corner and a three man crew climbed out. Two more squad cars and a fire truck arrived as the ambulance carrying Tommy Brody departed.

Dillon and Suel answered questions for the next hour and a half. They told the officers that DI Walsh from the Mountjoy Garda Station was investigating the earlier assault on Aideen. Eventually, Dillon was allowed to go home. By the time he opened his front door, he was too tired to care about the mess Lucifer had left in the kitchen. He stumbled up the stairs. Still dressed, he fell into bed, and immediately went asleep.

FIFTY-EIGHT

Lucifer woke him the following morning. Dillon was dressed in the same clothes he'd worn the day before and slept in. He stumbled out of bed and let Lucifer out the front door. The cellphone in his front pocket rang while he was spooning coffee grounds into the coffee maker.

"Jack Dillon," he answered in a raspy voice, then cleared his throat.

There was a chuckle on the other end. "Sounds like I woke you, Dillon. Your email said to phone you no matter the time," Ronnie Maxwell said.

"No problem, appreciate the call, Ronnie. You're just catching me before my first cup of coffee. You get the images I sent?"

"Yes. Two emails, as a matter of fact. One from you and the other from your forensics section, a woman named Ina Nolan. Based on the time these were sent, I'd say you were both burning the midnight oil."

"Oh, you don't know the half of it, Ronnie. A crazy late night, but in the end worth it. You notice anything on those images?"

"Notice anything? If I had to take a wild guess, I'd say your man looks one hell of a lot like he might be the Otis lad. Is that what you're thinking?"

"Yeah. They got a fifty-nine point something percent match with the images in forensics. They can't ID the woman, but her clothing matches the description the roommates gave as to what Madeline Keller was wearing. You notice the way he's got hold of her?"

"You mean his arm around her shoulder?"

"That's part of it. If you enlarge the image with his head turned like he's talking to her, you can also see a bit of his left hand holding onto her left forearm. We're thinking Otis drugged her, probably Rohyponl, the same thing he slipped into Colin Cominsky's pint. I'm wondering if you found anything on the phone records?"

"As a matter of fact, we did. I was planning to call you anyway."

"What'd you find?"

"McKenzie and Otis were the only ones who made phone calls after seven that evening."

"McKenzie told us he phoned that woman, Molly. She's the one who grabbed their money and threatened to call security if they didn't leave," Dillon said.

"Her name is Molly Patrick, by the way. I've got two lads giving her a ride in as we speak. We want to get her statement," Maxwell said.

"Wonderful."

"Yeah. Records indicate that was the only call McKenzie made. The other two calls were made by Darren Otis, one to Molly Patrick about half past eight. That call was made from Dundalk."

"Dundalk? But that's across the border."

"Yes, it is. His second call was made to Madeline Keller's number, a call that lasted two minutes, and it was made from Dublin."

"Dublin?"

"Yes, from the north side on the M1 just opposite the airport. Apparently, he called while driving."

"On the phone while driving, sounds like grounds for an arrest," Dillon said.

"I'm not sure—"

"I was joking, Ronnie. Jesus, and I'm the one going on two hours sleep. This helps to confirm it was him in the images."

"I've a request in for a subpoena to get official copies of the Otis phone records from his service provider, Verizon. I'll have the subpoena before the noon hour and the records within twenty-four hours. If we rely on the unofficial records we copied, there's always the chance they could be thrown out of court."

"I've got one more thought," Dillon said.

"Which is?"

"Those two images where you're just seeing the backside of the both of them. If you blow them up, it looks like he's wearing a brown leather jacket and there's a tear or maybe a scrape about three inches long on the back of his upper right shoulder. Check that out on the images we sent you. And, can you check on your images from the Empire Pub? I can't recall, but I think he may have had that jacket on in the images as they were leaving the pub. On those images, as they're driving out of the Empire parking lot, I'm betting the compact car belonged to Darren Otis. There was only a partial on the license plate. If you can check and see if he has a vehicle registered to him, I can check CCTV down here for the license number."

"You're going to check the entire city?"

"Those images you received were taken on the Ha'penny Bridge. She can barely walk at that point. I'd say there's a halfway decent chance he parked just on the other side of the Liffey. Either on or somewhere close to Bachelors Walk. We locate his vehicle down here, we got this little prick by the short hairs."

"You coming up today?"

"I'd hoped to, but we were involved in a shooting and an arrest last night. We'll be talking to internal affairs and one of the local precincts regarding an earlier assault."

"Everything okay?"

"Yeah, an assault investigation that was going nowhere and now, suddenly after last night, it looks like we got the guy."

"Never enough of those."

"You're preaching to the choir on that, Ronnie. But, it's going to hold us up for a day or so until we can get back up there. In the meantime, if you can check those images to confirm the jacket and get the license number to the car Otis may have been driving that'll help. We'd like to be there when you make an arrest."

"It would help if we had a body. In all honesty, he could testify that he just helped her to the bus stop and, at this stage, there really isn't anything we can do to dispute that," Maxwell said.

"Hey, we were treading water for over a week and a half with no progress. At least now, it looks like we're beginning to get somewhere."

"Long may it last. Let me know when you're heading back up."

"Tomorrow, at the earliest," Dillon said.

Once they hung up he opened the front door and Lucifer hurried back in and ran to his empty food and water dish.

"I know the feeling, pal," Dillon said as he filled both dishes. As Lucifer attacked his food dish, Dillon slowly climbed the stairs toward the bathroom for a hot shower.

FIFTY-NINE

It was early afternoon. Dillon and Suel had been sitting in DCI McCabe's office for over an hour. Along with them were two humorless investigators from internal affairs asking questions regarding the assault on Suel's sister, Aideen, and the previous night's *'involvement'* with Tommy Brody.

"We were only allowed five minutes with Mr. Brody. He seemed to be in a good deal of pain," Officer Higgins said. "He states that you did not identify yourself as An Garda Síochána, Marshal Dillon. You did not issue a warning. And, it would appear, you displayed a callous disregard for public safety when firing your weapon." He looked up from his notes and stared at Dillon.

Dillon smiled and looked around the room, before he focused in on Higgins. "No offense here, I mean, I get you're required to ask these questions, but you're kidding, right? Or is your head that far up your ass?"

His partner, a thin man with pale skin, a heavy dark beard and lifeless grey eyes, aptly named Dullden, shifted in his chair and said, "You fired your service weapon and an individual is now lying in Saint James hospital with burns over sixty percent of his body and a crushed right hand. Those are the facts and, I have to say, I find your attitude and explanation rather unsatisfactory."

"Which part is unsatisfactory? The part where he's ready to throw that Molotov cocktail through the front window and incinerate the two individuals inside? The part where I didn't try to *'negotiate'* with him? Or the part where I dragged him from the fire and the burning liquid, extinguished the flames on his body and saved his worthless ass? Sixty percent burns, the bastard is lucky to even be alive. If nothing else, he's hopefully learned not to play with fire."

"Do you find this funny, Marshal?" Dullden said.

"You fired your weapon which led to Mr. Brody being consumed by flames," Higgins said.

"You're right, I did. And, in so doing saved the lives of at least the two individuals in the home not to mention the damage to the unit and attached units. Brody wants to file a lawsuit against me? I welcome it. He's now been identified as the individual who assaulted and raped Aideen Suel almost two weeks earlier. His assault put her in the hospital for three or four days. He'll be charged with that assault and rape before the day is over. Apparently, he has a history of assaults on women. He has an arrest record that stretches back fourteen years. So, I just want to make sure I got this right. You're questioning me because I raised my voice to him. What would you have me do? Talk nicely?"

"Now really. We're questioning you because—"

"I think we've heard just about enough," DCI McCabe said, looking at Dillon.

"Thank you, sir," Dullden said. "For the life of me, Marshal, apparently you simply don't realize that we adhere to the law over here. This is not your American wild west where you can just ride in and—"

"Excuse me," McCabe said. "Apparently, you simply don't realize. The Marshal was faced with a life or death situation last night. I hasten to add, the lives were those of DI Suel and his sister. Given the split second option, he had no choice but to act as he did and then, in my humble opinion, went beyond what was required and sought to save this completely worthless individual's life. In the process risking his own. Gentlemen, thank you for your time. Rest assured, I intend to file a complaint within the hour to the office of Commissioner Harris. Good day, gentlemen."

"DCI McCabe, I realize you may find—"

"Stop right there. You don't seem to realize one blessed thing. You clearly have had zero experience out on the street. But then, why should that come as a surprise? You both lack a modicum of common sense. Now get out."

Higgins and Dullden looked at one another and slowly rose. As they headed for the door Higgins said, "This isn't the last you're going to hear from us."

McCabe looked around, picked up a tea mug from his desk and made like he was going to throw it. Higgins and Dullden ran out the door and kept going, running through the Special Branch office.

"God give me strength. All right. First, both of you, good work last night. Well done. You are suspended from duty within the city limits of Dublin with pay pending our investigation of the incident. This should take twenty-four to forty-eight hours."

"Within the city of Dublin?" Suel asked.

"Got it, sir," Dillon said, suddenly realizing what McCabe was saying and jumped to his feet. "Come on, Paddy. Let's get out of the Chief Inspector's hair."

Dillon walked over to his desk, turned off his computer, bussed three plates, a bowl, and two tea mugs from his desk, bringing them to the break room. He pulled the Madeline Keller file from his file drawer, locked the drawers on his desk and walked over to Suel who was in the process of just hanging up the phone.

"Two days with pay," Dillon said and smiled. "Any plans?"

"Just on the phone with DI Walsh at Mountjoy. He said Tommy Brody is hand cuffed to a hospital bed in James's burn unit. He's got a severely broken hand and burns over sixty percent of his body. He's going to be there for a while. Charges will be filed tomorrow. Assault, rape, attempted murder, resisting arrest. Walsh has a laundry list of charges along with two other women who'll testify that he assaulted them as well. Oh, and get this, he had eleven stitches across his nose and left cheek from an earlier injury. They're in the process of doing a blood match on some broken glass from the crime scene evidence they gathered at Aideen's."

"How's she doing?"

"Relieved. She didn't want to press charges because she was afraid he would kill her, or I'd kill Brody. I never thought about it, but I can sort of see her point."

"So, you're not going to be staying at her house anymore?"

"Tell you the truth, I'm looking forward to getting back to my place."

"Think you might fancy a little trip?"

"Up north to Belfast?"

Dillon nodded and brought Suel up to date with the images, potential facial ID, Otis's phone records and the suspected drugs in Madeline and Cominsky's drinks.

"This is the same bollocks we were calling the Golden Boy?"

"'Fraid so."

"And you're going up there?"

"Maxwell's just waiting for the official phone records to come from Verizon and then he'll arrest Otis. I'd like to be there for that and sit in on the interview if Ronnie will let us."

"We could grab the first train in the morning. We'll be in Belfast before ten," Suel said.

"Call Ronnie Maxwell and tell him we're coming up. See if there's anything he needs from us to make the arrest."

As Suel reached for his phone he said, "You thinking of interviewing any of the others?"

"You mean Cominsky? No, I don't see any benefit. Plus, I'd just as soon not ruffle his uncle's feathers. With the images and the phone records, I'm hoping we can pressure the Golden Boy to fess up and tell us what the hell happened. A body would put the bastard away for a long time."

"Damn bloody shame," Suel said as he punched in the numbers for Ronnie Maxwell.

SIXTY

Dillon and Suel were on the early morning train heading up to Belfast. Suel had just handed Dillon a medium sized coffee before he sat down in the seat across from him.

"I'll be waiting for you out on the Albert Bridge Road," Ronnie Maxwell said into his phone.

"Good Ronnie, once we link up are you going to arrest Otis?"

"I have someone watching him now. He's still at home, but he has a class early this afternoon at Queen's. I'd like to grab him as he's getting into his car to attend class."

"This wouldn't happen to be a finance class, would it?"

"Afraid not, I believe it's Elizabethan literature or some damn thing. Why do you ask?"

"Just something in the back of my mind. Listen, we'll see you in little more than an hour."

"I'll be waiting," Maxwell said and hung up.

Dillon opened his computer bag and pulled out the Madeline Keller file. He paged through the interview notes until he came to their interview with Darren Otis. He skimmed forward running a finger down the page until he came to the name he was looking for. He pulled his cellphone out and called the general number for Queen's University.

"Professor Winton Varley, please," he said, once the phone was answered.

"One moment, please, while I connect you."

The phone rang five times and Dillon was expecting to be dumped into voice mail when a man answered, half shouting, "Varley."

"Is this professor Winton Varley?"

"Yes, but whatever you're selling, I'm not interested. Thank you," Varley said.

"Professor, my name is Jack Dillon. I'm a United States Marshal attached to An Garda Síochána in Dublin. We're working a case in conjunction with the PSNI and your name came up."

"My name? What on earth for? I haven't been down to Dublin in two, no, make that three years. In fact—"

"I'm sorry, professor, perhaps I misspoke. My question merely regards a course you're teaching. I just wish to confirm the attendance at an exam by one of your students."

"An exam?"

"Yes, a student by the name of Darren Otis. I believe he took an exam about two weeks back in your finance course."

"Otis? Darren Otis? Oh, yes, I have a third year class with young Otis, a good student almost always in attendance if that's your question. But there wasn't an exam. In fact, there won't be an exam throughout the entire third year course."

"No exam?"

"That's correct. There is, however, a fairly stringent term paper, minimum fifteen thousand words dealing with investments and stock ratios on which the students will be graded. I've seventeen individuals in that particular class. The Otis lad is one of them."

"And his grade in the class is based entirely on this paper, fifteen thousand words."

"Fifteen thousand words, at a minimum. However, that is not the entire grade. The paper will reflect ninety percent of his grade, attendance, participation, and overall attitude make up the remaining ten percent."

"And no exam?"

"That is correct."

"Thank you for your time professor."

"Wait a moment. Is the lad in some sort of trouble?"

"No sir, just confirming that he was indeed in your class."

"Well, yes. As I said, he's one of seventeen in the third year class," Varley said, sounding just a little confused.

"Thank you for your time, professor," Dillon said and quickly hung up.

"Let me guess, going home to study for an exam turns out to be complete and utter bullshit," Suel said and slurped some tea.

"Pretty much."

SIXTY-ONE

The train began to slow as they entered the outskirts of Belfast. Suel sat with his arms folded across his chest staring out the window. "What do think the chances are of finding the Keller girl alive?" He asked the question without turning to look at Dillon.

Dillon closed the Keller file and placed it back in his computer bag. "The chances of finding her alive? At this stage, I'd have to say just about zero. I think the chances of finding her at all are extremely slim and growing more so by the day."

Suel shook his head and continued staring out the window. "Such a shame. A young person, hell, any person with their life ahead of them and it's cut to the quick like this. Something I'll never get used to. Never understand."

"Not to mention what it does to those around her, family, friends, the ripple of pain and incredibility, thinking this couldn't possibly happen to someone you know. Unless you've had the experience, it's impossible to realize how this affects people, literally for generations. Her roommates, those three young women. Odds are at some point, they'll tell the story to their children and grandchildren. It will definitely affect how they raise their kids. Madeline's parents will be forever known as the couple whose daughter was murdered. No one is the same after an event like this. How could you be?"

Suel shook his head and absently said, "As a lad growing up during the troubles my uncles used to tell us the best place to hide a body was in a graveyard."

"Were they involved?"

"In the politics? No, in fact the entire family, along with most of the families around us, worked very hard to protect us kids from anything political, conversations, the constant bad news. We weren't allowed to play with toy guns. My mother wouldn't have them in the house. Which, of course, made the idea all the more appealing to her thick headed sons. There were things in those days you didn't do, mmm, like traveling north," he said and indicated the train car. "My mother was in a bombing."

"A bombing? Was she up north?"

Suel shook his head and looked at Dillon. "No. Actually, there were a number of bombings in Dublin. The one she was in happened on her birthday, as a matter of fact. A car bombing on Sackville Place, January twentieth, nineteen seventy three. Happened on a Saturday at three in the afternoon in the midst of weekend shopping. She was just eighteen, in the city center with a couple of girlfriends. They were heading down O'Connell Street, just ready to turn onto Sackville when the bomb went off. It was horrific, knocked the three of them to the ground. Sent some poor soul through a window, blood and panic all over the place. You can just imagine.”

“Jesus Christ, was she injured?”

“Not physically. She said they got to their feet and just started running. About an hour later they found themselves in Drumcondra, scared out of their minds. I guess she didn’t go into the city center for years, still doesn’t fancy the place almost fifty years later.”

“They ever arrest anyone?”

Suel shook his head, “No, I’ve read and reread the files. At least, what I could get my hands on. Most of it was made public in the late nineties. No one’s ever claimed responsibility.”

“Any clues on who did it?”

“All sorts of rumors, anonymous tips, and plenty of suspicions. The UVF, the IRA, the Brits, but nothing concrete.”

“How many people were killed?”

“One man. Actually, he was a Scottish lad, I believe. Lots of people injured. It all sounds so crazy now, but those were the times.”

“Puts things in perspective, I guess.”

The announcement came over the loudspeaker system that they were coming into Belfast Central Station.

“Where are we meeting Ronnie?” Suel said getting to his feet.

“He said he’d be waiting for us on Albert Bridge Road.”

SIXTY-TWO

onnie Maxwell was waiting for them on Albert Bridge Road. As they stepped onto the sidewalk, he flashed the lights on the black SUV and they hurried over. The road and sidewalks were wet and there was a light mist. Just enough moisture in the air to cause one to occasionally have to turn on the windshield wipers.

"Hi, Ronnie, so nice to have a chauffeur," Suel said climbing into the front seat.

"It's only for the protection of our citizens. We wouldn't want the likes of either of you two behind the wheel with innocent people out on the streets. How was the train ride?"

"Wonderfully uneventful," Dillon said.

"We've the Otis phone records from Verizon. I've subpoenas for the lad's jacket and basically anything else we want. I've a team parked outside the house, his parents place by the way. No activity and we don't really expect any for another hour until he's scheduled to leave for his class. If he does attempt to leave they'll arrest him, but we can take our time heading over."

"Would we have time to go to Belfast City Cemetery?" Dillon said from the back seat.

Maxwell looked at him in the rearview mirror and Suel turned around.

"The cemetery? What do you want to do there?" Maxwell said.

"We were there, compliments of Calvert Cominsky and his nephew. They played us a bit, telling us we could meet the young woman friend of Colin. Something has been bothering me ever since that visit and it came back stronger while we were riding up on the train. I just can't quite put my finger on it."

"Something I said? The bombing?" Suel said.

"No. I don't think so. It's just something nagging me, but I can't quite get it. It's just below the surface."

"And you think going to the cemetery will suddenly enlighten you?"

"Maybe, I just don't know. If it's a hassle, we can do it later."

"The city cemetery is a big place. They're slowly in the process of restoring a lot of the grave markers that were destroyed over the years. But, if you think it will help we can drive through and hopefully, the light will come on," Maxwell said.

"If you wouldn't mind. I just want to check something out. Humor me, it'll only take a minute."

Maxwell put the car in gear and pulled away from the curb. "We're only ten maybe fifteen minutes away. Suit yourself."

"I told you he was loco," Suel said to Maxwell and settled into the front seat.

SIXTY-THREE

The green wrought iron gates stood open and Maxwell took a right off of Falls Road. He drove past the stone pillars marking the entrance to Belfast City Cemetery, past the dressed stone structure.

"Veer to the right, Ronnie, and stay on this lane until it curves around to the left," Suel said.

They passed two cars parked off to the side. One was an elderly couple carrying a bouquet of flowers. The other was a younger woman, with a small, white dog. The dog was on a leash.

"Pull over up there behind that dark green Mercedes," Dillon said.

"A Maybach S-class. That probably cost more than a year of my salary," Maxwell said.

"Huh? I'd say more like two years for any of us," Suel said.

"Four doors and dark green. Just a wild guess. I'd be willing to wager a pint that Calvert Cominsky is here," Dillon said.

"That bollocks," Suel said. "What do you say we follow the lane all the way around and come back another time?"

"No, actually this might just work in our favor. Park it for a minute, Ronnie. You two can stay in the car if you want."

"And miss all the fun? Not on your life," Maxwell said.

"Oh, for God's sake, I'm saddled with idiots," Suel said and opened the passenger door before Maxwell had even stopped the car.

The weather had begun to clear. The mist had stopped, at least for the moment, and there was a small patch of thinning clouds with just a hint of blue sky off to the west. Dawn Davies' grave site was maybe fifty yards away. Two individuals were busy encircling the grave site with a coil of wire fencing. The fencing was green and maybe three feet high. The white cross Colin made had been repositioned to accommodate the fencing. Colin and Calvert Cominsky appeared engrossed in their task and failed to notice the three officers until they were almost on top of them.

"Gentlemen," Calvert said, rising to his feet. He handed a hammer to Colin and issued some instructions before approaching the group. He shook his head in a disappointed fashion and said, "Is this really necessary? Here? At this time?"

"Actually, we had no idea you were even here," Dillon said.

"Oh, I see," Calvert said, sounding like he didn't believe a word.

"Honestly, we didn't. You're stringing that fencing, is that to keep the dogs away?"

"As if her death at such a young age wasn't tragic enough, we've got these idiots around here letting their dogs off the leash. The first thing the damn things do is run over and start to dig up Dawn's grave. Colin's ready to stand guard over the site. Hopefully, this fencing will bring the problem to a close. Now what is it you want?"

"Actually, nothing. Like I told you, we had no idea you were even here. So, the dogs continue to be a problem?"

"There was a hole almost six inches deep when we arrived a half hour ago. Right in the middle of the grave. Would you not think people might, at least, have the decency after being stupid enough to have the damn dog off the leash in the first place. That they'd fill in the damage the damn animal created?"

Colin began pounding a stake into the ground and the noise caught their attention. All four turned to watch for a moment.

"Hopefully, this will address the problem. We've mentioned it innumerable times to the staff but it seems to fall on deaf ears. Such a shame and so unnecessary." He turned back to look Dillon in the eye. "And how goes your investigation?"

Dillon flashed a quick smile. "Moving along. Never as fast as we would like, but moving. Would you mind if I spoke with Colin?"

"As a matter of fact, yes, I would."

"You could join us, I certainly don't have an objection."

"I would prefer that you not speak with him. The death of Dawn and now the disappearance of the Keller girl have really taken a toll on him. In fact, it's why we're here this morning. This is finally something positive he can do here."

"The dogs digging? Has that been an ongoing problem here?"

"Colin noticed it maybe two weeks ago. He's been out here every day since. Sometimes twice a day."

"Strange, isn't it? The staff wouldn't have some method of enforcement or if it's such a problem they would just ban the dogs entirely," Dillon said.

"Initially, they told us it was the first time they've ever experienced it. Frankly, based on what we've seen, I'm having a tough time accepting that explanation."

Dillon held his hand out for Calvert to shake. "I'd like to thank you for your time. I hope that fence does the trick."

Calvert waited a long moment before he shook Dillon's hand. "Let's hope it works. Wishing a safe and speedy journey back to Dublin for the both of you."

SIXTY-FOUR

Once they were back in the car Suel said, "What the bloody hell was that all about, Dillon?"

"Just being a gentleman," Dillon said.

"How did you know that legal plonker was even going to be here?"

"Actually, he's very highly regarded, has a sterling reputation," Maxwell said as they drove around the bend and headed back toward the front gate.

"Oh, well, excuse me. Dillon, how did you know that legal *bastard* was even going to be here?"

"Honestly, I didn't. Say, Ronnie, pull over for a moment."

"Everything okay?"

"Yeah, hang on," Dillon said opening the car door. "I just want to take a picture."

He ran toward a three man grounds crew. One of them was in the process of reversing a backhoe. As soon as he backed up, the other two jumped into a gravesite, at this point only about two feet deep, and began shoveling dirt. "Excuse me, you guys mind if I take your picture?" Dillon said.

"You American?"

"Yeah, just visiting a grave site. Can I take your picture digging?"

They smiled at one another and the one who'd asked if he was American said, "Yeah, sure, I guess. Billy's just off to refuel and then he'll be back if you want a shot of the backhoe."

"No, I'd just like a picture of you two using the shovels."

They sort of chuckled and the one said, "Okay, here, Brian you get down to the end so he can get both of us." They proceeded to toss shovels full of dirt onto the small pile as Dillon clicked away.

He quickly took a half dozen photos with his cellphone. "Okay fellas, thanks, much appreciated."

"Let us know when we're famous," one of them said.

"I'll be sure to do that. Let me ask you something. Two guys over on the other side are stringing some fencing around a recent gravesite. They told me they were having trouble with dogs digging up the site. Is that a problem?" Dillon said.

They exchanged looks and the one who'd been doing the talking hopped up out of the partially dug grave, rammed his shovel into the pile of dirt and said, "It shouldn't be. Problem is, people let their dogs off the leash and the dogs run. Tell you the truth, we've not had the problem before, least wise that I can recall. I don't know if it's something with the site. At first we were thinking maybe a dog in heat left something there and it attracted the males, but it's been going on far too long. We offered to place the fencing around the gravesite, but they said they would do it. Hopefully, it'll work. We're going to be seeding a number of recent grave sites at the beginning of next week and it would be nice if the dogs didn't dig it up."

"What in the hell was that about?" Suel said as Dillon climbed back into the car.

"Anything else you want to see here before we pick up the Otis lad?" Maxwell said.

"They're planning to put grass seed on the gravesite next week."

"Yeah?" Suel said not following.

"They just said it would be nice if the dogs didn't dig it up. Guess I'm ready if you two are. Let's go get Darren Otis and see what he has to say this time."

Suel seemed to think for a moment then nodded. "CCTV tapes, phone records, the jacket, the McKenzie lads testimony that Otis drugged Colin Cominsky's pint. I think it's starting to lean in our favor."

"Yeah. Well, let's see how all that works on Otis. Only one way to find out," Dillon said.

Maxwell pulled his phone out and placed a call. "Yeah, we're just leaving the city cemetery. We'll see you in about fifteen minutes."

SIXTY-FIVE

The Otis home was on Demesne Road in an area on the edge of Belfast called Holywood, almost next to the Holywood Golf Club. The house was partially hidden from the road by a trimmed hedge and trees. The brick home was two stories tall with a slate roof and a front door centered between two large windows. Three large, evenly spaced windows with white curtains ran across the second floor. A winding gravel drive ran from Demesne Road up to the house. A compact car, blue with a white roof and fancy wheel rims, was parked at the front door. Two men were busy cutting the grass and trimming the hedge.

Maxwell pulled in behind a car parked on Demesne Road. Dillon could see two silhouettes in the front seats. Maxwell took his phone out, placed a call and put it on speaker so they could all hear. Someone answered just after the first ring.

"We were starting to worry, Ronnie. Everything okay."

"Just a quick stop at the city cemetery."

"Get your prayers said," one of them replied and both laughed.

"What's the news here?"

"That's your man's car parked at the front, the Opel Adam. A two thousand sixteen model. Two doors and a hatchback. Pretty nice ride for a lad. I'd say looking around the car, the lawn crew, and the mansion, money doesn't seem to be an object."

"Any sign of him yet?" Maxwell asked.

"No, sir. We expect him in the next fifteen or twenty minutes if he's going to be on time to his class. Other than the gardeners, there's been no sign of any activity."

"I think we'll just wait. I'd like to have him pull out of the drive and you can pull him over just down the lane. Away from the house. Tell him it's just some more questions. Don't mention our friends from Dublin. We'll let that be a surprise. I've an interview room scheduled at Musgrave. Offer him a water and we'll let him sit for fifteen or twenty minutes. I want him thinking it's somewhat casual. So, no restraints."

"And if he refuses?"

"Put the bangles on him and haul his privileged ass in. Once he's processed, secure him to the chair in the interview room."

"Carrot and the stick," one of them said and laughed.

"Hopefully, it won't come to that. Any problems let us know."

Maybe ten minutes later, Darren Otis came out the front door. He was wearing a brown leather jacket. He opened the driver's door, tossed what appeared to be a computer bag in behind the driver's seat and climbed behind the wheel. He started the car, calmly turned the car around then gave two toots on the horn as he passed the gardeners now standing and chatting. They both gave him a slight wave, and one of them clearly made some sort of comment to his partner. Otis stopped at the end of the drive, checked for traffic and made a left hand turn headed in the general direction of Queen's University.

A moment later, the car in front of them pulled away from the curb, followed Otis over a slight rise and disappeared. Maxwell waited a few minutes before he turned the car on. It felt like an eternity before he pulled away from the curb. When they reached the top of the rise they could see both vehicles pulled over to the side. The two officers were in plain clothes and at the moment, they were in the process of helping Otis into the back seat.

Maxwell gave an audible exhale. "That seemed to go all right. Twenty minutes to Musgrave station. Give him some time to think about things."

"How long will the processing take?" Dillon said.

"As long as he apparently came along without a problem, we're not going to process him. They'll just set him in the interview room, let him think for a bit and then, we'll go in. He hasn't been arrested. We're just going to have a nice little conversation," Maxwell said as they drove past the cars parked along the side of the road.

"They're going to wait there for a bit, just to make sure we're in the building before they arrive."

SIXTY-SIX

Darren Otis sat at the metal table with both hands wrapped around a plastic water bottle. His brown leather jacket was draped over the back of his chair, one of four chairs around the table. Occasionally, he looked around, but otherwise seemed to focus on the water bottle. The walls were painted a light grey and the floor looked to be a light green linoleum edged with a white mopboard at the base of the wall. Dillon, Suel and Maxwell had been watching Otis for the better part of fifteen minutes through the two way mirrors.

"What do you think?" Maxwell said.

"I think he's looking too calm, like he's working at it. You notice the right foot," Suel said.

"Yeah, nervous, he hasn't stopped tapping that foot since he sat down. I'm going to head in there. You two wait here until I give you a signal then come on in. Let me get him started. I'm not going to mention the jacket until you come in. You've got the CCTV images on your computer," he asked Dillon.

"Yes, and you've got them loaded in the room, right?"

Maxwell nodded.

"I'm going to load a couple more images on my computer, depending on how it goes, I may not use them," Dillon said.

"Wish me luck, gents," Maxwell said and left the room. A moment later there was a loud knock on the steel door that seemed to echo in the room. Darren Otis looked up as Maxwell entered the room.

"Let's see how this goes," Suel said.

"Mr. Otis, we've met before. Detective Inspector Maxwell. Thank you for coming down to chat," Maxwell said pulling a chair out and sitting down across from Otis.

Otis simply nodded then made a few nervous swallows.

"I want to assure you. You are not under arrest," he paused as he set a laptop and a thick file on the table and sat down. "All right now, let's get started, shall we? I'll be recording our conversation for future reference." Maxwell clicked some keys on the laptop as he looked across the table at Otis who gave a frightened sort of nod. "I'm Detective Inspector Ronnie Maxwell . . ." He went on to list location, date, time and that he was interviewing Darren Otis.

"Now then, Mr. Otis, you are here of your own free will, correct?"

"Yes."

"And we are here to discuss the disappearance of an American student, Miss Madeline Keller. Had you ever met Miss Keller?"

"No," Otis replied in barely a whisper.

"I'm sorry, would you mind repeating that and speaking up just a bit louder. We'll need these tapes for future reference, you know, should we have any questions or want to review what, exactly was said. Now then, did you ever meet Miss Madeline Keller?"

"No, I did not."

"And you knew of her how, exactly?"

"She was dating a friend of mine, Colin Cominsky."

"And do you know how they met?"

"They met in Dublin at Trinity college. I believe it was some sort of social hour the school set up for students but I can't be sure."

"Can't be sure it was at Trinity, or that it was a social hour set up by the school?"

"I'm not sure if it was at the social hour. I'm pretty sure they met at Trinity."

"Ever been there, at Trinity?" Maxwell said in a tone that suggested it was just a casual question, not really part of the official interview.

"I was once, four years ago, I was on a rugby team for my school and we had a match on the Trinity field."

"What school was that?"

"Ashfield."

"Oh, really, a fine reputation. Well done, you. Did you happen to win the match?"

"As a matter of fact, yes, we did."

"Ahh, fair play to you. And you graduated from there?"

"Yes, sir."

"And then where?"

"I'm third year at Queen's."

"Get down to Dublin often?"

"No sir."

"When was the last time you were down there?"

"Last time, umm, I don't know exactly. Last summer, early summer, actually May, I think. I was with me mam."

"Visiting friends?"

"No, shopping on Grafton Street."

"Interesting, just outside of Trinity, isn't it?"

"Yes, but we didn't go there, to Trinity. We took the train down and then a taxi to Grafton Street and took the train back up here all on a Saturday afternoon."

Maxwell nodded like it made sense and changed course. "Who is Molly Patrick?"

"Molly?"

"Yes."

"I don't think I know anyone by that name."

"Oh," Maxwell flipped through a few pages in his file and said, "Hmmm, interesting. You see? James McKenzie testified that you gave him Molly Patrick's phone number the night you met up at the Empire Pub."

"He, ahhh, must have made a mistake. I don't know anyone by that name."

"A mistake? Interesting," Maxwell said and nodded. "Mr. Otis, this is going to go a lot better for you if you tell us the truth. If you lie to us, we'll certainly find out, if we don't already know."

"I wouldn't lie to you. I'm not that kind of person," Otis said gesturing with his hands.

"So, you don't know anyone named Molly Patrick? You never gave James McKenzie her phone number?"

"No, I didn't. Why would I give Jimmy her phone number? How many times do I have to say it before you believe me?"

"Apparently quite a few more, because we have your phone records and they indicate you called her number four separate times over the past five weeks."

"What? I . . . I must have misdialed, I don't know. All I know is, I don't know anyone named Molly and anyway, I'm not crazy enough to go into Towerview. It's full of nothing but knackers and gobshites."

"How did you know she lived in Towerview? I never mentioned it."

"Yes, I think you did."

"Actually, no. I didn't, and for the record, let me remind you, your last call to her was on the night Madeline Keller disappeared. You phoned Molly at half past eight from just outside of Dundalk as you were heading south to Dublin."

"That's, that's impossible. She's telling you lies. She always lies. I never called her. I was home studying for a finance exam."

"Really? Interesting because we spoke with Professor Varley and he was adamant that there was no, nor will there be, any finance exam. He's requiring a term paper, at least fifteen thousand words, that will make up ninety percent of your grade."

"I was home, studying finance, I meant to say working on my term paper. I don't know who told you that shite, but I never called that Molly person."

"You must be referring to Verizon. Because your phone records show that you made the call to Molly while driving just outside Dundalk. And then, amazingly, even though you haven't been down there in months, you phoned Madeline Keller while driving on the M1 just outside of Dublin airport."

The color seemed to drain from Otis's face. "There must be some mistake," he said, sounding as though he realized the jig was up.

"Now, one thing at a time. We have testimony from Molly Patrick that you were a somewhat regular *client*. Darren, she even described your car and didn't she spend an evening with you at home recently, while your parents were in London for the weekend? She mentioned you were rather familiar with her on the sitting room rug. In front of the fireplace, if I remember correctly. I think it's time you stop trying to fool us Darren. We know what happened. We know it wasn't your intent, things just sort of got out of hand. Believe me, I know, it happens. I deal with it every single day."

"She lies. I told you, she never tells the truth and okay, I talked to her once or twice, but I never did anything with her. She was too far gone to go home so I let her spend the night, but nothing happened. She was so high she couldn't possibly remember. Honest."

Maxwell gave a nod and signaled Dillon and Suel to join them.

"Here we go," Suel said.

SIXTY-SEVEN

Suel gave a forceful knock on the interview room door. Almost, but not quite pounding and stepped back. Dillon opened the door and stepped into the interview room, Suel followed.

Darren Otis looked up and grew a pained expression on his face.

Maxwell turned as if to see who had entered and feigned surprise. "Oh, gentlemen, just in time. Please, take a seat. You remember Mr. Darren Otis, I believe. Darren, Detective Inspector Suel and US Marshal Dillon, both with An Garda Síochána."

Otis suddenly placed both hands in front of his face, "No, no, no," he pleaded and started to cry.

Maxwell gave a nod to the two empty chairs. Suel settled into the chair next to Maxwell. Dillon took hold of the empty chair next to Otis and pulled it over and turned it around next to Suel. All three officers were now facing Otis. Dillon pulled his laptop out, placed it on his lap and opened it. A moment later the images of the gravediggers at Belfast City Cemetery appeared on the screen.

"Darren," Maxwell said in a soft tone. "Why don't you tell us what happened?"

Otis, sniffled and wiped the tears from his cheeks. Maxwell reached to the shelf behind him, pulled a number of Kleenex from a box and handed them to Otis. He blew his nose, wiped more tears away and took a deep breath.

"I didn't mean for anything to happen. I just thought, well, since I saw the selfies she sent Colin, and I knew they broke up, I thought, you know, maybe she'd be, umm, be interested, sort of. You know? So, I called her, told her I was in Dublin and that Colin gave me some things that belonged to her and I was going to return them."

"And she agreed to meet you?"

"She was out with some friends but they were getting ready to go home. I told her to hang on, I could be there in twenty minutes and she said okay."

"And where was this?" Maxwell said.

"You already know."

"That's right, we do, but it's better if you tell us, Darren."

"She was in Temple Bar, a pub called the Quays."

"You met her there?"

"Yeah, she was sitting at a back table, all alone. I bought a pint and a glass of Guinness and we just chatted, drank, listened to the music for a bit. I told her everything was in my car and then we went to my car."

"You happen to add anything to her glass?"

Otis looked wide eyed at Maxwell and slowly nodded.

"What was it?"

"I put two roofies in her glass. I didn't think they would affect her all that much, just help her relax. You know? But I literally had to drag her the last bit to my car. She could barely walk. I didn't know what to do. I couldn't just leave her, she wouldn't be safe. So, I drove back up here thinking she could sleep if off at my house, only when I got here she was, umm, was sort of unresponsive and her lips were purple. I checked, but she didn't seem to be breathing. I . . . I didn't know what to do. So, I just hid her," Otis said and began sobbing again.

"We should get her, Darren, rescue her . . . so she's not alone. Let us help, tell us where you hid her, Darren?"

He shook his head no.

"Darren, let's make this part right. Tell us where she is and we'll get her."

"It's too late, it's too late, it's too late," he sobbed.

Dillon lifted his computer from his lap and turned it toward Otis. "Darren, it would be better for you if you told us, even if we already know the answer. We took this picture this morning."

Otis looked at the image of the two gravediggers on the laptop and then at Dillon. His eyes grew wide. "But, no one saw me, no one knew. How, how did you know?"

"She's with Dawn Davies, isn't she?" Dillon said.

Otis nodded slowly and whispered, "I'm sorry, I didn't mean for it to be like this."

"We're sorry, too," Dillon said and looked at Maxwell.

Maxwell slowly shook his head, pulled a card out from his file and began to read. "Darren Otis, I'm placing you under arrest for the kidnapping and murder of Madeline Keller. You do not have to say anything. But, it may harm your defense if you do not mention when questioned something which you later rely on in court. Anything you do say may be given in evidence . . ."

* * *

They were standing around Maxwell's desk, finishing up the paperwork. "Dillon, how in the hell did you know?" Maxwell said.

"Paddy told me."

"Me? What did I ever tell you?"

"On the train, you said the best place to hide a body was in a graveyard. It didn't come to me until we saw them putting the fence around the gravesite. One of the gravediggers I photographed made a comment. It was the dogs, they knew Madeline was there. Out of all the possible places in that cemetery, it's why they kept digging there."

Suel shook his head. "My uncles, when they'd say it, we were never quite sure if they were joking or not."

"You ready to head back to Dublin," Maxwell said.

"We've got one more stop, but we should probably get going if we're going to still make our train."

SIXTY-EIGHT

The taxi pulled up in front of Ian Cominsky's home. Calvert Cominsky's dark green Mercedes was parked along the curb. "This shouldn't take long, if you wouldn't mind waiting for us. We'll be headed to Belfast Central next," Suel said.

The driver nodded and they left the taxi, walked through the squeaky iron gate, climbed the front steps, and rang the doorbell. Eventually, Calvert Cominsky opened the massive oak door with a disgusted look on his face.

"I'm going to tell the both of you right now, this is all wrong. We fully intend to fight this until Colin is vindicated and then, I plan to see that you are both dismissed and jailed for abuse of power. Colin had nothing to do with this incident. Now, where's your lackey, DI Maxwell? Neither of you have the authority to make an arrest here."

Suel exhaled loudly, taking a big breath to calm himself down before he spoke.

"We're not here to arrest Colin. We're here to simply bring you up to date and remove any thoughts you or his father may have had in regard to this situation."

"So, you've finally come to your senses. I have to say it's about damn time."

"Is Colin here?" Suel said, in a tone that suggested some colorful names for Calvert.

"He's with his father in the study. You can follow me," Calvert said and walked down the hallway, Dillon and Suel followed. They passed the two massive sliding doors, both now closed, and headed for the study. Dillon remembered the creaky wooden floor, the eight panel door and the antique brass door knob that led to the study.

Calvert stepped into the room and held the door for them. "Of course, you know Colin, and you've met Reverend Cominsky."

Colin and his father were seated across from one another. The reverend sat behind his massive antique desk in his office chair that somehow gave the impression of a throne. The worn Bible sat just off to his left on the embossed leather desktop.

"Good afternoon," Dillon said. "We won't take up much of your time. We wanted to let you know we've made an arrest in the disappearance of Madeline Keller."

A collective sigh seemed to escape into the room.

"No doubt some pathetic, sinful, brute in Dublin. Have you any idea the pain and stress you have caused our family? To all the families? Attacking Colin? Accusing his friends?" the reverend said.

It was Dillon's turn to take a deep breath and exhale.

"Actually, we've received a confession from Darren Otis. He's now under arrest with the PSNI at Musgrave station."

"That is absolutely idiotic," the reverend shouted. He jumped to his feet and slammed his fist on the desk. "I happen to know the lad."

"Which still makes him guilty," Suel said stepping forward, eyes glaring. "He confessed to driving down to Dublin the night the lads met at the Empire Pub. We've his phone records, he called a prostitute as he drove past Dundalk. Seems he gave the lads her number and they paid her a visit that night. And, he phoned the victim, the Keller girl, while driving on the M1 just outside of Dublin Airport."

"That . . . that's impossible," the reverend said, suddenly not sounding all that sure.

"He made the phone call, drugged her, just like he drugged you that night, Colin. Only she never recovered. Never knew he slipped two roofies into her glass of Guinness. We've got him on CCTV tapes if you'd care to view them, Reverend. We usually keep that sort of thing sealed, but I'd gladly make an exception in your case."

"Is there a body?" Calvert asked.

"Oh, yes. Indeed," Suel said. "He buried her that same night, care to ask where? I'll save you the trouble, Belfast City Cemetery. As it turns out, in the grave of Dawn Davies. That's why all the dog activity. The PSNI and our *lackey* friend DI Maxwell are in the process of recovering the body as I speak. Now, if you'll excuse us. We've got to get back down to Dublin and inform the girl's parents that all hope has been dashed by a lad that you personally know, reverend."

Suel turned and stormed out of the room leaving Dillon to face the Cominskys. "Forgive my partner, but it's been trying on our side, as well. Colin, if you can do anything to take something positive from these past few weeks, stick to your goal of finding a cure for the cancer that took Dawn's life. I firmly believe you can accomplish that and she would be so pleased. It's been an experience, reverend. I'll show myself out."

Dillon closed the study door behind him, let himself out of the house and walked out through the squeaking iron gate. Suel was waiting for him in the back of the taxi. "I had to leave before I strangled that self-righteous bastard. I'm not even sorry I said that. So, don't start in on me. What a bleeding bollocks," Suel said.

"I thought you were rather to the point," Dillon said.

Suel's phone rang, he glanced at the screen then answered. "Yes, Ronnie. All right, no, we were just about to head to the station, but we can be there shortly." He leaned forward and said, "Change of plans, Belfast City Cemetery. Okay, Ronnie, we'll see you shortly." He hung up then said, "They have a crew about to begin recovery. They could use us for identification."

Dillon nodded and just stared out the window. When they arrived at the cemetery there were a half dozen cars and a yellow ambulance with reflective green squares along the sides. They paid the taxi driver and hurried over to the gravesite. The wire fence had been removed, rolled up, and placed off to the side along with the wooden cross Colin Cominsky had made. Two men in white hazmat suits and gloves were carefully scraping shovels full of dirt from the grave. They were maybe a foot down. Ronnie Maxwell stood off to the side. Four other people, all PSNI with hands in their pockets stood watching, no one spoke. A black body bag was stretched out on the ground in front of Maxwell. Standing maybe ten feet behind him, Dillon recognized the three men who had been digging the grave earlier that morning. One of them gave him a nod and a slight wave.

"How's it going?" Suel asked.

"Should be anytime now." Maxwell said and held up a plastic evidence bag containing a silver watch with a black leather strap. Bits of dirt clung to the watch and the clasp was still hooked to the strap. The end of the strap appeared to have torn from the small silver watch. "Came across this just a few minutes ago."

Dillon flashed back to the CCTV images of Otis leading Madeline across the Ha'penny Bridge and the wrist watch around her right wrist. He knew for certain it was her they were about to recover and yet there was a subconscious, automatic response that he wanted to be wrong. Wanted Madeline to somehow still be alive.

"Oh, here we go," one of the men in a hazmat suit said as a bit of white cloth suddenly appeared. A portion of a butterfly tattoo was exposed below the seam on the cloth . . . just in case Dillon had any doubts.

As small as the exposed area was, any sense of a lingering hope was immediately dashed. Dillon knew the cloth was silk. Knew they would uncover the spaghetti string straps and the jeans. A lump suddenly developed in his throat and his eyes began to tear. "God damn it."

Madeline Keller was eventually placed in the body bag, then lifted onto a gurney and rolled back to the ambulance.

SIXTY-NINE

They were on the last train headed to Dublin. It was after nine when Dillon pulled his phone out and called Eric Bergman. Suel continued to stare out the window into the dark. Neither one had spoken in the past hour.

After five rings Dillon was dumped into Bergman's voice mail. "You've reached Eric Bergman. I can't take your call just now. If you'd please leave a message I'll get back to you as soon as possible." Dillon listened to the automatic message telling him to speak after the tone.

"Hi, Eric. Jack Dillon. I'm on the train from Belfast heading back to Dublin. We recovered Madeline Keller's body. The PSNI have a confession and have made an arrest today. Call me when you have a chance."

"You going to have to tell the family?" Suel said, still staring out the window.

Dillon took a deep breath and thought about it for a moment. "I'd prefer not to. I hate having to do that. But, I suspect he'd like me with him, and I'll go if he wants me to."

"It's a tough business," Suel said shaking his head.

They sat in silence for the next fifteen or twenty minutes, Suel staring out the window, Dillon looking at nothing in particular, just thinking about Madeline Keller and her parents. When Dillon's phone rang, Suel looked over and mouthed the words, "Good luck."

"Eric, thanks for calling me back," Dillon answered. He didn't sound eager to have the conversation.

"They made an arrest?"

"Yeah. Turns out to be a friend of the former boyfriend, Colin Cominsky. Cominsky's not involved. Well, except that he was the former boyfriend and that's how this bastard knew of Madeline."

"What's his name?"

"Otis. Darren Otis. Third year student at Queen's University."

"What the hell happened?"

"He drove down from Belfast the night she went missing. Apparently, phoned her and said he was returning some items from the former boyfriend. Meets her in the Quays Pub, places roofies in her drink and drives her back up to Belfast. When he finally stops, she's dead. I'm guessing died of an overdose, but the medical examiner has only just gotten her body. I would expect to learn official cause of death sometime late tomorrow."

"And you're thinking drug overdose as the cause?"

"That would be my guess, at this stage. Her parents still over here?"

"Yes and no. The mother was just incapable of dealing with all this. Basically, had a mental breakdown. A sister flew over yesterday and escorted her back to the US on a flight this morning. Once they get back to the states, she'll go into the hospital. The father's scheduled over here for four more days."

Dillon was suddenly deep in thought.

"You still there, Jack?"

"Oh, yeah. Sorry, this has been a tough one. Madeline didn't deserve this and then that stupid bastard that killed her will be locked up for life, which he deserves, but Jesus. There just are no winners here. You going to call her father?"

"You know, it's late. I'm thinking I might just give him one more night of not knowing she's gone. He's still holding out hope and with the wife basically having a breakdown, he's got a hell of a lot on his plate just now. I'll pay him a visit tomorrow, best to tell him in person. Would you be interested in coming with me?"

There it was, sort of the icing on a shit sandwich. Dillon wished he had the backbone to say no, no way. "Yeah, sure. If you want me there, I'll go." He held his breath, praying Bergman would say something like, *Thanks, but I'll deal with it.*

"Thanks. I'll give you a call, once I line something up. I'll drive. Talk to you then, Jack, and thanks again," Bergman said and hung up.

"Want me to join you?" Suel said.

Dillon thought for a moment and shook his head. "No, Paddy, there's no use in both of us being miserable."

SEVENTY

Eric Bergman's call came through early the following afternoon, he picked up Dillon thirty minutes later. He was driving a black Mercedes, *Fittingly morbid*, Dillon thought as he climbed in.

"I really appreciate you coming with me," Bergman said as they crossed the Liffey, drove past O'Sheas and the Brazen Head Pub and up the hill past Christ Church Cathedral. They drove down College Green and pulled up on the sidewalk in front of the Westin Hotel.

Dillon looked at Bergman for a moment questioning the parking on the sidewalk.

"Diplomatic plates on the car. They can't tow or clamp me. One of the few benefits."

Once inside the Westin, they made a B-line toward the front desk. Bergman flashed his ID and asked the woman behind the desk for the room number for Madeline's father.

"I'm afraid I can't give you that," she said, shaking her head, not sounding all that sure.

Dillon flashed his An Garda Síochána badge and ID card and said, "We're here to inform the gentleman of a death in the family. The privacy of his room would probably be the best place to do that. Both for him and your other customers."

"Oh, umm, yes, yes of course. He's in room number four-twelve. You can take the elevators just over to your right. Once you step off on the fourth floor his room will be to your right and down the hall."

"Thank you," Dillon said. He flashed a quick smile, turned and headed toward the elevators. "He knows we're coming?" Dillon asked as they stepped onto the elevator. It was the third time he'd asked since Bergman had picked him up.

"Yeah, he's expecting us."

"Does he know why we're here?"

"I didn't tell him, specifically, but I'd say he knows. He sounded resigned to the fact on the phone."

Dillon nodded and they stepped off the elevator and walked down the hall. Keller's room was just two doors away from the elevator and Bergman knocked softly.

Keller opened the door a moment later and nodded. "Please, come in, gentlemen," he said and held the door for them. "Have a seat. I'm afraid you'll have to use the bed," he said and indicated the kingsize bed with a wave of his hand.

Dillon sat down on the corner of the bed, closest to the door. Bergman sat next to him as Keller walked to the desk with a tv sitting on it and a bottle of Jameson Whiskey. He undid the seal on the bottle, poured maybe a quarter of an inch into three glasses then handed a glass to Bergman and Dillon.

"I'd like to propose a toast to my wonderful daughter, Madeline. May the good Lord comfort her soul until we all get to Heaven." He took a tiny sip and set his glass down, then sat in the chair in the corner, pulled it an inch or two closer to Dillon and Bergman and said. "Let's hear it, gentlemen."

Dillon and Bergman sat quietly for a moment before Bergman said, "I'm afraid, Mr. Keller, the news isn't good. Yesterday, in Belfast, the authorities arrested a young man in connection with the kidnapping and murder of your daughter. Her body has been recovered and is currently in the Belfast City Morgue. They are in the process of performing an autopsy to determine cause of death."

"And what," Keller cleared his throat a couple of times. "What have they determined was the cause of death?"

Bergman looked at Dillon. "We haven't heard, officially, but we believe it will be due to a drug overdose." Keller's eyes grew wide. "We believe she was the victim of the individual slipping a drug into her drink and that was the cause of the overdose."

"And was she raped?"

"Not that I'm aware of and we've heard nothing at this time to indicate that was the case."

"And the, the, individual who is responsible, who confessed?"

"A young man from Belfast. Third year college student at Queen's University."

"Belfast? Was it that damn Cominsky kid?"

"No sir, he knew nothing about this and both he and his family were visibly upset when they were informed by the police. He's quite innocent."

"But then how did she . . . How did this person choose her? She was out with friends."

"The PSNI, the Belfast Police, obtained his phone records. Apparently, he phoned Madeline, told her he wished to return some items to her. She agreed to meet and he drugged her drink."

Keller sat and seemed to think for a long moment. "Thank you for telling me, I know how difficult it can be. Mr. Bergman, would you be able to help us. I'm going to want to, to take Madeline . . ." His voice began to tremble and a tear suddenly ran down his cheek. "I'm going to want to take her back . . . to escort—. Oh my God," he suddenly cried and began sobbing uncontrollably.

SEVENTY-ONE

s Dillon entered the office, Suel said, "How'd it go? You look like you survived."

"About like you'd expect," Dillon said. "In the end, I'd say Madeline's father held up as well as can be expected, maybe even better as a matter of fact."

"A damn awful part of the job," Suel said.

"You'll get no argument from me."

Dillon finished up the paperwork as best he could on the Madeline Keller file. He checked in with Ronnie Maxwell, but he had yet to receive a definitive cause or time of death from the Belfast coroner and didn't expect anything until the following day at the earliest.

There was a letter addressed to him from Commissioner Harris's office, the head of An Garda Síochána. Dillon was invited to an interview in two days regarding the Internal Investigation dealings they'd had with officers Higgins and Dullden in DCI McCabe's office. Apparently, McCabe really did file a complaint.

His phone rang a little after six. Suel, McCabe, and most everyone else had already gone home for the day.

"Jack Dillon."

"Just calling to say that you owe me and it might be a nice night to pay up."

"Is this Teresa?" Dillon joked.

"No, you right plonker, it's me, Ina. Oh, the price you're going to pay after that comment."

"Ina, great to hear your voice, but it's been a bit of a tough day. I wonder if I could get a rain check and—"

"Actually, I talked to Paddy, earlier. He told me a bit about the last few days. I'm so sorry. I'm thinking dinner, nothing crazy, and maybe a nice back rub might be just what you need."

Dillon seemed to think about that for a long moment and suddenly saw the wisdom of her suggestion. "You want to meet me somewhere and—"

"Actually, no, I don't. My car is in the shop. I'm thinking you give me a lift, we stop and have dinner, I'll buy and then you come over to my place for a night cap, or whatever."

"You ready to go now?"

"Give me fifteen minutes. I'll call you and meet you at the back door."

He ended up waiting thirty minutes before Ina called, but it was worth it. He took the stairs as opposed to the elevator and came around the corner just as she was adjusting her dress. She looked beautiful in the dark green dress that stopped about mid-thigh and displayed just a hint of her deep cleavage. Her auburn hair was perfectly arranged down and over her shoulders.

"Well, I have to say, you're certainly worth the wait," Dillon said.

"Thank you, you're not so bad either. At least nothing that couldn't be fixed, given some time."

"I'll take that as a compliment. You have any place special in mind?"

"No, not really. What are you feeling like?"

"I've got a place I was in once and want to try, interested?"

"Let's do it."

Dillon drove down to Bachelors Walk. They chatted about everything and nothing along the way. Ina seemed fixated on the Irish rugby team playing New Zealand's All Blacks in two weeks time and Dillon was more than willing to let her go on about it. He gave a nod, the odd comment or a smile from time to time. Her voice and laughter somehow seemed to begin to release the stress of the past days. Once he parked, they crossed the Ha'penny Bridge and walked up the steps and into the Merchants Arch.

SEVENTY-TWO

Ina looked out the window. "You know, I've been past this place countless times, but I've never been in here."

"Well, if it isn't Marshall Dillon. Finally come to join us," Jerry O'Hara yelled from behind the bar.

"I thought you said you were only here once before?" Ina said.

"Honest, just the one time."

"Apparently, you made quite the first impression."

O'Hara stepped out from behind the bar and shook Dillon's hand as he looked at Ina. "Oh, now who's this? A daughter?"

"Oh, I'm liking it here already," Ina said.

"Come on, let me take you to a table in the back room, be a bit more quiet for you and you won't miss a word your man is saying."

"Mmm," Ina said. "I'm thinking we'd be better off if he was listening to me."

"That's true of all us men, my dear. Here you go," O'Hara said and pulled a chair out for her. "Now, let me just get a server for you and Marshal, remember our deal. This one is on the house.”

“Then, we’ll start with a bottle of your most expensive wine,” Ina said.

They ordered dinner and a bottle of wine. Dillon kept Ina’s glass filled, telling himself it was because he would be driving. More than once, she placed her hand over his and gave it a squeeze as they chatted. They had finished their meal and were considering a dessert when Dillon noticed a familiar face at the bar.

“Damn it,” he said staring over Ina’s shoulder.

“What’s wrong,” she said turning around.

“A guy named Riley Dempsey. I don’t believe it. Paddy and I have been trying to get him for weeks. He’s into everything. Last time we almost had him, he crawled out of a pub on his hands and knees and got away. There’s a good chance he’s looking the place over to rob it. I’m going to have to deal with this.”

“No,” she said and turned back to face Dillon.

“Ina, it’s not that simple. I can’t just—”

“Do you have a phone? We’re on the edge of Temple Bar, there’s Garda all around. Call it in, tell them to hurry, and when you hang up, I’ll do the same.”

“That’s not how it’s done.”

“Oh God, American’s. What? You’re suddenly a one man army? Look around, the place is crowded. Get some back up in here. Good Lord, he just ordered a pint. He’s here for at least fifteen minutes, if not longer. If he gets up to go, we can get him outside.”

"Your not going to—"

"Make the phone call, sweetheart. So then, we can go to my place and enjoy whatever might happen," she said and raised her eyebrow.

Dillon didn't have to think very hard. He phoned in the sighting of Riley Dempsey, mentioned that he was probably armed and waited.

Ina phoned next, giving almost identical information with the exception of her stating that she thought she could see a pistol stuck in the back of his belt.

Dillon saw the first two officers about four minutes later talking to the security man at the passageway door. A moment after that, two men he recognized as undercover walked into the bar. They stood on either side of Riley Dempsey and ordered pints of Guinness.

A moment later two uniformed officers suddenly charged in the front door, one of the men next to Dempsey shoved him off his stool and onto the floor. He was handcuffed and pulled to his feet before most of the people in the barroom knew anything had even happened.

Dillon and Ina walked out to the barroom. "Well, if it isn't Riley Dempsey. Pleasure seeing you again and in cuffs," Dillon said just as Dempsey was hauled out of the bar.

"You the one who called this in? You're Dillon, right? The US Marshal," the man who'd cuffed Dempsey asked.

"Yeah, we were seated in the backroom. I was afraid if he recognized me, he might start shooting."

"Smart move, you were right," he said and displayed the pistol in his hand. "Bollocks had it stuck in his belt, there was bound to be some sort of incident, none of it good. Timmy McGovern, I've heard about you, nice to meet you," he said and held out his hand.

"You're responsible for getting that guy?" Jerry O'Hara said to Dillon.

"They called it in," McGovern said, "Given the man's history there's a good chance he came in here to help himself to your cash."

O'Hara looked at Dillon and Ina and said, "You two can eat here anytime you want. It'll be on the house, always."

Later that night Dillon sat on the leather couch with Ina curled up against him. Soft music was playing some sort of song in French. Both candles on the fireplace mantel were lit and there was a fire burning in her fireplace. They each held a glass of wine in their hand, not the first.

"You know, it just dawned on me, with my car in the shop, I don't know how I'm going to get to work tomorrow. I think it might be a good idea if you spent the night," Ina said and then clinked her glass with Dillon's.

THE END

Thank you for taking the time to read <u>Madeline Missing</u>. If you enjoyed the read and have a moment please leave a review, it really helps. Thank you.

Check out this sample of the next book in the Jack Dillon Dublin Tales series, <u>Mistaken Identity</u>.

ONE

The voice on the loudspeaker said, "Ladies and gentlemen, as we start our descent, please make sure your seat backs and tray tables are in their full upright position. Make sure your seat belt is securely fastened, and all carry-on luggage is stowed underneath the seat in front of you or in the overhead bins. Thank you."

Kate Murray reached over and squeezed Megan Gaffney's hand. This was it. An eight-hour flight that seemed to have taken eight days was almost over. They'd watched movies, eaten two meals, drank wine, and never slept. Now, finally, they were descending into Dublin airport.

They didn't just smile. They grinned at one another. After two years of Kate waitressing in a St. Paul bar and Megan working a checkout lane in the grocery store, they were here. Add to that graduating last week after four years at the U of M. And they'd pulled it all off, the celebratory trip to Ireland. They held hands as the plane descended over the ocean, passed a small island just off the left side of the aircraft, and flew over a housing estate where all the houses appeared to be white with reddish roofs. Suddenly, they were just feet off the ground with the runway directly below them.

The plane seemed to skip for a second or two and began to slow as the engines roared. A moment later, a voice came over the intercom. "Ladies and gentlemen, on behalf of Delta Airlines, we'd like to welcome you to Dublin Airport. The local time is seven forty-five am, and the temperature is sixty-six degrees Fahrenheit, 18 degrees Celsius. For your safety and comfort, please remain seated with your seat belt fastened until the captain turns off the Fasten Seat Belt sign."

"Oh, we made it, Megan. After everyone said we'd never be able to do it."

"Well-earned, Kate. I can't wait. I've got the maps in my suitcase. We'll get the car and be on our way. As soon as the plane stops, let's grab our stuff and hurry off."

They weren't about to hurry. Since they were flying coach, they were seated in the back of the plane. Not so amazingly, once the plane stopped and the fasten seatbelt sign was turned off, everyone stood in the aisle. And that was all they did. No one moved. After fifteen minutes, they could detect some movement up in the next section. Eventually, it was their turn to pull bags from the overhead compartment and exit the plane. They walked along a mile or two of hallways with large black and white pictures of famous Irish people they didn't recognize. They were on the second floor of the concourse, and occasionally they passed windows that looked down onto departure gates filled with people flying out of Dublin.

A sign ahead signaled a ladies' room. They nodded at one another and hurried in, only to wait in line. The passport control area was huge, with a very short line, until they realized the short line was for people with EU passports. The non-EU passport line, meaning the rest of the world, wound back and forth for a mile or two and didn't appear to be moving very fast, if at all.

Forty-five minutes later, they stood nervously in front of a uniformed woman seated behind thick glass. "Passports," she said.

They placed their passports on the counter and smiled nervously.

She paged through the blank pages of both passports before looking up at the girls. "Purpose of your trip?"

"We're going to visit where our families came from," Kate said.

"We're Irish, Westmeath and Cork," Megan added with a smile.

"You were born here?"

"No, in Minnesota. St. Paul."

"So, you're American, which is why you have American passports."

"Well yeah, but my name is Kathleen, and she's Megan."

The officer didn't seem to be impressed. "How long are you staying?"

"One week," they replied in unison.

That seemed to bring a smile to the officer's face. She stamped both passports and pushed them back across the counter. "Enjoy your stay and drive carefully."

"We will," Kate said.

"Thank you," Megan said. They grabbed their passports and hurried to baggage claim.

It took over an hour by the time they had their luggage, exchanged dollars for euros, and signed the paperwork for their red Nissan Micra rental car. But finally, they were driving out of Dublin airport. Kate was behind the wheel, thankful for her father's insistence they pay the extra cost for an automatic transmission on the car rental.

"We follow this Swords Road to a stoplight and take a right onto Old Airport Road. That brings us to the M50 that's like the interstate at home, and we take that to the M4 and Westmeath," Megan said.

"This driving on the wrong side is weird," Kate said.

"I think that stoplight up ahead is the Old Airport Road," Megan said.

Kate stopped at the red light. After a minute, a green arrow flashed, but the red light remained on. Three seconds later, a horn honked, and then another.

"I think we're supposed to go," Megan said.

"But the light is still red," Kate said. More horns honked behind them. "I don't know," Kate said. As she began to make a right-hand turn, the green arrow turned yellow, and two cars suddenly screeched around her, leaning on the horn as they sped past. The woman driving the second car gave them the finger as she passed.

"Welcome to Ireland," Megan said, and they both laughed.

TWO

Marshal Jack Dillon, and Detective Inspector Paddy Suel, both with An Garda Síochána Special Branch, sat next to Eric Bergman from the US Embassy. All three men occupied the last bench in the rear of the courtroom in Dublin's Criminal Courts of Justice building. They'd been in the courtroom for the past two and a half days at the request of the prosecution. Dillon and Suel had been the arresting officers in the Sands brothers drug case. Bergman was representing the US Embassy since the two brothers were Americans. Mercifully, none of the three had been called to testify, which, on the one hand was good, but on the other, made for two and a half very long, boring days. Not a complaint from any of the three.

At 11:38 am, according to the large clock on the courtroom wall, both Sands brothers were found guilty of possession with intent to sell and led out of the courtroom without uttering a word. Under Irish law, they were liable for a prison sentence of no more than 14 years. The prosecuting solicitor, a somewhat unpleasant blonde woman, named Caoilfhoinn O Tighearnaigh, packed her briefcase, flashed a quick smile in the direction of the three men, and walked out of the courtroom.

"You're welcome," Bergman said just under his breath as she walked past and stepped into the hallway.

"What are you on about? It's probably more excitement than the likes of you have seen in the last month," Suel said. Both he and Dillon laughed.

"What do you think the Sands brothers will get?" Dillon asked.

"Their sentence?" Suel said. "Hard to say. First-time offenders over here, but Keylin Tierney, that's Caoilfhoinn O Tighearnaigh to the likes of you two, had their histories back in the States entered into the records if you caught it yesterday. They've both done time. I'd say it's possible they'll get a minimum of five years here, but the full fourteen may be more like it. Thirty kilos of coke in their possession and an unwillingness to cooperate, hell, they'll be locked up in Mountjoy for a good long while. Be interesting to see how the lads fair after keeping their mouths shut."

"Whoever it is they're protecting, they'll run into his rivals in the Joy. Oh, to be a fly on the wall," Dillon said.

"Idiots came over here, thinking it would be an easy mark. They'll have plenty of time to examine their mistakes."

"Mistake number one was traveling with the girlfriends," Dillon said. "They're back in the States?"

"Yeah, they will be later today. They'll be met this afternoon, the moment they step off the plane in New

York. DEA took them into custody last night and quietly put them on a flight this morning." Bergman looked at his watch. "Right now, they've been over the Atlantic for about ninety minutes. They're theoretically looking at five years, but after their cooperation, there's a good chance that will be reduced to maybe two to three years probation, maybe some community service. Hell of a stupid move for a couple of college girls. Nice looking girls too, a blonde and a redhead. One can only hope they'll learn. I'm told the father of one has political connections. So, I'm sure he's been on the phone," Bergman said.

"Hell of a stupid move for anyone," Suel said and shook his head. "The world at their fingertips and they shit the bed."

"I'll never understand the attraction to bad guys that some women seem to have. It's like a phase or something they seem to go through."

"They're young, dumb, looking for some excitement, or maybe just doing something to piss their mothers off. Used to be, in my day, they were wearing short skirts or leaving the condom wrapper where their mother would find it. A simpler time, I guess. It all looks like so much child's play compared to what those two young ladies are going to be dealing with," Suel said.

"A week of parties and being stupid and they're going to pay for it for the rest of their lives. Think of all the job opportunities that just went out the window. It's a damn shame," Bergman said.

"It's damn stupid is what it is. Job opportunities are the least of their problems. They'll be fair game for pals of these two guilty knackers."

"Enough," Dillon said, rising to his feet. "Eric, you got time to join us for lunch? We can grab something just around the corner in Phoenix Park."

Bergman looked at his watch. "I can. You thinking the Tea Rooms?"

Dillon shook his head. "No. You know where the Phoenix Cafe is?"

"At the far end of the park, near the Ashtown Demesne?"

"Yeah. It's one of those rare, lovely afternoons in Dublin, not a cloud in the sky, or at least there wasn't an hour ago. There's an outdoor courtyard in the back. First one there grabs a table. You coming, Paddy?"

Suel nodded as he stood. "If memory serves, Dillon, you owe me a meal or two. You best follow me and stay close, so you're able to pay when the time comes."

"I'll see you two over there," Bergman said and headed out the door.

THREE

Megan folded the map resting on her lap in half and looked up just in time to see the sign announcing the town of Mullingar in thirty kilometers. "I don't get it. We were driving on the M4 for most of the way, and now, all of a sudden, it changed to the N4. I wonder what the difference is. It all looks the same to me."

"Thirty kilometers? How many miles is that?"

"I think about twenty, but I'm not sure."

"Let's stop and ask directions to the B&B when we get to the town. I don't know about you, but I'm getting tired. A little nap might do the trick. Maybe close my eyes for a half-hour."

"A nap? Kate, it took us twelve hours to get over here, and now you want to go to sleep?"

"Thirty minutes, Megan. I'll do a power nap. Otherwise, I'll be absolutely worthless. Besides, we can still do stuff today. It's just a little after noon."

Fifteen minutes later, Kate pulled to a stop in front of a two-story, white stucco building that looked at least two hundred years old. She was parked between two picnic tables. The sign above the door read 'The Swordsman Pub.' "I'm just going to get directions to the B&B. Be back in a minute," she said.

"I don't think this is for cars, Kate. They've got those picnic tables and chairs laid out. Maybe pull into the parking lot over there and let me go in with you. I need to stretch and use the bathroom."

"Yeah, now that you mention it."

The inside of The Swordsman was dark, nearly empty, with wooden tables and paneling that confirmed at least a century, if not two, of existence. Two men sat at the bar, five stools apart from one another. Neither one looked at the other, nor at Kate or Megan for that matter. They simply sat and stared at their half-finished pints, either asleep or deep in thought.

The back of the bar was filled with at least a hundred different bottles of liquor. The only name the girls recognized on the beer taps was Budweiser. The dark-haired woman behind the bar was wrapping black napkins around a knife, fork, and spoon and placing them in a small bucket. She smiled as the girls approached and said, "What can I get you, ladies?"

"Directions," Kate said. "We're looking for McGovern's Guest House. Have you heard of it? It's a B&B."

"Oh yeah, I know it. You're only about ten minutes away. Were you planning to check-in."

"Yeah, just for the night," Megan said.

"Well, they'll let you drop off your bags. But they're pretty strict about no check-ins until three. Whoever was there last night has to be out by noon, and they clean the room, make the beds with fresh sheets, and place clean towels in the bath. Mrs. Brady runs it. She's pretty strict. I suppose you could call her, see if you could drop your bags off."

"Three o'clock?" Kate said.

"Sorry, but like I said, she runs a tight ship, which is a good thing. But only three hours to clean the rooms and the bathrooms, you can see her point. Why don't you grab a table and have some lunch? My name's Megan, by the way," she said and held out her hand to shake.

"That's my name, too. Without the 'H'," Megan said, shaking hands.

"Same here. Grab a table and have some lunch. Best to get your order in before the noontime crowd arrives."

"I'm Kate," she said, holding out her hand.

"Let me guess; you're Americans, and you're coming from Dublin."

"Right on both counts. We needed to flee the city. A moving target is harder to hit," Kate joked.

A man sitting across the way, alone in a booth, listened to the conversation. After Kate's moving target comment, he pulled his cellphone from his pocket and hit the speed dial button. After two rings, someone answered. "Yeah Toby, what'd ya got?"

"Brennan, you're never gonna guess what just fell into my lap."

"I don't know, based on the disgusting muppet you are, I'd guess it was a bowl of stew," he said and laughed.

"Very funny. Not. What if I told you I know where to find the two bitches what turned on the Sands brothers and gave the Guards all that information? Showed the coppers where your thirty kilos were hidden."

"The first thing I'd say is you're one stupid bastard if you're thinking I'm finding this the least bit funny. The next thing I'd say is you better get your ass in gear because, when I get my hands on the likes of you for making a joke of it, you're gonna wish you was dead."

"Stop yelling and listen to me for a minute. For fuck's sake. I'm sitting down here at the Swordsman, minding me own business. When who should walk in but two American bitches."

"You stupid bastard. Have you any idea how many Americans come into this country every day? God save me, there'll probably be a dozen just in the Swordsman tonight."

"Oh really, Americans? A blonde and a redhead? And they just told Megan behind the bar that they had to get out of Dublin on account of a moving target is harder to hit. Said they left this morning, which means they was waiting around for the Sands brothers' trial to end before they hightailed it out of town. Probably left so you and your ilk wouldn't find 'em."

"A blonde and a redhead, you say?"

"Yeah, and most definitely American. I put their ages at maybe twenty-two, twenty-three. You ever meet 'em, Brennan?"

"No, but Kevin told me a little about them. Describe them to me."

"Describe 'em? Blonde and a redhead. Shoulder length hair on the both of them. Both about the same height. The blonde's a little heavier, but you'd never call her fat. The redhead's got the tighter ass. Blonde has the bigger boobs. Nice big ones, Brennan. Both wearing jeans and nice tops. Maybe looking like they've been on the run for a couple of days. You know, the hair ain't quite done up. Tops are a little wrinkled."

"Toby, that sure as hell sounds like them."

"You ready for the best part? They introduced themselves to the woman working the bar. Know what their names are?"

"Don't fecking tell me."

"Exactly. Megan and Kate. The one named Megan said it's spelled without the 'H.'"

"Oh, sweet Jesus. They drinking or what?"

"They both just went into the loo. Brennan, I bet they're in there doing a line of coke. Probably some of the stuff what belongs to you."

"You keep an eye on them. They go anywhere, you follow. Got it?"

"Yeah, I guess I can do that. What do want me—"

"I'm heading out there now. Be there in a bit."

"Don't get the Guards after you, Brennan. They got speed traps set up all along the way."

"Don't you worry none about me. You just stay on their ass, and I'll make it worth your while. I'm heading out now."

"Drive careful," Toby said, but Brennan had already hung up.

FOUR

Dillon walked up the street to his car. He pulled out of his parking place on Conyngham Road, drove past the Criminal Courts of Justice building, and turned onto Chesterfield Avenue in Phoenix Park. Suel had stopped at the light a few cars behind him. The park was the largest urban park in Europe, dating all the way back to the seventeenth century. Among other things, along with being home to the headquarters for An Garda Síochána, it was home to a large herd of fallow deer.

Once in the park, it was a long, straight shot along Chesterfield Avenue. He passed the Wellington Monument, the Phoenix Tea Rooms, and the Dublin Zoo. He had to stop and let a car pass at the roundabout encircling the Phoenix Park Monument just opposite the entrance to the American Ambassador's residence before turning off Chesterfield and onto the road leading to the Phoenix Park Cafe. He parked close to the entrance, climbed out of his car, and waited for Paddy Suel to join him.

Once Suel climbed out of his car, Dillon glanced across the field and down the road looking for Bergman but didn't see his car. "I don't see Bergman. We might as well go in and get lunch, hopefully, he'll be able to join us."

"He probably stopped at the Ambassador's Residence to raid the refrigerator, so he doesn't have to pay for a meal. Not that I'm worried about paying. Good thing, too, 'cause I'm fecking famished. Starving as a matter of fact," Suel said.

"Well then, let's get you fed."

They walked into the Phoenix Park Cafe and stood in line. The food was served cafeteria style. Grab a tray, slide it along the rail, and point to whatever you want. Dillion grabbed a panini sandwich and a decaf coffee. Suel smiled at him, pointed at a salad, a slice of quiche, a pot of tea, and a slice of yellow cake with what looked like strawberry jam drizzled over it.

"You sure you got enough?"

Suel flashed a quick smile across the counter, nodded towards Dillon, and said, "He's paying for me."

The woman glanced at Dillon just to make sure.

"Yeah, against my better judgement, I'll pay for both of us."

"Let me find us a table while you settle up," Suel said and carried his tray out to the courtyard.

Dillon had about two bites left in his sandwich when Bergman sat down. He had a small salad and a mug of coffee on his tray.

"Sorry I'm late, fellas. Ended up stopping at the Ambassador's Residence for what I thought would be just a moment and, well, you know how that goes."

"Sure you don't want more than just that salad? Dillon's buying," Suel said.

For a moment, Bergman seemed to be considering the offer then shook his head. "No, I better not. I grabbed a chocolate brownie just out of the oven over at the residence."

"See, what'd I tell you?" Suel said to Dillon.

"What?"

"Ignore him, Eric. You have to do anything else regarding the Sands brothers?"

"No, basically, we filed paperwork in support of the prosecution. Nothing more than a formality in this case. I guess the only thing that was kind of surprising is that they even had passports in the first place. We've already sent both passports on to the State Department. Given their criminal records, neither one should have been able to hold a passport. Either someone at state was asleep at the switch or paid off, both slim chances. More likely, the passports are fake, but that sort of begs the question. With all the technology involved, if they were fakes, they were damn good. State's on it, and they'll find out."

"And the girlfriends?"

"Like I said, they'll be escorted off the plane and in the custody of the DEA. You guys find any connection with the Sands brothers prior to the girls coming over here?"

Dillon and Suel shook their heads. Suel took a large bite of his panini and wiped some sauce off his chin.

Dillon said, "Both girls are from wealthy families. They've known one another since nursery school. Apparently, they came over here to party for a couple of weeks and ended up with a lot more than they bargained for."

Bergman shook his head. "Too bad, they were both nice looking and supposedly smart, but they were in way over their heads."

"Like we were saying before, Eric. Some pretty serious probation and a record that's going to disqualify them from a lot of future job opportunities. If they ended up having to do a chunk of time in some rehab facility, it wouldn't surprise me."

"They're lucky they aren't going to be locked up over on North Circular Road," Suel said and took another bite of his panini.

"You mean the Dochas Centre?"

Suel nodded and continued chewing.

"Sex and coke seemed to be the main items on their agenda," Dillon said. The only thing that saved them is they somehow knew the Sands brothers kept the stash in paint cans. The girls had no idea there were thirty kilos there, but then again, they were so high they didn't know their own names when they were arrested."

Suel popped the last of the panini into his mouth and licked his fingers. "They showed us the empty paint can with the coke hidden inside. We were looking at maybe forty different paint cans—"

"Forty-five to be exact," Dillon said.

"Yeah, and the cans looked brand new. No paint spilled around the edges or anything. I pick one up, and I can sense something solid inside the can. We open it up, and there's a neatly wrapped kilo. Open the next one, same thing. We get thirty kilos and an extra fifteen empty cans, probably just waiting for the next shipment. It was like something out of a movie," Suel said. He stabbed his fork into the slice of yellow cake, shoved a forkful into his mouth, and grinned.

"Yeah, well, finish up. God only knows you need sweetening, and we need to get back to work," Dillon said.

TO BE CONTINUED . . .

Things are about to go crazy. Better grab your copy of <u>Mistaken Identity</u>, the eighth book in the Jack Dillon Dublin Tales series.

Don't miss the list of Mike Faricy books.

BOOKS BY MIKE FARICY
CRIME FICTION FIRSTS

A boxset of the first four books in four crime fiction series:
Russian Roulette; Dev Haskell series
Welcome; Jack Dillon Dublin Tales series
Corridor Man; Corridor Man series
Reduced Ransom! Hot Shot series

The following titles comprise the Dev Haskell series:
Russian Roulette: Case 1
Mr. Swirlee: Case 2
Bite Me: Case 3
Bombshell: Case 4
Tutti Frutti: Case 5
Last Shot: Case 6
Ting-A-Ling: Case 7
Crickett: Case 8
Bulldog: Case 9
Double Trouble: Case 10
Yellow Ribbon: Case 11
Dog Gone: Case 12
Scam Man: Case 13
Foiled: Case 14
What Happens in Vegas… Case 15
Art Hound: Case 16

The Office: Case 17
Star Struck: Case 18
International Incident: Case 19
Guest From Hell: Case 20
Art Attack: Case 21
Mystery Man: Case 22
Bow-Wow Rescue: Case 23
Cold Case: Case 24
Cash Up Front: Case 25
Dream House: Case 26
Alley Katz: Case 27
The Big Gamble: Case 28
Bad to the Bone: Case 29
Silencio!: Case 30
Surprise, Surprise: Case 31
Hit & Run: Case 32
Suspect Santa: Case 33
P.I. Apprentice: Case 34
Rebel Without a Clue: Case 35
Puppy Love: Case 36

The following titles are Dev Haskell novellas:
Dollhouse
The Dance
Pixie
Fore!
Twinkle Toes
(*a Dev Haskell short story*)

The following are Dev Haskell Boxsets:
Dev Haskell Boxset 1-3
Dev Haskell Boxset 4-6
Dev Haskell Boxset 7-9
Dev Haskell Boxset 10-12
Dev Haskell Boxset 13-15
Dev Haskell Boxset 16-18
Dev Haskell Boxset 19-21
Dev Haskell Boxset 22-24
Dev Haskell Boxset 25-27
Dev Haskell Boxset 28-30
Dev Haskell Boxset 1-7
Dev Haskell Boxset 8-14
Dev Haskell Boxset 15-19
Dev Haskell Boxset 20-24
Dev Haskell Boxset 25-29

The following titles comprise the Jack Dillon Dublin Tales series:
Welcome
Jack Dillon Dublin Tale 1
Sweet Dreams
Jack Dillon Dublin Tale 2
Mirror Mirror
Jack Dillon Dublin Tale 3
Silver Bullet
Jack Dillon Dublin Tale 4

Fair City Blues
Jack Dillon Dublin Tale 5
Spade Work
Jack Dillon Dublin Tale 6
Madeline Missing
Jack Dillon Dublin Tale 7
Mistaken Identity
Jack Dillon Dublin Tale 8
Picture Perfect
Jack Dillon Dublin Tale 9
Dublin Moon
Jack Dillon Dublin Tale 10
Mystery Woman
Jack Dillon Dublin Tale 11
Second Chance
Jack Dillon Dublin Tale 12
Payback Brother
Jack Dillon Dublin Tale 13
The Heist
Jack Dillon Dublin Tale 14
Jewels To Kill For
Jack Dillon Dublin Tale 15
Retirement Scheme
Jack Dillon Dublin Tale 16
The Collector
Jack Dillon Dublin Tale 17

Jack Dillon Dublin Tales Boxsets:
Jack Dillon Dublin Tales 1-3

Jack Dillon Dublin Tales 4-6
Jack Dillon Dublin Tales 1-5
Jack Dillon Dublin Tales 1-7
Jack Dillon Dublin Tales 6-10

The following titles comprise the Hotshot series;
Reduced Ransom! Second Edition
Finders Keepers! Second Edition
Bankers Hours Second Edition
Chow Down Second Edition
Moonlight Dance Academy Second Edition
Irish Dukes (Fight Card Series)
written under the pseudonym Jack Tunney

The following titles comprise the Corridor Man series:
Corridor Man
Corridor Man 2: Opportunity knocks
Corridor Man 3: The Dungeon
Corridor Man 4: Dead End
Corridor Man 5: Finger
Corridor Man 6: Exit Strategy
Corridor Man 7: Trunk Music
Corridor Man 8: Birthday Boy
Corridor Man 9: Boss Man
Corridor Man 10: Bye Bye Bobby

Corridor Man novellas:
Corridor Man: Valentine

Corridor Man: Auditor
Corridor Man: Howling
Corridor Man: Spa Day

The following are Corridor Man Boxsets:
Corridor Man Boxset 1-3
Corridor Man Boxset 1-5
Corridor Man Boxset 6-9

THANK YOU!

Contact the author:
- Email: mikefaricyauthor@gmail.com
- Twitter: @Mikefaricybooks
- Facebook: Mike Faricy Author
- Website: http://www.mikefaricybooks.com

Published by

MJF Publishing

Mike Faricy ♦ 358